Martha Finley

The Thorn in the Nest

Martha Finley

The Thorn in the Nest

1st Edition | ISBN: 978-3-75234-163-8

Place of Publication: Frankfurt am Main, Germany

Year of Publication: 2020

Outlook Verlag GmbH, Germany.

Reproduction of the original.

THE THORN IN THE NEST

BY

MARTHA FINLEY

CHAPTER I.

"A malady

Preys on my heart, that medicine cannot reach."

Our story opens in spring of 1797, in a sequestered valley in Western Pennsylvania. On a green hillside dotted here and there with stately oaks and elms, and sloping toward the road, beyond which flowed the clear waters of a mountain stream, stood a brick farm-house—large, roomy, substantial; beautiful with climbing vines and flowering shrubs. Orchard, meadow, wheat and corn fields stretched away on either hand, shut in by dense forests and wooded hills; beyond and above which, toward the right, towered the giant Alleghenies; their summits, still white from the storms of the past winter, lying like a bank of snowy clouds against the eastern horizon.

But night drew on apace, the light was fast fading even from the mountain tops, and down in the valley it was already so dark that only the outlines of objects close at hand were discernible as our hero, Kenneth Clendenin, mounted upon Romeo, his gallant steed, entered it from the west and slowly wended his way toward its one solitary dwelling. The road was familiar to both man and horse, and ere long they had reached the gate.

A negro boy perched on the top of the fence, with his hands in his pockets, whistling softly to himself in the dark, broke off suddenly in the middle of his tune, sprang nimbly to the ground and took the bridle, exclaiming, "Ki, Massa Doctah! t'o't dat you and ole Romeo comin' up de road. Ole Aunt Vashti she tole me watch out hyar an' ax you ef you's had yo' suppah, sah?"

"Yes, Zeb, tell her I have and shall want nothing more to-night," answered the traveller, alighting. "Rub Romeo down and give him a good feed."

"Dat I will, Massa Doctah; I neber 'glects ole Romeo," returned the lad, vaulting into the saddle and cantering off to the stable, while the gentleman walked quickly up the path leading to the house.

Within a wood fire burned brightly in the wide chimney of the living room. An arm-chair stood on each side of the hearth, the master of the house occupying one, his wife the other, she with her knitting, he half crouching over the fire, watching the flickering flames in moody silence.

At a table on the farther side of the room, a little girl was poring over a book by the light of a tallow candle. She had seemed very intent upon its pages, but at the first sound of the approaching footsteps sprang up and ran to open the door.

"At last, Kenneth!" she cried, in a joyous but subdued tone.

"Yes, little sister," he said, laying his hand caressingly for an instant on her pretty brown hair, and smiling into the bright, dark eyes. "I'm glad to find you up, I thought you went to bed with the chickens."

"Not to-night—the last—O Kenneth! Kenneth!" and she burst into passionate weeping.

"Marian, my little pet sister," he whispered, sitting down and drawing her to his breast with a tender caress, "try to be cheerful for mother's sake."

"I will," she answered, hastily wiping away her tears. "I have a parting present for you, Kenneth," she went on with a determined effort to seem bright and gay; "a pair of stockings made of my own lamb's wool, and every stitch knit by my own fingers—I took the last to-night, and you're to travel in them."

"Many thanks," he said, "my feet will surely keep warm in such hose, though the nights are still very cool."

"Yes, come nearer to the fire, Kenneth," said the mother, who had been watching the two, silently, but with glistening eyes.

She was a woman of middle age, gentle mannered, with a low and peculiarly sweet-toned voice, a tall and stately figure, and a face that told a story of trial and sorrow borne with patience and resignation.

Kenneth resembled her strongly in person and manner, he had the same noble contour of features—the broad high forehead, the large dark gray eye, keen yet tender in expression.

"Thank you," he said, coming forward and taking his stand upon the hearth, where the firelight fell full upon his tall, manly form, "its warmth is by no means unpleasant."

"Sit down, Kenneth; sit down, and take me on your knee," said Marian, bringing him a chair.

"Are you not growing rather large and heavy for that?" the mother asked with a slight smile, as Kenneth good-humoredly complied with the request.

"I'll be bigger and heavier before he has another chance," remarked the child, putting an arm about Kenneth's neck and gazing wistfully into his eyes.

"But not too big, never too big, to take your seat here," he responded, drawing her closer. "Ah, there will be many a lonely hour when I shall long for my little sister, long to feel her weight upon my knee, her arm about my neck, just as I feel them now."

"Why do you all talk so much?" queried the older man sharply, speaking for the first time since Kenneth's entrance, and turning somewhat angrily toward the little group. "You leave me no peace of my life with your incessant gabble, gabble."

With the last word he rose and withdrew to an inner room.

No one answered or tried to detain him: the shade of sadness deepened slightly on the mother's calm face, and Marian's arm tightened its hold on Kenneth's neck, but no one spoke and the room was very still for a moment.

Then the mother, glancing at the dial-plate of a tall old-fashioned clock, ticking in a corner, said, "Marian, my child, it is growing late, and you will want to be up betimes in the morning."

The little girl, heaving a sigh, reluctantly bade them good-night and retired.

Kenneth looked after her.

"What a sweet creature she is! what a lovely woman a few years will make of her," he said; but catching the expression of the mother's countenance, he ended abruptly, with almost a groan.

She had dropped her knitting in her lap, her face had grown very pale, her lips quivered, and there was a look of anguish in her eyes.

Kenneth longed to comfort her, but could find no words. He brought a glass of water and held it to her lips.

She swallowed a mouthful, and as he set the glass down on a stand by her side, took up her work again with a slight sigh. The spasm of pain seemed to have passed, and her face resumed its accustomed expression of patient endurance.

4

He stood gazing down on her, his eyes full of a wistful tenderness.

"Mother," he said, bending over her and speaking in a voice scarce raised above a whisper, "our God is very good, very merciful, surely He will hear our united prayers that it—that fearful curse—may never light on her."

"His will be done with me and mine," she answered low and tremulously. "Though He slay me, yet will I trust in Him."

He turned and paced the room for several minutes, then came back to her side.

"And I—am I right to go and leave you thus?—alone—unprotected, if—"

She looked up with a great courage in her noble face. "Yes, go, Kenneth; I do not fear, and it is best for you and for him. You forget how fully we have both been convinced of that."

"How brave you are, how strong in faith!" he cried admiringly.

She shook her head in dissent. "You do not know how my heart fails me at times when I think of my dear boy far away in that Northwestern Territory fighting his battle with the world among strangers, often exposed to the pitiless storms, or in danger from wild beasts or savage Indians; coming home from his long rides over prairies and through forests, wet, cold, and weary, and finding no one to cheer him and comfort him."

There were tears in her eyes and in her voice.

"Don't be troubled about me," Kenneth said cheerily, "I am young and vigorous, and shall rather enjoy roughing it, in the pursuit of my calling?"

"A noble calling to one who follows it in the right spirit, Kenneth. Your arrangements are all completed?"

"Yes; we meet at the cross-roads an hour after sunrise."

She gave him a troubled, anxious look, opened her lips as if to speak, then closed them again.

"What is it, mother?" he asked. "Why should you hesitate to say to me all that is in your heart?"

"Miss Lamar! I saw her the other day. She is sweet and fair to look upon, and very winsome in her ways, but—"

The sentence was left unfinished, while her eyes sought his with a yearning, wistful look.

"I will be on my guard," he said, huskily. "I know that marriage is not for me —as a physician I am convinced of it as another might not be—unless—oh, there will come to me, at times, a wild hope that there may one day be an end to this suspense—this torturing doubt and fear!"

"Too many years have passed," she answered sadly. "I have no longer any expectation that it will ever be cleared up this side the grave."

"Do not say it," he entreated, "it must be done! I shall never resign hope till— I have attained to some certainty; and yet, and yet—in either case it must be grief of heart to me."

"My poor boy!" she murmured, regarding him with tenderly compassionate gaze; then after a pause, "Kenneth," she remarked, "there is little Clendenin about you except the name; you strongly resemble my mother's family in both disposition and personal appearance."

"And yet," he said, with a melancholy smile, "there is nothing more certain than that I am a Clendenin."

"Well," she said, gazing upon him with loving pride, yet with eyes dim with unshed tears, "it is a family of no mean extraction; and an honest, pious ancestry is something to be thankful for."

CHAPTER II.

Kenneth Clendenin, having completed his medical studies at Philadelphia, graduated with honor, and afterward spent a year in the hospitals there, was now about emigrating to Chillicothe, a town recently laid out by General Nathaniel Massie, in what was then the Northwestern Territory; now the state of Ohio.

None of his family were to accompany him, but he was to act as escort to two ladies, who, with their children, were also going thither to join their husbands. One of them had under her care a young orphan girl, bound to the same place, where she was to make her home with a married brother, Major Lamar.

The Clendenin household were early astir on the morning succeeding the events related in the former chapter. Before the sun had peeped above the mountain tops they were summoned to a savory and substantial breakfast, prepared by old Vashti, who had been cook in the family since Kenneth's earliest recollection.

He was the first to answer the call; coming in from a farewell tramp about the premises, to find the faithful old creature in the act of setting the last dish upon the table.

"I'se done my bes', honey," she said to him, with tears in her eyes. "It mos' breaks dis ole heart to tink you won't eat no mo' dis chile's cookin'."

"I don't know that, Aunt Vashti," he responded, smiling, "I'm not going quite out of the world."

"'Pears mighty like it, honey," she said; then seeing his eyes wandering uneasily about the room and the porch beyond, "You's lookin' for ole marster?" she whispered, coming close to his side. "He was off to de woods wid his gun 'fore daylight. 'Spect he didn't want to say good-by."

"Probably," he answered, with a slight sigh; then turned with an affectionate greeting to his mother and Marian, who entered the room at that instant.

They sat down at once to their repast, without the husband and father, no one remarking upon his absence, or asking any questions in regard to it; the meal was, indeed, almost a silent one; the hearts were too full for much speech.

Kenneth's saddle-bags and portmanteau were in readiness, packed by the mother's loving hands, and Romeo stood pawing at the gate. Zeb's horse, too, was there, tied to the fence near by, while its rider was eating his breakfast in the kitchen.

The travelers had no time for loitering, for many miles of rough road must be passed over that day.

The adieus were quickly spoken, and the windings of the road soon hid master and servant from the view of the weeping, disconsolate Marian and her sorrowful-faced mother.

Kenneth's heart, too, was heavy, spite of the cheerful air he had assumed for the sake of the dear ones he was leaving behind; but Zeb seemed in fine spirits. He was young and light-hearted, had no relatives to leave, in fact loved "de doctah" better than any other human creature.

And he was going to see the world, a prospect which thrilled him with delight.

The sun was now shining brightly, birds sang cheerily in the trees that bordered the roadside, the morning air was fresh and exhilarating, and Zeb's spirits rose high as he cantered along at a respectful distance behind his master.

A mile away from Glen Forest, as the Clendenin place was called, they came out upon a cleared place where stood a little country church in the midst of an enclosure, whose grass-covered mounds, with here and there a stone slab, proclaimed it the settlers' last resting place.

Here Kenneth drew rein, and calling to Zeb bade him ride on to the cross-roads and there await his coming; and if their fellow travellers should arrive first, tell them he would join them in a few moments.

"Yes, sah," returned the lad, whipping up his horse, while Kenneth dismounted and made his way to a spot where four or five little graves, and one somewhat longer, were ranged side by side.

Giving only a glance at the others, the young man turned to this last and stood for some moments gazing down upon it with a look of grave, sad tenderness upon his noble, manly face.

"Angus Clendenin, aged fourteen," he murmured in low, moved tones, reading from the inscription on the headstone. "Ah, brother beloved, why were we so soon parted by grim death? We whose hearts were knit together as the hearts of David and Jonathan!"

But time pressed and he must away. Plucking a violet from the sod that covered the sleeping dust, and placing it carefully between the leaves of his note book, he remounted and pursued his journey.

As he reached the place of rendezvous, where Zeb was lazily sunning himself, seated on a fallen tree, with his horse's bridle in his hand, three large wagons came toiling along the intersecting roads; beside the foremost a graceful girlish figure, tastefully attired in riding hat and habit, and mounted upon a beautiful and spirited pony, which she was managing with the utmost apparent ease and skill; curbing its evident impatience to outstrip the slower and more clumsily built animals attached to the vehicles.

At sight of Kenneth, however, she loosened her hold upon the rein, and came cantering briskly up with a gay "Good-morning, Dr. Clendenin."

The face that met his gaze was so fair and winsome, so bright with youthful animation, that the grave young doctor could not forbear a smile as he returned her greeting with courtly grace.

Nellie Lamar's beauty was of a very delicate type—a sylph-like form, delicately moulded features, a sweet, innocent expression, complexion of lilies and roses, a profusion of pale golden hair, beautifully arched and pencilled brows, large melting blue eyes, "deeply, darkly, beautifully blue," and fringed with heavy silken lashes, many shades darker than the hair.

She was but fifteen, just out of school and quite as guileless and innocent as she looked.

A charming blush mantled her cheek as she caught the admiring glance of

Kenneth's eye.

"So, so, Fairy, be quiet, will you?" she said, tightening her rein with one hand, while bending low over her pony's neck she softly patted and stroked it with the other. "If those clumsy, slow-moving creatures would but travel faster!" she exclaimed with pretty petulance, lifting her head again and sending an impatient glance in the direction of the approaching wagons. "Neither Fairy nor I can well brook having to keep pace with them."

"They are somewhat more heavily laden than she," he said smilingly, with some difficulty restraining the impetuosity of his own steed, as he spoke; "she should have charity for them. But I fear Romeo is disposed to join her in leaving them behind. We will lead the van, however, Miss Lamar, and sometimes indulge these restless spirits in a run of a few miles ahead; if it is but to return again."

"Ah, that will be delightful!" she cried with almost childish vehemence. "I have fairly dreaded the thought of travelling at this snail's pace all the way to Chillicothe."

The wagons had now come up, and from the foremost peered out two chubby, rosy boy faces.

"O Doctor Clendenin! won't you take me up behind you?" shouted the owner of one, the other chiming in, "Me, too, doctor, me too!"

"Hush, Tom! hush, Billy! you should not ask such a thing. Doctor, don't mind them," quickly interposed the mother, showing her cheery, matronly face alongside of theirs.

"Good morning, Mrs. Nash," Kenneth said, moving to the side of the wagon. "We have an auspicious day for starting upon our long journey."

"Yes, indeed, doctor; and how thankful I am that we're all well and so comfortably accommodated."

"You don't seem to care at all for the old home scenes and friends we're leaving behind, Sarah," whined a woman's voice from the second vehicle; "but for my part I shall never, never forget them, and I think it's dreadfully hard I should have to go away from them all into that howling wilderness, as one may say," and the voice was lost in a burst of sobs.

"But we're going to our husbands, Nancy, and they ought to be more to us than all the world beside," returned Mrs. Nash, cheerfully. "Dear me, I'm just as glad as can be to think that in a few weeks my Robert and I will be together again for good and all."

It was characteristic of the two, who were sisters-in-law, the one always looking at the bright side of life, the other at the dark; the one counting up her mercies, the other her trials.

"It'll be a rough, hard journey, and some of us will be sure to get sick," sighed Mrs. Barbour. "Flora's always been a delicate child, and I'll never take her there alive."

"She's looking well," remarked Kenneth, glancing in at the bright eyes and pink cheeks of a little girl, sitting contentedly by Mrs. Barbour's side.

"And we'll have the doctor handy all the way, you know," suggested Mrs. Nash. "Tom, Tom, be quiet," for the boy was still clamoring for a ride on Romeo.

"So you shall," Kenneth said, lifting him to the coveted place, "and, Billy, you shall have your turn another time."

The third wagon carried no passenger; its load consisting of baggage, household stuff, a tent and provision for the way, for there were few houses of entertainment on the route and it would often be necessary to camp out for the night.

The roads were new and rough; in many places in very bad condition. Sometimes there was a mere bridle path, and bushes and branches must be cut away, or fallen trees removed, to allow the wagons to pass.

At noon of this first day they halted on the banks of a bright little stream, dined upon such fare as they had brought with them, and rested for an hour or two; allowing their horses to graze and the children to disport themselves in racing about through the underbrush in search of wild flowers, in which Miss Nell presently joined them.

Kenneth, leaving the two women sitting together on a log, strolled away in another direction, toward Zeb and the drivers who were keeping guard over the horses and wagons.

"Dear me!" sighed Mrs. Barbour, "what a journey we have before us! how we're ever to stand it I don't know; I am tired already."

"Already!" echoed her sister; "why I don't intend to be really tired for a week."

"I'd like to know what intentions have to do with it," returned the first speaker, rather angrily.

"A good deal, I assure you," asserted Mrs. Nash, with decision. "Make up your mind to be miserable and you can't fail to be so; resolve to enjoy yourself, and you're almost equally sure to do that."

"Humph!" grunted her companion, turning away with a scornful toss of the head.

"What's wrong?" asked Miss Lamar, coming toward them with her hands full of delicate spring blossoms.

"Wrong! where?" returned Mrs. Barbour, sharply, thinking the query aimed at her.

"Yonder," Nell answered, gazing anxiously in the direction of the group about the wagons; "they all seem to be busying themselves about that wheel."

"There, I knew it!" cried Mrs. Barbour, "something's broken, and we'll be kept here all night; and we'll be having such accidents all the way. Nobody ever was so unfortunate as I am."

"Why you more than the rest of us?" asked her sister, dryly. "If one is delayed, we all are."

"It was only a broken linchpin, already replaced by another," announced Kenneth a few moments later; "and now, if you please, ladies, we will go on our way again."

At dusk the party arrived at a lonely log cabin in the woods, where they found shelter for the night.

Fare and accommodations were none of the best—the one consisting of fat pork, hominy, and coarse corn bread, the other of hastily improvised beds, upon the floor of the lower room for the women and children; upon that of the loft overhead for the men.

Mrs. Barbour, according to her wont, passed the time previous to retiring in fretting and complaining; talking of herself as the most ill-used and unfortunate of the human race, though no one else in the company was in any respect faring better than she, and all were not only bearing their discomforts with patience and resignation, but cheerfully and with an emotion of thankfulness that they had a roof over their heads; as a heavy rain storm had come on shortly after their arrival, and continued till near morning.

But that was another of the complainer's grievances; "The roads would be flooded, the streams so swollen that it would be impossible to cross with the wagons."

Nell, hearing these doleful prognostications, turned an anxious enquiring look upon Kenneth.

"Do not be alarmed," he said, leaning toward her, and speaking in an undertone of quiet assurance: "the rain is much needed and therefore a cause for thankfulness; and if streams cannot be forded immediately, we can encamp beside them and wait for the abating of the waters."

"But our provisions may give out," she suggested.

"Then we will look for game in the woods, and fish in the streams. No fear, little lady, that we shall not be fed."

Nell liked the title, and felt it restful to lean upon one who showed so much quiet confidence in—was it his own powers and resources or something higher?

The journey was a tedious and trying one, occupying several weeks; and Kenneth's office as leader of the party was no sinecure.

There were many vexatious delays, some occasioned by the wretched state of the roads, others incident to the moving of the cumbrous and heavily laden wagons; which latter might have been avoided had he travelled alone, or in company with none but equestrians.

But Kenneth was of too noble and unselfish a nature to grudge the cost of kindness to others.

And on him fell all the care and responsibility of directing, controlling, and providing ways and means; settling disputes among the drivers, and attending to the safety and comfort of the women and children.

These various duties were performed with the utmost fidelity, energy, and tact, and all annoyances borne with unvarying patience and cheerfulness; even Mrs. Barbour's peevish complainings and martyrlike airs failing to move him out of his quiet self-possession, or goad him into treating her with anything but the greatest courtesy and kindness.

He showed the same to all in the little company, and to those with whom they sought temporary lodgings here and there along the route; more especially to any who were sick, exercising his skill as a physician for their relief, and that without charge, though sometimes it cost him the loss of a much needed night's rest.

Mrs. Barbour was too completely wrapped up in herself and her own grievances, real or imaginary, to take note of these things beyond a passing feeling of wonder that Dr. Clendenin should bestow so much attention upon people who were not likely ever to make him any return; but ere the journey's end they had won for him a very high place in the respect and esteem of the other adults of the party, and in the hearts of the children.

Nell, who was often sorely tried by these same vexations and delays, formed an unbounded admiration for Kenneth's powers of forbearance and self-control.

She gave expression to it in talking with Mrs. Nash, as they found themselves alone for a few moments on the evening previous to their arrival at their destination.

"Yes," was the reply, "I am astonished at his patience; particularly with Nancy. She exasperates me beyond everything—she is such a martyr. Yes, always, in all places, and under all circumstances, she's a martyr."

CHAPTER III.

Within five or six miles of Chillicothe an approaching horseman was espied by our travellers, and, as he drew near, Mrs. Nash and her two boys recognized him with a simultaneous cry of delight.

"Robert!"

"Father, father!"

To which he responded with a glad "Hurrah! so there you are at last!" as he put spurs to his horse and came dashing up to the side of the wagon containing his wife and children.

There was a halt of several minutes while joyous greetings, and eager questions and answers were exchanged; then leaving Mr. Nash in charge of the slow-moving vehicles, Kenneth and Nellie rode on toward the town.

It was the afternoon of a perfect day in May. Their path led them, now through the depths of a forest where grew in abundance the sugar maple, black walnut, buckeye, hackberry, cherry and other trees which give evidence of a rich soil; now across a beautiful prairie covered with grass from four to five feet high, and spangled with loveliest wild flowers, which with the blossoms of the plum tree, mulberry, crab apple and red and black haw, fringing the outer edge of the prairies, filled the air with delicious perfume, and feasted the eye with beauty.

Nellie was in ecstasies. "It is a paradise, Dr. Clendenin! is it not?" she cried.

"An earthly one," he answered with his grave kindly smile. "May you find much happiness in it, little lady."

"And you too, doctor," she said gaily, turning her bright, winsome face to his. "I'm sure you ought."

"You think it a duty to be happy? and you are right."

"A duty? I never thought of it in that light," she said laughing lightly.

"Ah! are we not bidden to be content with such things as we have, and to be always rejoicing?"

They had become excellent friends—these two—as day after day they rode side by side a little in advance of the wagons.

There was some ten years difference in their ages, a good deal seemingly at Nell's time of life. She looked up to Kenneth as to one much older and wiser than herself, and won by his ever ready sympathy and interest, talked to him with the charming frankness of her confiding nature and extreme youth. She told the history of her past years, particularly the last five, which had been spent in a boarding school in Philadelphia, and about the brother she was going to:—how he fought bravely for his country in the Continental army, had been taken prisoner by the British, what he had suffered on one of those dreadful prison-ships, till peace at last set him free, that he had married since and now had a family of children.

He was very much older than herself, she explained, being the eldest born while she was the youngest, and as both parents had died while she was a mere infant, he was like a father to her. Kenneth seldom spoke of himself, but she sometimes led him on by her questions to talk of his home at Glen Forest, his mother and Marian, for both of whom he evidently cherished a deep and tender affection.

Nell remarked that she had seen them at church once or twice, had thought Mrs. Clendenin very sweet and noble looking, and Marian the loveliest of little girls.

"You read them both aright," was Kenneth's answer, with a look and smile that made him, Nell thought, the handsomest man she had ever seen.

"If he were not quite so old," she said to herself, "perhaps, I don't know, but perhaps I might fall in love with him. It would be very foolish though, for of course he could never care for such a silly young thing as I am."

She had observed that he seemed a skilful physician and surgeon, and had discovered that he could tell her a vast deal about trees and plants and the birds and wild animals of the woods through which they passed.

They had never met in Philadelphia though living there at the same time, but it was pleasant to talk with him about the city and its various attractions.

So they had not been at a loss for subjects of conversation, nor were they to-day.

Silence fell between them for a few moments after Kenneth's last remark, then Nell said, with a saucy smile, "So you, I suppose, are never sad, Dr. Clendenin."

"Alas, Miss Lamar," he answered with a far away look in his eyes, an expression of keen anguish sweeping across his features, yet passing away so quickly that she could hardly feel sure it had been there, "my theory and practice do not always agree."

"Well," said she, "I don't believe there is anybody in the world who is not sad at times. Yet we have a great deal to make us glad, and just now I feel as blithe as a bird. We are coming to a river."

"Yes, the Scioto."

"Oh, then we must be near Chillicothe, are we not?"

"Yes, here is the ferry, and yonder, on the farther side, lies the town."

"That! I see only a few log cabins scattered here and there in a dense forest."

"True, miss, that is just what it is," said the ferryman, pushing off, for they were already on board his flat boat; "but you'll find more houses than you'd think, and the streets marked out quite straight and wide."

"And can you tell me in which Major Lamar lives?" Nell asked eagerly.

"Certainly, miss, there are not so many of us that we don't all know each other's faces, and houses too. The major lives on Walnut Street, but a step from where I shall land you. And yonder he comes," he added as the boat touched the bank and Romeo and Fairy bounded ashore.

Another moment and the girl was in her brother's arms, weeping for very joy, as if her heart would break, he soothing her with caresses and tender, loving words.

"There, there, Nell, darling, my sweet little sister, we're together at last, and don't mean to be parted ever again. Come, come, don't spoil your pretty eyes with crying."

She brushed away her tears at that, raised her head, saying, "O Percy, I'm so glad, so happy! How are Clare and the children?"

Then without waiting for an answer, "Oh how forgetful I am!" she cried turning to Kenneth, who with half averted face and dewy eyes, was thinking of Marian, and could almost feel the clinging of her arms about his neck. "Percy, this is Dr. Clendenin, who has cared for me like a brother, through all this long, tiresome journey."

The two grasped each other's hands warmly, and the major insisted on carrying Kenneth off with him to share the hospitality of his house.

It was a pleasant home circle into which he was presently introduced,—Mrs. Lamar, a fair, graceful, bright-faced lady, still young, and three or four rosy, bright-eyed boys and girls.

He received a warm welcome, while Nellie was embraced, kissed and rejoiced over to her heart's content, a heart that went out in strong affection to her kindred and craved a full return.

The evening meal was already prepared, the table set in the living room. Its snowy linen, delicate china and shining silver would not have disgraced a much more lordly dwelling; and the viands which presently came in smoking from the kitchen, fresh fish, game and hot corn-bread, might have tempted the appetite of an epicure; much more that of our travellers, who had fared but indifferently well for some days past.

The major's house was but a log cabin, the only kind of building in the settlement at that time, simply furnished, and consisted of only three rooms beside kitchen and garret; yet a great deal of comfort and enjoyment were to be found there, and Kenneth was not ill-pleased to be tendered the freedom of the house, and accepted the offer with hearty thanks.

"We elect you our family physician, sir, if you will not decline the office," said the major, as they rose from the table; "and as such you will of course consider yourself perfectly at home among us."

Kenneth was beginning to express his sense of his host's kindness when he was interrupted by a hasty summons to the bedside of a sick woman at the other end of the village.

"Come, Nell, and take a look at Chillicothe," the major said, leading the way to the grass plot in front of the house, where they seated themselves upon a log.

There were many such lying about the streets, many trees and stumps of those which had been felled, still standing; in fact nearly the whole town was still a wilderness; yet though not a year old, it already contained, beside private dwellings, two taverns and several stores and shops of mechanics, but among them all there were but four shingled houses, and on one the shingles were fastened with pegs. The streets were very wide and straight, crossing at right angles; not all cleared yet, but marked out by blazing the trees of the thick wood in whose midst the town was located.

There were many Indians in the vicinity. They had a town not far away, on the north fork of Paint Creek, and here in Chillicothe their wigwams were interspersed among the dwellings of the whites as Nellie noticed with some uneasiness.

But her brother reassured her. "There is no danger," he said, "they are perfectly friendly."

"Ah, but they are a treacherous race," she sighed with a dubious shake of the head.

"Quite a change from Philadelphia, Nell," Clare remarked, joining them with her knitting in her hand.

"Yes, but it is many weeks since I left there."

"Is it nice in Philadelphia, Aunt Nellie?" asked Bess, the eldest of the children, hanging affectionately about the young girl. "Do tell us what it's like, and about the pretty things in the shop windows."

"Another time, Bess," interposed the major. "Run away to your play now, and let older people talk. Nell, you saw Washington more than once?"

"Ah yes! many times—and he asked for you, Percy, in the kindest way, speaking in the highest terms of your services to the country."

"It is like him," the major exclaimed with emotion.

"And this young doctor, Nell," pursued Clare, with a meaning smile, "what is he like?"

"Just what he has shown himself to-night," the girl answered, blushing slightly, as she had a trick of doing, the rich blood showing readily through the clear, transparent skin.

"A handsome, polished, courteous gentleman, intelligent and well informed above the generality, that is about all one could learn in so short an interview," and Clare laughed low and musically. "But you have had an opportunity to study his character pretty thoroughly."

"A thing I never thought of doing," returned Nell, with some annoyance; "but I can tell you that he is very patient and very kind."

"Any one might well be that to you, Nell," remarked her brother, regarding her with a proud, affectionate smile.

"But it was not only to me, but to everybody, and to the very horses and dogs. He seems to be always thinking of others, never of himself, and to have a kind look or word or smile for the humblest and meanest creature that crosses his path, and," low and hesitatingly, "I believe it's because he is a real, true Christian."

"I know it, one can read it in his face," said the major heartily, "and I am rejoiced; for such men are needed here."

"There they are!" cried Nell, starting up. "See! the wagons are just crossing the ferry!"

The Nashes and Barbours had been old friends and neighbors of the Lamars before the emigration of the latter to Ohio, and the major and his wife now hurried to meet and welcome them; Nell and the children following.

Kenneth, having bestowed all needed attention upon his patient, was hurrying toward the ferry also, as indeed was nearly every man and women in the village, all alike rejoicing in every new accession to their numbers, and eager for news from the older settlements.

There were joyous greetings, hearty handshakings, and quite a crowd gathered around Kenneth, giving him welcome, expressing unfeigned satisfaction with the advent among them of a good physician.

"Why, hollo! I recognize an old friend! Kenneth Clenendin, I was never more surprised and delighted in my life!" cried a familiar voice, and our hero's hand was warmly grasped in that of a former schoolmate, a young man of pleasing, open countenance, and bluff, hearty manner.

"Is it you, Godfrey Dale?" Kenneth exclaimed, shaking the hand cordially, his face lighting up with pleasure. "Why, where did you come from?"

"From Tiffen's tavern over yonder, the sign of the General Anthony Wayne," returned Dale, laughing.

"You are here as a settler?"

"Yes, and as land agent and lawyer. It's a fine country, Kenneth, and men of both your profession and mine are needed in it. Come, let me show you my quarters. You must share them for the present, at all events."

And linking his arm in that of his friend, he led the way, nearly all the men of the crowd following.

The General Anthony Wayne was no spacious modern hotel, but like its neighbors a log building with windows of greased paper, its accommodations of the plainest.

A cheerful wood fire blazed in its wide chimney, but the evening was a warm one for the time of year, and the company preferred the outer air.

They grouped themselves about the door, sitting on stumps and logs, or leaning against the trees, while Kenneth, the centre of the throng, patiently answered questions and gave all the information in his power regarding matters of public interest both at home and abroad.

The sun went down behind the hill overlooking the valley on the west, the stars shone from a clear sky overhead, and lights twinkled here and there among the trees.

Nell, standing in the doorway of her brother's house, asked what they were, remarking:

"They are many more in number than the cabins."

"Yes," answered Clare, "do you not know that the Indians have a way of lighting up their wigwams with torches made of the splinters of birch and pine?"

"I wish," murmured the girl, with a slight shudder, "that they could be kept away—miles away from the town."

CHAPTER IV.

Early hours were the rule among the settlers in those primitive days, and by nine o'clock all was darkness and silence in the dwelling of the Lamars.

A bed stood in one corner of the large family room, a trundle bed beneath it, which was drawn out at night; and here slept the parents and younger children.

One of two smaller apartments between this and the kitchen was appropriated to Nell; the other occupied by the older children.

The young girl was roused from her sleep in the middle of the night by something falling down the wall close to her side.

"Percy! Percy!" she screamed in affright.

"What is it, Nell?" answered the major, springing out of bed.

"Oh, I don't know, I don't know! It's too dark to see! But, oh, come and bring a light quickly!"

That was more easily said than done; friction matches were as yet an unknown luxury; the choice was between flint and steel and the fire covered upon the kitchen hearth.

He chose the latter, but it was a work of time to hunt out a coal from the ashes, and blow it into life till it would ignite the wick of a candle.

The thing was accomplished at last, however, and the light revealed a viper beneath Nell's bed.

The major succeeded in killing it, and soothing his sister's alarm with a few kindly reassuring words, again retired to rest.

It was some time before Nell's fears were forgotten in sleep, and a grumbling voice from the kitchen woke her early in the morning.

"Dear me, who's been rakin' ober dis fire? It's clar out, every spark of it; an', Tig, you'll have to run over nex' do' for a bran' to start it wid."

Silvy the cook was evidently very much out of humor.

"Pshaw! you didn't cober it up right," returned the boy.

"You git along!" was the wrathful answer. "I reckon you done raked it ober yourself; and I'll tell de major ef you don' quit cuttin' up sech shines. Be off after dat bran' now, fast as you kin go."

Nell turned over on her pillow and listened.

"Percy must have forgotten to cover up the coals again," she said to herself. "What a narrow escape I had! What with Indians and vipers in the town, bears, wolves and panthers in the woods, I seem to have come into a dangerous place."

She sighed rather drearily, a homesick feeling creeping over her, spite of her love for Percy and the rest.

But that presently vanished before the beauty of a balmy, sunshiny May morning, the sight of the well-spread breakfast table, and the affectionate greetings of her brother and the children.

"I'm going shopping, Nell," announced Mrs. Lamar two hours later, when the house had been set to rights, and Silvy given her orders for the day; "will you go with me?"

"Shopping!" echoed the young girl in incredulous surprise.

"Yes; do you think Philadelphia is the only place where one may shop?"

"No; but here in the woods?"

"Yes, here in the woods we can shop; we have already three stores."

So they donned their bonnets and sallied forth.

It was pleasant walking in the shade of the great forest trees, traversing at the same time woodland paths and village streets, the twitter of birds and rustling of leaves in the breeze mingling with the busy hum of human voices and the sound of the woodman's axe; for men were engaged here and there in laying the foundations for new dwellings or clearing spaces preparatory to doing so.

Not many rods from the General Anthony Wayne they came upon Dr. Clendenin and his friend Godfrey Dale, standing together in earnest conversation, while some workmen stood near apparently awaiting their directions.

The gentlemen lifted their hats, Kenneth with the grave, quiet smile Nell had learned to know so well, Godfrey saying "A pleasant morning, ladies."

"Are you going to build?" asked Mrs. Lamar, nodding in return.

"Yes; a double office with a hall between," said Dale. "We think it will be sociable."

A man came staggering up axe in hand. "I—I'm after—a job; and you—you wa—want these trees cut down?"

"We do, Davis, but you're in no condition to wield an axe at present," returned Dale; and growling out an oath the fellow staggered away.

"It's perfectly dreadful the amount of drunkenness we have here of late!" remarked Mrs. Lamar looking after him.

"Yes, whiskey's too cheap," said Dale; "men, women and children are getting drunk."

"How is that?" enquired Kenneth, "there is no distillery in the vicinity?"

"No; but since keel boats have begun to run on the Scioto the Monongahela whiskey manufacturers have rushed their firewater in here in such quantities that the cabins are crowded with it and it has fallen in price to fifty cents a gallon."

"They'll be making work for you, doctor," said Mrs. Lamar, "and I hope you'll try to convince the people that whiskey taken in such quantities is ruinous to health."

"Ruinous to body and soul," he said. "You may rest assured, Mrs. Lamar, that my influence will be decidedly against its use."

"We will take a stroll round the town, Nell, before making our purchases," Clare said, moving on. "What a grave, quiet manner Dr. Clendenin has, for so young a man!"

It was a new phase of life now presenting itself to the young girl, and she found it interesting. Her attention was presently attracted by a squaw walking a little distance ahead of them, wearing a shawl completely covered with silver brooches.

"They get them at Detroit in exchange for furs, moccasins and baskets," explained Clare. "You know, I suppose, that they are quite skilled in ornamental work with beads and porcupine quills."

The major joined them and they extended their walk for a mile or more through the woods, climbing the hill that forms the western boundary of the valley, from which they had a birdseye view of the village and the surrounding country, a beautiful landscape, in all its native wildness, diversified with hill and valley, forest and prairie, traversed by streams of living water.

Returning, they called upon Mrs. Nash, whom they found in excellent spirits, full of enthusiastic delight with her new home and her restoration to the companionship of her husband, after months of separation. That seemed to make amends for everything: accustomed comforts could be done without, inconveniences easily borne, they would soon be remedied, and in the meantime were mere subjects for mirth.

"She's a cheery and wise little woman," was the major's remark, as they went on their way again.

"Yes; always the same," assented his wife; "but we'll hear a different story here," as they approached another cabin. "This is where the Barbours live, Nell, and I know Nancy of old."

"So do I, and we part company here," said the major laughingly, lifting his hat to his wife and sister, and hurrying on his way, while they drew near the open door of the dwelling.

"Walk in, ladies," said Mr. Barbour, putting his little girl off his knee, and trying to give them seats.

"How do you do?" said his wife, coming forward. "I was just wondering if you two were going to be formal with an old friend like me. How fortunate you are in being able to run about enjoying yourselves, while here I've been hard at work since daylight; no time to rest after my long journey, but I must go to work washing up our dirty clothes the first thing."

"No, now, Nancy," expostulated her husband, "you needn't have done it. I told you there were camp-women about, from Wayne's army, that would be glad of the job."

"And I wouldn't have one of them near me if I never have any help," she retorted; "but I never get any thanks from you, work as hard as I will."

"Father's been at work too," put in Flora, leaning up affectionately against him; "and so have I, and we've got most everything fixed now."

"Yes, you look quite settled already," Mrs. Lamar remarked, glancing round the room.

"It needn't take long for that when you've but one room and next to nothing to put in it," whined Mrs. Barbour. "But perhaps it's just as well not to have much, or it might be stolen from you; for I dare say those camp-women and soldiers are thievish; and I don't suppose there's any sort of government here yet, to protect property."

"I've never heard of anything being stolen here," said Mrs. Lamar; "though to be sure the town is not a year old yet."

"Well, there was a suspicious looking woman prowling about here last night; she came in making an excuse that she wanted to light her pipe at the fire, and stared round as if she was taking note where things were, in case she should get a chance to help herself."

"Pooh! only idle curiosity," said Mr. Barbour. "You're always meeting trouble more than half way, Nancy."

"We're out shopping," remarked Nell, willing to change the subject of conversation.

"Shopping!" echoed Mrs. Barbour with a derisive laugh.

"Yes," said Mrs. Lamar, rising; "and that reminds me, Nell, that we should be attending to it at once."

It was no very arduous undertaking; in the first store they entered they were promptly supplied with the darning needle and skein of thread they were in search of. Change was made in a novel way; literally made by cutting a silver dollar into halves, quarters and eighths.

The merchant, an unmarried man, was extremely polite and courteous, and while waiting upon the ladies cast many a furtive, admiring glance at the slight, graceful figure and fair face of the major's young sister.

Kenneth had a call that afternoon to a case of delirium tremens, which took him past the dwelling of the Barbours.

He knew they were not in, having seen them but a few moments before strolling in the opposite direction, and was therefore surprised, within a few yards of the cabin, to see a man issue from the back door, with a bundle under his arm, and disappear among the trees.

The doctor paused for an instant, with the thought of giving pursuit, but the call for his services was urgent, and he hurried on again.

Turning a corner the next moment he came suddenly upon a man and woman conversing together in low tones, who at sight of him shrank guiltily back into the shadow of the trees; but not before his quick eye had caught a sight of their faces in the gathering gloom, for twilight had already set in, and his ear a few words of their talk.

"A pretty good haul considering."

"Yes; and now we'd best be off."

Suspicious words enough, but Kenneth had no time to think of them then, nor for hours afterward—so critical was the condition of his patient. It was only when on returning about sunrise the next morning, they were recalled to his mind by the sound of Mrs. Barbour's voice lifted up in scolding and lamentation.

"Yes, they're gone, every one of them;—that overcoat, just as good as new, the shirt I finished only the day before I started from home, and that elegant bandanna handkerchief. I told you somebody would get in and rob us in our sleep, if you didn't fasten the door well. Perhaps you'll believe another time that my opinion's worth something."

"There, there, Nancy, don't go on as if everything we had was lost. The town isn't so large that a thief can keep himself hid very long in it," Mr. Barbour was replying as the doctor stepped up to the open door.

"Good morning," he said, "I accidentally overheard Mrs. Barbour's lament, in passing, and I think I can throw some light on this matter," then went on to tell of what he had seen and heard the previous evening.

"So you see, Nancy, we weren't robbed in our sleep after all," was Mr. Barbour's comment, addressed to his wife.

"No thanks to you, anyhow," she retorted; "and it's your fault all the same; because I wouldn't have gone out and left the house alone if I'd had my way."

Mr. Barbour subsided. Why could he not learn how utterly useless it was to attempt to justify himself under the accusations of his wife?

"And there you sit never moving hand or foot to find the thief and get your own out of his clutches!" she whined, moving about with disconsolate and martyrlike air at her work of preparing the morning meal.

"Well, well, I'll go and see what can be done," he said, rising and putting on his hat. "Doctor, would you recognize the thief?"

"I am quite sure I should know again the suspicious looking persons I have been telling you of," Kenneth answered as they stepped out together.

"Now don't be gone all day, Mr. Barbour; breakfast will be on the table in half an hour," his wife called after him.

"Very well," he said looking back, "am I to let the thief escape rather than keep you waiting for an hour?"

"Of course you'll do one or the other—probably both," she fretted, as he walked on without waiting for an answer, "though it needn't take half that time to scour this wretched little town from end to end."

It did not; scarcely ten minutes had elapsed before it was known by every inhabitant that a theft had been committed, and that a man named Brannon and his wife, people of low character, whose absence would be gain to the place, had absconded during the night. They were not desirable citizens, but the stolen property must be recovered, and the larceny punished.

A hot pursuit was immediately begun, and before noon the culprits were taken and brought back in triumph.

But as yet the town had no constituted authorities. What was to be done?

The citizens gathered together on the river bank, chose one of their number, a Mr. Samuel Smith, as judge, and proceeded to try Brannon in due form; a jury was empanelled, the judge appointed Godfrey Dale as attorney for the prosecution, and another young lawyer, Maurice Gerard by name, for the defence.

Witnesses were called and examined. The goods had been found in possession of the accused, but he stoutly affirmed that they were his own.

Barbour, however, was able to prove property, and Dr. Clendenin's evidence was strong against the prisoner, whom he identified without hesitation as the man he had seen carrying away a bundle from Barbour's cabin the previous evening.

There was other testimony, but Kenneth's was the most conclusive.

The judge summed up the evidence, the jury retired to a short distance, and in a few moments returned with the verdict of guilty, and that the culprit be sentenced according to the discretion of the judge.

The latter presently announced his decision:—ten lashes upon the naked back of the prisoner, or that he should sit upon a bare pack-saddle on his pony, while his wife taking it by the bridle should lead it through every street of the village, pausing before the door of each house with the announcement, "This is Brannon who stole the great-coat, handkerchief, and shirt."

Brannon chose the latter horn of the dilemma, and a responsible person was appointed by the judge to see the sentence immediately and faithfully executed.

The crowd waited to see the man mounted upon the pony, then scattered to their homes or other positions favorable for watching his progress through the town.

He submitted to his punishment in dogged silence: glancing about him with an air of sullen defiance as he took his seat. Then his eye caught that of Kenneth fixed upon him in grave pity, and the look was returned with one of bitter hatred and revenge.

"Curse you!" he muttered under his breath, "the day will come when you'll repent of this."

CHAPTER V.

The Brannons fled immediately upon being released, after the carrying out of the sentence. No one mourned their departure: but Nell Lamar, having heard from Dale of the look the culprit had cast upon Kenneth, rejoiced not a little in secret that they were gone.

"Dr. Clendenin had been so kind to her on her journey," she explained to herself, "that in common gratitude she must care for his safety."

Naturally, being both friend and physician to the major's family, Kenneth was a frequent visitor at their house. Though noticeably quiet and undemonstrative in manner, he soon became a great favorite with them all, from the parents down to the youngest child; and Nell saw no reason to appropriate his visits to herself, even when unprofessional.

Nor had she any desire to do so; and in fact his conversation was seldom directed to her. Yet it did not escape Clare's quick observation that the calm gray eye saw every movement of her young sister, and that no tone of the sweet girlish voice ever fell unheeded upon his ear.

She was well pleased, Nell could not help loving such a man, or being happy with him, so would soon be provided for, and the major relieved of her support.

That last would never have been the major's thought, his darling little sister was esteemed no burden by him. He was one of the wealthiest men in the place, held a highly responsible office under the general government, and had received large grants of land in compensation for his services in the Revolutionary war.

Nell was fond of her brother, yet stood somewhat in awe of him. He was a reserved, rather taciturn man, and military life had increased a natural tendency to sternness of manner toward those under his authority which belied his real kindness of heart. He had never a harsh word or look for Nell, yet she dared not lavish upon him the demonstrations of affection her loving young heart longed to bestow; dared not offer him a caress; and he rarely gave them unasked to her or to any one else except the youngest of his children.

Clare was more demonstrative and really meant to be very kind, but was as dictatorial and domineering in her way as the major in his, and before many days had passed she began to treat the young girl as a child, checking, criticising, reproving, and directing with the most exasperating persistency, and as having an undoubted right.

This was very trying to Nell's sense of womanly dignity; and though by no means an ill-tempered little body, she sometimes found it difficult to possess her soul in patience.

"Where now?" asked Clare one morning, addressing her.

"To the woods with the children, after wild flowers and mosses," returned the young girl gaily.

She was standing in the doorway swinging a broad-brimmed hat by its strings, her beautiful uncovered hair glittering like burnished gold in the sunbeams sifting down upon it through the leaves of the overshadowing trees, as they stirred restlessly to and fro in the pleasant summer breeze.

She was in a happy mood, light-hearted and free from care as the birds warbling overhead, and had been humming snatches of song till interrupted by Clare's question.

"You have been here nearly a week now," pursued that lady in precisely the tone she would have used to one of her children, "don't you think it is time to begin to make yourself useful? Life was never meant for a perpetual holiday."

Nell's cheek crimsoned.

"What would you have me do? offer my services as assistant to Silvy the cook, Maria the nurse-maid, or Tig the stable boy?" she asked in a slightly sarcastic tone.

"Silvy is an excellent cook, and it might not be at all amiss for you to take some lessons of her," said Clare. "But there are other employments. The children need instruction, and you ought to be able to give it. Then there are spinning and sewing."

"I don't know anything about spinning."

"I'll teach you, in return for the lessons you give the children in spelling, reading and writing."

"Very well, we'll talk of it when I come back from my walk," Nell answered, tying on her hat.

She was willing enough to make herself useful, but Clare's manner was irritating.

Her annoyance was, however, soon forgotten in the prattle of the children, and the beauty of the woods.

They wandered about till weary, then sat down on a log to rest.

"Now if I only had a book," remarked Nell.

"Why didn't you bring one?" asked Bess.

"I don't mean a Sunday book, such as those on the shelves in the sitting-room," was the half scornful reply.

"Aunt Nell, there are some other kinds of books up in the garret."

"What kinds?"

"Oh, I don't know; stories, I believe, but not fit for me to read, mother says."

Nell rose eagerly. "Come, let us go back," she said, "I must see those books. But how came they there?"

Bess explained as they wended their homeward way, she walking soberly by her aunt's side, the boys racing on before, climbing and jumping over stumps and logs.

The major had formerly been in the mercantile business, and in the garret were stowed away boxes of goods—a medley of many odds and ends which had fallen to his share in the division of unsold stock made by himself and partner in the winding up of the joint concern.

The garret was the favorite resort of the children when kept within doors by stormy weather, and Bess had made herself well acquainted with the contents of the boxes, turning them over and over in search of "pretty things" with which to bedeck her dolls and herself.

The books proved to be novels—"Claremont" complete in several volumes and an odd volume of "Peregrine Pickle."

Nell seized upon them with delight and carried them off to her bed-room. Books were rare luxuries in those days, there were no newspapers or magazines published in that region of country, and as yet there was no regular mail.

Nell read and re-read "Claremont," devoting to its perusal every spare moment when she could steal away unobserved to the solitude of her room, and carrying a volume with her in her rambles with the children.

Then she took up "Peregrine Pickle," but with sore disappointment that the first volume was missing; so much so that she at length plucked up courage to ask her brother what had become of it; though quite fearful that he would disapprove of her reading it.

"Well," he said with a smile, "I suppose my former partner has it, and somebody is probably as anxious for this as you are for it. I'm sorry, for your sake, that we were so careless in dividing our stock."

"It is just as well," said Clare; "time can be more profitably employed than in the reading of such trash."

"I consider it a very innocent amusement," replied the major, shortly; not over-pleased with the remark, seeing that it called a flush of wounded feeling to Nellie's fair cheek. "I remember that I enjoyed reading it myself. If it were in my power to get it for you, Nell, you should have it."

She thanked him with a look, then rose and left the room.

"This is but a dull place for her after Philadelphia," he said to his wife. "I have no doubt she misses the weekly newspaper and many another source of entertainment which she enjoyed there, but must do without here."

"Probably; but she is no worse off in regard to those things than any of the rest of us," said Clare coolly.

"You forget, my dear, that you have me," returned the major with playful pleasantry. "And the children," he added, taking his youngest on his knee. "We're worth a good deal, aren't we, Ralph?"

The major so sincerely regretted his sister's disappointment that it was frequently in his thoughts during the next week, and he was seriously considering the feasibility of sending to Philadelphia or New York for a box of books such as she would find both entertaining and instructive, when the want was supplied in an unlooked for manner.

Dr. Clendenin and his friend Dale had pushed forward their office building as fast as possible and taken possession.

Making a call upon Kenneth one afternoon, the major found him unpacking books and arranging them upon shelves he had had put up along the wall.

"Books!" cried the major. "You have quite a library. All medical works?"

"Oh, no," said Kenneth. "Will you step up and look at them? My stock is not large, but valuable, to me at least, and I hope to add to it from time to time."

"Valuable! yes, indeed, to a lover of literature," remarked the major running his eye over the titles. "Shakespeare, Milton, Pope, Dryden, Gray, Goldsmith, Gibbon, Plutarch, Rollins, etc., etc. Poetry, history, fiction are well represented, and I see you have a goodly supply of religious works of the best class, also. Medical books, too, in plenty, but of their quality I am no judge."

"Yes, I shall not want for good companionship here in my somewhat rough bachelor quarters," Kenneth answered, surveying his treasures with an air of quiet content. "But I do not mean to be selfish, major, make yourself at home among my friends."

"Thank you," returned the major heartily, wishing that Nell had been included in the invitation; when Kenneth, as if in answer to his thoughts, said, "The ladies of your family, too, might find something here to enjoy."

Then the major told of Nell's disappointment, and half an hour later was on his way home, carrying her the "Vicar of Wakefield," and the assurance that Dr. Clendenin's entire library was at her service.

Nell's face sparkled with delight at the news, and the sight of the book.

"How kind in him!" she said. "I'll handle them with the greatest care."

For many months those books and the talks with their owner which naturally grew out of their perusal, were her greatest enjoyment; for as yet she had very few companions near her own age.

But as the town grew there was a corresponding increase in its young society and in the sources of amusement and entertainment open to her. She had many admirers and Kenneth stepped quietly aside, as one who had no desire to win the prize.

Mrs. Lamar did not understand it, no more did Dale, or Nell herself, though Kenneth had never comported himself as a lover and she had not consciously thought of him.

There were other things about Kenneth that puzzled Dale. He seemed to have some secret grief; there were times when his look and manner betokened inexpressible sadness, though he always shook it off and assumed an air of cheerfulness on being spoken to.

Dale's curiosity was piqued, and indeed he would have rejoiced to give all the sympathy and comfort that might be in his power; but there was a quiet, reserved dignity about Kenneth that forbade any intrusion into his private affairs.

He rarely spoke of himself or his own concerns; he sometimes mentioned his mother or sister, always with the greatest respect and affection, but his talk when they were alone together was of literature, of the interests of the community in which they lived, the state, the country, the acts of the government, and what was going on in foreign lands, or of Dale's own plans and prospects, in which Kenneth took the most generous, unselfish interest.

As a physician he was untiring in his efforts to relieve, patient and sympathizing, in manner gentle even to tenderness with the aged and with the little ones.

He soon came to have great influence in the community and it was always cast on the side of right. A man of pure morals and an earnest Christian, he was as ready and competent to pray with the sick and dying, and to point out to the troubled soul the paths of peace, as any minister could be.

These offices were performed as simply and easily as those others in which the healing of the body only was concerned.

Another thing Dale noticed, with the thought that it was decidedly odd, that Kenneth took evident pains to make acquaintance with all the Indians in the vicinity, and of every white man who had visited their tribes, whether near or far off, or had had much to do with them in any way: that he asked many questions, wording each with care to avoid arousing suspicion in regard to his motives, and that invariably his main object seemed to be to gain information in regard to whites living among the Indians.

Once Dale ventured to ask if he had ever had a friend or relative carried off by them; but the answer was a quiet "No," that while it left his curiosity entirely unsatisfied, gave no encouragement to further questioning.

They were in Dale's office; Kenneth had come across the connecting hall with some enquiry in regard to a piece of land for the disposal of which Dale was the agent, and a casual mention of the Indians had made a favorable opening for his query.

A moment's silence followed Kenneth's reply, then Zeb came rushing in.

"Somefin goin' on down to de rivah, sahs, Squire Smith goin' for to hol' court, dey say. Sent de constable to cotch the tief an' fotch him along double quick."

Dale sprang from his chair and caught up his hat.

"My services may be needed," he said, laughing, "though the squire doesn't make much account of law. Come on, doc; if the sentence should be flogging you may be needed too."

A man named Adam McMurdy, who cultivated some land on the station prairie below the town, had come in to Squire Smith with a complaint that during his absence the previous night, some one had stolen his horse collar; that he had examined the collars on the horses of the ploughmen at work this morning, recognized one of them as his, and claimed it of the horse's owner, Bill Slack.

That Slack had not only refused to restore it, insisting that it was his own, but used very abusive language toward him (McMurdy), and threatened to whip

33

him for accusing him of the theft.

On hearing the story the squire immediately despatched his constable in search of Slack, with strict orders to bring him and the collar at once into court.

The court had already convened under the trees by the river side, and the constable was hurrying toward it with the collar in one hand, the accused tightly grasped in the other, as Dr. Clendenin and Dale stepped into the street.

They followed quickly on the heels of the constable. Life had so little of the spice of variety then and there that even so trivial an affair created some stir and excitement.

Also the squire had an amusing method of dealing out justice that made a trial conducted by him somewhat entertaining to those who were spectators.

Nearly all the men of the town were there.

The prisoner being arraigned at the bar of justice, the squire turned to McMurdy and asked, "How can you prove this collar to be yours?"

"If the collar is mine," he replied, "Mr. Spear, who is present, can testify."

Mr. Spear, the Presbyterian minister, stepped forward.

"If the collar is McMurdy's," he said, "I wrote his name on it, on the inner side of the ear."

"Hand it to me," said the squire. Taking it from the constable and turning up the ear, "Yes, here's the name. No better proof could be given, and my sentence is——"

"If the court will excuse the interruption," began Dale, a mischievous twinkle in his eye; "let me say that according to law, as——"

"No, the court won't be interrupted," returned the squire, frowning him down. "All laws were intended for the purpose of enforcing justice. I know what's right and what's wrong as well as the man that made the laws; therefore stand in no need of laws to govern my actions.

"My sentence is that the prisoner be tied up forthwith to your buckeye and receive five lashes well laid on."

It was done and the crowd dispersed. The trial had occupied scarcely five minutes and every one was satisfied except the culprit.

CHAPTER VI.

"There's even-handed justice for ye, stranger?"

A stalwart backwoodsman in hunting garb of dressed skins was the speaker, and the words were addressed to Kenneth, near to whom he had stood during the brief trial of Bill Slack.

Dale had walked away in company with a brother lawyer, and Kenneth was turning from the unpleasant scene with a thought of pity for the weakness and wickedness of the unhappy criminal.

"Yes," he answered, "Squire Smith is a man of discriminating mind and judgment, very impartial in his decisions, and prompt in seeing them carried out. But what a happy world this might be if all were honest and upright!"

"That's true; but we've got to take it as it is.

"Got quite a town here," pursued the hunter, moving along by Kenneth's side as he walked up the street. "Last time I was round here in these parts, there wasn't so much as an Injun wigwam to be seen; nothin' but the thickest kind o' thick woods."

"I thought your face was quite new to me," said Kenneth. "May I ask where you are from?"

"You kin ask, sir, and I haven't the least objection in life to tellin'. I've been huntin' and trappin' all through this Northwestern Territory, along the Ohio and the Little Miami, and away up north by the great lakes; and even as far as the head waters of the Mississippi. And I come back with a lot of furs and skins. Sold 'em mostly in Detroit."

"Ah!" exclaimed Kenneth, with interest. "You must have had an adventurous life, and fallen in with many tribes of Indians."

"Humph! yes, young man; saw a good deal more of the ugly, treacherous varmints than I cared to. I hain't no love for 'em, and no more have they for me."

"You have had some encounters with them?"

"More'n a few, stranger. I've taken their scalps, and been mighty near losin' my own; have been in their clutches several times, run the gauntlet twice, and would have been burnt at the stake if I hadn't made my escape. However, I haven't any more to tell than any other man that's been huntin' and trappin' for ten or a dozen years."

Kenneth invited him into his office, set food and drink before him, and by dint of adroit questioning drew from him a good deal of information in regard to the various tribes among whom he had been.

"Have you ever met with any whites living with them?" he asked at length.

"Yes, occasionally. There's Simon Gerty; I saw him, and he's a worse savage than the redskins."

"But any others? Any women?"

"I met another man that was a prisoner, got away afterwards; and saw children at different times, girls and boys, both, that they'd stole away from their folks and adopted. And I saw a white woman a few weeks ago, that's been with 'em for years, and is married to an Injun; got a family of pappooses."

In reply to further questions he went on to describe the situation of the Indian village where he had seen this woman, but could give no description of her, except that she was very much tanned, dressed like the squaws, and had scarcely a more civilized look than they.

"I hope she's no kin o' yours?" he remarked, looking keenly at his questioner.

"No; I never had friend or relative taken by them," Kenneth answered, "though our family were pioneers, and several of them lost their lives by the Indians."

"Humph! then I reckon you hain't no love for 'em either?"

"Not so much as I ought to have, I'm afraid."

"How's that? Can't say as I see any call to love 'em at all."

"They are human creatures, and Christ died for them as well as for the white man. Doubtless they are equally dear to Him," Kenneth answered, with gentle gravity, fixing a kindly look upon his rough companion.

"Well, now, that may be," the man returned thoughtfully. "Fact is, I've never paid much attention to those things. Minister, are ye?"

"No; a doctor."

"Find much to do about here?"

"Not just now," Kenneth answered aloud, adding to himself, "Happily I can very well be spared for a few days."

Upon the departure of the backwoodsman from the office, Zeb was summoned and directed to saddle Romeo and have him at the door by the time his master should return from a round of visits among his town patients.

"I am going off on a hunt, Zeb, and shall want my gun, blanket and some provisions; get me some parched corn, bread and a little salt, and pack them in one end of my saddle-bags," was his final order.

"Yes, sah. You'll take me 'long, I s'pose?" interrogatively.

"No, Zeb, I'm going alone; I must leave you to take care of the office and see who calls. I shall be away for two or three days, or longer, and shall want to know when I return who have been wanting the doctor, that I may go to them at once."

"'Tain't jes' the very bestest time ob yeah for a hunt," muttered the boy, watching his master as he strode rapidly down the street. "Wondah what sort ob game Massa Doctah's gwine arter."

By noon of that day Kenneth had put several miles of hill and valley between him and Chillicothe.

He had gone, telling no one whither, or on what errand he was bound, and those who saw him leaving the town took it for granted that he had had a call to some sick person in the country.

His course was northwesterly, and for days he pressed on sturdily in that direction, taking an hour's rest at noon, subsisting on the provisions in his saddle-bags, and such small game as came in his way, at night kindling a fire to keep off the wild beasts, and sleeping on the ground, wrapped in his blanket, with his horse picketed near by.

His way lay through pathless forests and over trackless prairies where perhaps the foot of white man had never trod; the solitude was utter and the compass his only guide; not a human creature did he meet; but during the hours of darkness his ears were greeted with the cry of the panther and the howl of the wolf, now far in the distance, now close at hand.

But brave by nature and strong in faith, Kenneth committed himself to the care of Him who neither slumbers nor sleeps, and there in the wilderness rested as securely in the shadow of His wing, as though in the midst of civilization and compassed by walls and bulwarks.

But in regard to the success or failure of the object of his journey he was not equally calm and trustful. How is it that our faith is apt to be so weak in respect to our Father's loving control of those things which affect our happiness in this life, even when we trust to Him unhesitatingly the far greater interests of eternity? Ah how slow we are to believe that word, "We know that all things work together for good to them that love God."

Such was Kenneth's experience at this time, earnestly striving, yet with but partial success, to throw off the burden of care and anxiety that oppressed him, now urging his steed forward with almost feverish haste, himself half panting with eagerness and excitement, and anon bringing it to a walk, while with head drooping and heavy sighs bursting from his bosom he seemed half inclined to turn and retrace his steps.

This hesitation, this shirking from the result of his quest, grew upon him as he advanced; but at length, "What weakness is this?" he cried aloud. "God helping me, I will throw it off and meet this crisis with Christian courage. Should the very worst come, it cannot peril that which I have committed to His hand. Blessed be His holy name for that gracious word, 'I give unto them eternal life: and they shall never perish, neither shall any pluck them out of my hand.'"

With the last words his voice rang out triumphantly on the silent air. Romeo pricked up his ears at the sound and quickened his pace to a rapid canter.

"Right, my brave fellow!" said his master, patting his neck; "on now with spirit, we are not far from the end of this long jaunt."

They were crossing a prairie, a sea of waving grass bespangled with flowers of many and gorgeous hues, beyond which lay a thick wood.

It was afternoon of the third day and the sun near its setting, as they plunged into the wood. Here the light had already grown dim, and soon darkness compelled a halt.

Kenneth dismounted, secured his horse in the usual way, gathered dry branches and leaves, and with the aid of flint and steel had presently a bright fire blazing.

A couple of birds which he had shot during the day, hung at his saddle bow. These he quickly stripped of their feathers and prepared for cooking, which he managed by suspending them before the fire, each on the end of a pointed stick whose other end was thrust well into the ground.

A bit of corn-bread from his saddle-bags, and water from a running stream near by, filled up the complement of viands that formed his simple repast.

He had but just begun it when a slight sound like the crackling of a dry twig, near at hand, made him look up.

The flickering firelight showed him a tall dark form creeping stealthily toward him, another and much smaller one close at its heels.

He instinctively put out his hand for his gun, lying by his side, then drew it back as he perceived that the approaching strangers were a woman and child. The former was wrapped in an Indian blanket, and carried a papoose on her back.

"Me friend," she said in broken English. "Me hungry; papoose hungry," pointing to the little one trotting at her side.

"Sit down and I will feed you," Kenneth answered, making room for her near the fire.

She seated herself upon the roots of a tree, the child crouching at her feet, laid the babe, which was sleeping soundly, across her lap, and taking the food he offered shared it with the other child.

Something in her look and manner half startled Kenneth. He hastily threw a pine knot upon the fire. It burst into a bright blaze, throwing a strong light upon the face and figure of the stranger, and Kenneth's heart throbbed as he looked keenly at her, at first beating high with hope, then almost it stood still in disappointment and despair.

"She is too young," he sighed to himself; then speaking aloud, "You are a white woman," he said.

"Squaw," she answered, shaking her head.

"You have grown up among the Indians and perhaps forgotten your own parents," he remarked, gazing earnestly upon her, "but your blood is white; you have not an Indian feature; your eyes are blue, your hair is red and curly."

She evidently but half comprehended what he was saying, gave him no answer save an enquiring bewildered look.

He called to his aid the slight knowledge he had gained of the Indian tongue, and at length succeeded in making himself understood.

At first she utterly denied that she belonged to the white race, repeating her assertion that she was a squaw, but finally admitted that he was right, acknowledging that she had a faint recollection of being carried away by the Indians in her very early childhood.

He asked if she would not like to go back; at which she answered very emphatically that she would not, she was the squaw of a young Indian brave, and the mother of these his children; loved husband and children dearly, and would on no account leave them.

She had strayed from her camp that day and lost her way in the woods, but would find it again and go back to the Indian village, distant not more than two or three miles, when the moon was up.

He ceased his persuasions, but regarded her with interest, thinking how sad it was that the child of civilized, perhaps Christian, parents should have become so entirely savage.

He asked if she knew of any other white woman among the Indians.

She did not.

He talked to her of God and of Christ, telling the sweet story of the cross, but was doubtful how much of it she was able to grasp.

She listened with a half interested, half puzzled air, a gleam of intelligence occasionally lighting up her somewhat stolid face.

But the silvery rays of the moon came stealing through the branches overhead, and, rousing the older child, who had fallen asleep on the ground at her feet, the woman arose, shouldered her still slumbering babe, and wrapping her blanket about her, gave Kenneth a farewell nod, and with the little one trotting at her heels as before, quickly disappeared amid the deep shadows of the wood.

The object of Kenneth's journey had been accomplished; the tiny flame of hope enkindled by the information gleaned from the hunter had gone out in darkness, and naught remained for him but to take up again his burden of secret grief and care, and go on with life's duties with what courage and patience he might.

Weary with the day's travel, he yet made no movement toward preparation for sleep. Long hours he sat over his fire in an attitude of deep despondency, hands clasped about his knees, head bowed upon his breast; then kneeling upon the ground he poured out his soul in prayer.

"Lord, the cross is very heavy, the cup very bitter, yet how light and sweet compared with what thou didst bear and drink for me! Forgive, oh, forgive the sin of thy servant! Who am I that I dare complain or murmur? Lord, hear the cry of thy servant! strengthen him that he rest in the Lord and wait patiently for Him; though it be till his feet stand upon the other shore."

CHAPTER VII.

There was as yet no post-office in Chillicothe, and no regular mail. One came occasionally, brought by a man on horseback, and its arrival was always an event fraught with deep interest to most of the inhabitants.

This occurred during Kenneth's absence, for the first time in many weeks. There was a letter for him from Glen Forest, of which Dale took possession, paying the postage.

"When will your master be home?" he asked of Zeb, who was lounging before the office door.

"Dunno, sah; he didn't say, sah."

"Where did he go?"

"Dunno, sah; said he gwine on a hunt; wouldn't be home for two or three days."

"Two or three days! and he's been gone nearly a week," exclaimed Dale, stepping into his office. "Nearly a week," he went on thinking aloud, as he seated himself at his desk and laid the letter on it. "I wonder if we shouldn't turn out in a body and hunt for him; he may have met with an accident or— the treacherous savage!"

He frowned anxiously at the letter for a moment, then with sudden recollection turned from it to busy himself with his own correspondence. Several letters had come for him, and they must be read, digested, and answered. They absorbed his attention for some hours, then came the call to supper, and still Dr. Clendenin was missing.

Dale was growing very uneasy; Kenneth had become as a brother to him. "I must do something," he said to himself on his return to his office, taking up the letter again and gazing earnestly at it. "What can have become of him? Where can he have gone? If he isn't here within an hour, I shall go and consult the major.

"Ah!" he went on musingly, still gazing at the missive in his hand, "wouldn't he put spurs to his horse, if he knew this was here waiting for him, that is, if he's alive and free? How eager he always is for these letters, yet never opens one before anybody, never alludes to their contents.

"And they always seem to increase that mysterious trouble that he keeps so carefully to himself, and tries so hard to throw off, even when he and I are quite alone together."

But at that instant there was a sound of horse's hoofs in the street without, then a glad exclamation from Zeb, "Ki, massa doctah! thought the Injuns got you dis time, suah!" and, throwing down the letter, Dale rushed to the door to greet his friend.

Kenneth was in the act of dismounting, saying in a kindly tone to Zeb, as he gave him the reins, "No; here I am quite safe. Has there been any letter or message for me?"

"Yes; there was a mail to-day," Dale said, stepping forward and grasping his friend's hand with affectionate warmth. "A letter for you. Come in, I have it here. But," with a look of surprise and concern at the haggard face and drooping figure, "you are ill, my dear fellow!"

"Not at all, only somewhat weary and worn," Kenneth answered, with a faint smile that had neither mirth nor gladness in it. "But the letter, Godfrey! Is it from—"

"Glen Forest? Yes; the superscription, I noticed, is in the usual hand, post-mark the same as on the others. Here it is. Take this chair, and while you read I'll run over and tell Tiffin to see that they get a hot supper ready for you."

Putting the missive into Kenneth's eager, almost trembling, hand, he hurried away before the latter could utter a word of thanks.

For weeks Kenneth had been hungering for this letter, yet now that he held it in his hand he seemed to have need to gather up courage for its perusal. For a moment he sat with closed eyes, lips moving, though no sound came from them; then he broke the seal and read; at first eagerly, hastily, with bated breath, then, turning back to the beginning, with more care and deliberation, dwelling upon each sentence, while the shadow deepened on his brow, and again and again his broad breast heaved with a heavy sigh.

At length, at the sound of approaching footsteps, he rose and retreated to his own office, at the same time refolding the letter and putting it in his pocket.

Dale had delayed purposely on his errand, stopping to chat now with one, now with another, in the tavern, then in the street.

At his own door he was met by Major Lamar with the question, "Any news of the doctor yet?"

"Yes, he's just back; looking quite worn out, too."

"Ah! I'm sorry to hear that. I can see him, I suppose?"

"Oh, yes; walk right in. I left him—why, no, he isn't here! Sit down, major, and I'll hunt him up."

But here let us go back and tell of some occurrences of the previous day in the major's family.

Early in the afternoon Tig was standing with elbows on the fence and chin in hands, lazily watching the sports of the children as they vied with each other in the agility with which they could leap over stumps and logs, when Silvy's voice came sharply to his ears, "Tiglath Pileser, you lazy niggah, what you doin' dar? Didn't I tole you to clean de knives? Now Miss Nell is ready for to go ridin' and you just go right 'long and fotch de hosses roun' soon's eber you kin git dem saddled."

"Am I to go 'long, mother?" queried Tig, turning with alacrity to obey; for the horses were the pride of his heart, a ride with Miss Nell his greatest delight, especially when he was her sole companion and protector; and to-day he thought he should be, as he knew of no other escort.

His mother's reply confirmed his hopes. "Course you is; you always gets dat honor when dar ain't no gentleman 'bout."

Tig made haste to the stable, saddled and bridled Fairy and a pony belonging to the major with unaccustomed speed, and led them round to the front door, where Miss Nell was waiting in riding hat and habit.

"You were very quick this time, Tig," she said with an approving smile.

"Ki! Miss Nell," he answered, grinning from ear to ear, "no wondah; I'se in a big hurry, les' some dem gentlemen mout be comin' 'long 'fo' we gets off."

"What gentlemen, Tig?" she asked, laughing, as she stepped upon the horse-block and sprang lightly into the saddle.

"Oh, de doctah, or Mistah Dale, or some dem other gentlemen. 'Tain't often dis chile gets a chance to take care ob you, Miss Nell."

"Do you think you can take care of her, Tig?" asked Mrs. Lamar, coming to the door with a basket in her hand.

"Guess I kin, mistis, I ain't 'fraid no Injuns, nor b'ars, nor painters!" cried the boy, straightening himself with an air of injured dignity.

"Don't boast, Tig, till your courage has been put to the test," answered his mistress. "Here, take this basket and see if you can get it full of ripe mulberries for tea. Nell, I really don't feel quite sure that I ought to let you go without a better protector."

"Nonsense, Clare! I've done it before," returned the young girl, her color rising. "And the responsibility is not yours, I'm old enough to decide such matters for myself." And with that she touched Fairy lightly with the whip and cantered off, Tig following close in her rear. It was a lovely summer afternoon, the heat of the sun tempered by a cool, refreshing breeze. Fairy had scarcely been out of the stable for a day or two and was full of spirit, and Nell reveled in the delight of dashing away at almost headlong speed through the forest and over the prairies.

So enjoyable did she find the swift movement, with the sense of wild freedom it gave her, the beauty of the landscape, the sweet scent of the woods and wild flowers, that she went much farther than she had at first intended, or, indeed, was aware of.

Then coming back she stopped with Tig under a cluster of mulberry trees on the edge of a prairie, to fill the basket with fruit.

Not caring to stain her pretty fingers, she left the boy to fulfil the task alone, while she wandered to and fro, gathering flowers.

The sun was getting low as they remounted.

"We must hurry, Tig," Nell said, glancing uneasily toward the west. "I did not think we had been here so long."

They sped across the prairie and entered the wood that lay between it and the town. Here it was already dusk, and Nell urged Fairy on, her heart beating fast, while she glanced hither and thither, seeming to see an Indian, a bear, wolf, or panther behind every tree.

Suddenly she caught sight of a pair of fiery eyes glaring upon her from an overhanging branch, and the next instant, with a low, fierce growl, something leaped upon the back of her horse, a huge paw was laid on her shoulder, a hot breath fanned her cheek, while a wild shriek from Tig rang in her ears, and Fairy reared and snorted with fear.

Oh, the mortal terror that seized upon Nell, almost freezing the blood in her veins! Closing her eyes she leant forward and threw her arms about the neck of her pony, clinging to it in frantic terror for what seemed an age of suffering, but was in reality scarcely a moment.

A bullet, sped by an unerring hand, struck the panther in the eye, and it fell to the ground dead.

A horseman, hurrying from the direction of the town, put spurs to his steed at sound of the report of the gun, and almost before its echoes had died away, Nell was in her brother's arms.

He soothed and caressed her, she lying on his breast, sobbing and speechless with fright.

"Ugh! big fellow!" grunted a voice near at hand, and Nell, looking up, saw a tall Indian standing over the prostrate wild cat, the outline of whose form could be dimly discovered in the fading light.

"Wawillaway," said the major, holding out his hand to the chief, "you have saved my sister's life, and I can never fully return the obligation! Come with us to Chillicothe. My house shall be your home whenever you choose to make it so."

Wawillaway grasped the offered hand in one of his own, while with the other he held the bridle of Fairy, who was shying at the dead panther, and trembling and snorting with fear.

"Indian good gun," he said. "Indian go to white man's wigwam. Come, white squaw very much 'fraid."

"Yes, Nell, we had better go; for it grows darker every moment. Can you sit your horse now?"

"Yes," she whispered, "I must. But oh, Percy, keep close to me!"

"As close as I can. I will lead your horse," he answered, as he placed her in the saddle. "But where is Tig? I thought he was with you."

Tig had fled in overpowering terror, at the instant of the discharge of Wawillaway's gun, and on reaching home they found him there, telling an incoherent story of attacking Indians and wild cats, that filled the household with alarm.

Great was their relief at the sight of the major and his sister, though Nell was in a state of nervous prostration and excitement that made it necessary to put her at once to bed and watch by her during the night.

The next day she was but little better, and on her account her brother had been anxiously looking for Dr. Clendenin's return, and had now come in search of him.

Kenneth was not long in making his appearance. His manner was calm and quiet as usual, and shaking hands with the major, who expressed hearty satisfaction at seeing him again, he asked if the family were all well.

"All but Nell," was the reply, "and I don't know that there's much amiss with her. But I should like you to see her. She had a terrible fright yesterday, and doesn't seem to get over it."

Kenneth's look was anxious and inquiring.

"I supposed you had heard—" the major began, but Dale interrupted, "No, no, he hasn't had time to hear anything yet, or even to eat; and here comes Zeb with his supper. I told him to bring it over to your office, doctor."

"Thank you," said Kenneth, "but it can wait. I will go with you at once, major."

But the major would not hear of it.

"There is no hurry," he insisted. "Besides you ought to hear the story of her fright before seeing her, and may as well do so while breaking your fast."

Kenneth yielded, for he had not tasted food since early morning, and felt in sore need of it.

"What can we do for her?" asked the major in conclusion.

"Divert her mind from the subject as much as possible," returned the doctor. "Dosing is not what she needs."

"My opinion exactly," responded the major, "but I must crave your assistance in applying your prescription."

"Certainly, my dear sir, I will do my best."

It was a fair summer evening, the sun just touching the treetops, as Kenneth left his office in company with the major.

People were gathered about the doors of their dwellings or places of business, the day's work done for most of the men, though the busy housewives still plied the needle, sewing or knitting; thus exemplifying the truth of the old adage, "Man's work is from sun to sun, but a woman's work is never done."

Children played hide and seek among the trees, their glad voices ringing out upon the quiet air in merry shouts and silvery laughter; but many of them, on catching sight of Kenneth, left their sport to run and take him by the hand, welcoming him with eager delight, and asking him where he had been so long.

Older people, too, crowded about him with a like greeting and the same question.

He parried it as best he might, not feeling disposed to be communicative on the subject, returned the handshakings and kindly greetings, and asked after the health of each family represented.

"You have won all hearts here, Dr. Clendenin," the major remarked, when at length they had parted with the last of the friendly interrogators and were drawing near his own door.

"Oh, I believe it is so!" Kenneth answered, with a glad lighting up of his grave, almost sad face, "and I sometimes wonder how it has come about."

"Love begets love, and so it is with disinterested kindness also," the major answered.

Mrs. Lamar, coming to meet them, caught the last words. "Quite true," she assented, holding out a hand to Kenneth, "and I know of no one else in whose case we see such an exemplification of that fact as in Dr. Clendenin's. Doctor, running away so suddenly and mysteriously, you left many an anxious heart behind you."

She gave him a look of keen curiosity as she spoke. But he would not take the hint.

"My friends are very kind and I would not willingly cause them a moment's uneasiness," was all he said. It was gently spoken, but tone and manner did not invite a further display of inquisitiveness.

Nell, seated in the doorway in a listless attitude, rose suddenly on perceiving her brother's approach and who was with him, and, overcome by an unaccountable fit of shyness, hastily retreated into the house, her heart beating fast, the hot blood dyeing her cheek.

Then, much vexed with herself, she turned at the sound of Kenneth's voice saying "Good evening," and gave him her hand with a murmured "How do you do, doctor?"

He made her sit down, and drew up a chair for himself close to her side.

"Don't be afraid of me because I come in my professional capacity," he said in a playful tone, again taking her hand and laying a finger on her pulse.

"You needn't," she said with a little pout, and seeming half inclined to jerk the hand away. "I'm not sick. I wonder what nonsense Percy's been telling you."

They were alone; the major and his wife had wandered on up the street; the children were sporting outside with their mates.

"None at all," he answered with his grave smile, "only that your nerves have had a shock from which they do not find it easy to recover."

"I'm not sick, and I won't be called nervous! I just wish people would let me alone!" she cried angrily, bursting into tears in spite of herself. "Oh dear! oh dear!" she sobbed, "I don't know what has come over me! I never was so ill-tempered or so babyish before!"

"Don't be vexed with me for saying it is because you are not well," he answered soothingly. "Let the tears have their way and they will relieve you greatly."

She cried quite heartily for a moment, then wiping away her tears, said with half averted face, and in a tone of suppressed horror, shuddering as she spoke, "Oh, I cannot forget it!—those fiery eyes gleaming out at me in the darkness, the heavy paw on my shoulder, the hot breath on my cheek! I seem to see and feel them all the time, sleeping or waking. What shall I do?"

"Try to forget it," he said gently; "turn your thoughts as much as possible to other things, and the effect of your fright will gradually wear away."

"I cannot forget it," she answered sadly. "I shall always be afraid to go into the woods now, and my walks and rides were the greatest pleasures I had."

"Ah, well," he said, "the wild animals will soon be driven from our immediate neighborhood; and in the meantime you must go well protected. My dear Miss Nell," he added in lower, sweeter tones, "you know there is One whose protecting care is over us at all times and in all places. Try to trust in Him with a simple, childlike confidence; such faith will do more to give you calmness and peace than anything else can."

A moment's pause; then turning the conversation upon other themes, he exerted himself for her entertainment till the major and his wife came in, when he shortly took his leave; for there were other patients requiring his attention.

CHAPTER VIII.

"How did you find Miss Lamar, doctor? Anything much the matter?" asked Dale, sauntering into his friend's office that evening, shortly after the return of the latter from his round of visits among his patients.

Kenneth sat at his table, spatula in hand, making pills, a slight cloud of care on his brow.

His reply was not a direct answer to the question.

"Sit down, Godfrey," he said. "I've been thinking of calling in your aid in the management of this case."

"Mine?" laughed Dale.

"Yes, as consulting physician."

"You are certainly jesting, yet you look as grave as a judge on the bench."

"I wish," Kenneth said, pausing for an instant in his work and looking earnestly at Dale, "that there was more young society here, more to amuse and interest a young girl like Miss Lamar. Can't you help me to think of something new?"

"Boating parties," suggested Dale.

"That will do for one thing. Now what else?"

"Get up a class in botany. I'll join it. You are quite an enthusiast in that line and know a great deal more on the subject than any one else about here."

"Thank you. I should enjoy it if others would. Anything more?"

"No, I should say I'd done my share of thinking, and you must finish up the job yourself, you who are to pocket the fee," returned Dale laughing. "Now I'm off, prescribing a night's rest for you, to be taken at once; for you are looking wretchedly worn out."

Very weary Kenneth certainly was, yet the friendly counsel was not taken. His work finished, he pushed his implements aside, and sat long with his folded arms upon the table, his head resting on them; not sleeping, for now and again a heavy sigh, or a few low breathed words of prayer came from his lips.

"Oh Lord, for them, for them, I beseech thee, in the midst of wrath remember mercy! Let them rest under the shadow of thy wing, till these calamities be overpast."

Both Dale's suggestions in the line of amusements were promptly carried out, and with excellent effect upon the patient. She was fond of plants and flowers, and Kenneth proved a capital teacher. Mrs. Lamar and several others, both married and single, joined the class and they had many a pleasant ramble over hill and valley in search of specimens.

The major provided a boat for the rowing parties and frequently made one of them himself, taking special care of his young sister.

When he was not present Kenneth took his place in this particular, but not at all in a lover-like way; his manner was fraternal, "sometimes almost paternal," Nell thought, with an emotion of anger and pique at "being treated so like a child."

"It is because I was so silly as to cry before him! He thinks me a mere baby," she said to herself now and again, in extreme vexation.

She was apt to be frank in the expression, or rather exhibition of her feelings, and Kenneth was at times not a little puzzled to understand in what he had offended. He never blamed her, however, but, attributing her displeasure to some fault or awkwardness in himself, redoubled his kindly attention, and his efforts to give pleasant and healthful occupation to her thoughts.

With this in view he would often take a book from his pocket, when he found himself alone with her, read aloud some passage that he particularly admired, and draw her into conversation about it.

Also he tried to interest her in his patients, occasionally taking her with him where he knew her visits would be welcome, and engaging her to prepare dainties to tempt the sickly appetites, and clothing for such as were poor enough to need assistance of that kind.

His only thought, so far as she was concerned, was to comfort and relieve, and it did not occur to him that there might be danger in the cure, for her as for himself.

Yet there was; for how could the girl gain such an insight into the noble generosity and unselfishness of his character, without learning to love him? It was not only his unvarying kindness towards herself, his patient forbearance even in her most petulant and unreasonable moods, but also his sympathy for, and gentleness toward, even the very poorest and most uninteresting and ungrateful of those who invoked his aid as a physician, his anxiety and untiring efforts to relieve suffering, and his unselfish joy when those efforts were successful.

Also his deep, humble, unassuming piety, and earnest desire to lead to the Great Physician, that there might be healing of soul as well as body.

Her admiration and respect grew day by day, until he seemed to her an example of all that was good and great and lovable.

Dale, too, unwittingly helped on the mischief. He had some notion of courting pretty Nell himself, so did not care to interest her too much in Kenneth; but his thoughts were often full of the latter, the strange secret that seemed to darken his life; and remembering Kenneth's expressed desire to engage Nell's thoughts upon matters that would take them from herself and the unfortunate occurrence that had shaken her nerves, and calling to mind also that she had come from the same neighborhood with Kenneth and would be likely to know the family history of the Clendenins, he deemed it no harm to broach the subject one day when alone with her, and ask if she could guess what their friend's sorrow was.

"No," she said in surprise. "I never heard of anything that could cause him such grief. They are well-to-do people, living on a lovely place of their own; they are most highly respected too. I frequently heard them spoken of, always in the highest terms, and never heard of any trouble, except that Kenneth's twin brother was drowned ten or twelve years ago. But surely he could not be grieving so over that now!"

"No, it can't be that," Dale said musingly, "it is evidently a deeper sorrow than any such bereavement could bring, or at least a grief and burden of a different sort."

"Are you not mistaken? May it not be a mere fancy on your part?" queried

Nell. "Dr. Clendenin has always struck me as a very cheerful person."

"He is not one to obtrude his griefs upon others," observed Dale in reply. "He forces himself to be cheerful when in general society, and seldom allows even me, his intimate friend, to perceive that he has a burden to bear; but I have reason to believe that he sometimes passes half the night pacing his office instead of taking the rest he needs after his day's toil."

From that, he went on to speak of Kenneth's late mysterious, lonely journey, and to describe the state in which he had returned.

Nell's heart was deeply touched. "How noble he is!" was her mental exclamation. "But Mr. Dale should not have told me, it seems almost like betraying his friend's confidence. I suppose he does not look upon it in that light, but I am quite sure Dr. Clendenin would never have done so by him."

"Of course," said Dale, breaking the momentary silence, "this is between ourselves. I have never mentioned these things to any one else, and never shall."

"Nor shall I, Mr. Dale," she answered.

She did not, but from that time she watched Kenneth more closely than ever before, and that with the growing conviction that Dale was right.

It became with her an absorbingly interesting subject of thought; her heart was more and more filled with pity for Kenneth's silent suffering, and pity is akin to love.

But what could be the cause of this strange, silent anguish? Was it unrequited love? She spurned the thought. What! he of all men to sue in vain? It could not be! What woman's heart could withstand such a siege?

She did not care for him in that way—oh no, not she; but that was quite another thing, he had not sought her, and she was not one to give her heart unasked.

The town was growing, the country rapidly filling up with settlers, mostly of the better class, refined, intelligent, educated and pious people.

Also many gentlemen from the older states, principally Virginia and Kentucky, came to look at land with a view to purchasing, and these always sought out Major Lamar and were hospitably entertained by him.

Thus Nell saw a great deal of society. She enjoyed it too, was a general favorite, and formed some pleasant friendships with these guests of the family; but half unconsciously she made Dr. Clendenin her standard of manly perfection, and found all others short of it.

While, however, in some of these visitors possible lovers might have been found, many were men in middle life, old companions in arms of the major. And these were not the least welcome to Nell, for she loved to sit and listen to them and her brother as they fought their battles over again around the fire in the cool spring or autumn evenings; or on the green sward before the door in the warm summer nights.

Few of them came in winter, and at that season boating, botanizing and long rambles into the country had of course to be given up, yet that less favored time was not without its quiet pleasures.

There was much spinning, weaving, sewing and knitting going on, the ladies often carried their work to a neighbor's house and spent a sociable afternoon together, winding up with an early tea. There were also social gatherings about the fire in the evenings, enlivened by cheerful chat, the cracking of nuts, several varieties of which were found in great abundance in the woods around the village, and scraping turnip, these last being used as a substitute for apples, until time had been given for their cultivation.

Thus had the summer passed, the autumn too, and midwinter had come, finding Nell fully recovered from the effects of her fright, her fears dispelled, her nerves as steady as ever they had been.

It was the second winter since her arrival in Chillicothe, and she had become really attached to the place and its cheerful social life, so free from formality and restraint.

Calling at the major's one evening, Kenneth found her alone in the sitting-room, quietly knitting and thinking beside the fire.

The wide chimney was heaped high with hickory logs, and the dancing, flickering flames filled the whole room with a cheerful, ruddy light.

Nell's back was toward the door and she did not perceive his entrance, till he spoke close at her side, his pleasant "Good evening, I hope I do not intrude?" rousing her from her reverie.

"Oh no, doctor, you are always welcome in this house," she said, rising to give him her hand, and inviting him to be seated.

"I knocked," he said apologetically, "but no one seemed to hear, so I ventured to admit myself."

"Quite right," she answered, "though I do not understand how I happened to miss hearing your rap."

"Preoccupation," he remarked with a half absent smile, gazing thoughtfully into the fire as he spoke. "You are all quite well?"

"Quite, thank you. My brother and sister are out spending the evening; and the children are in bed."

He did not speak again for several minutes, but sat watching the flames as they leaped hither and thither, but evidently with thoughts far away; and Nell, furtively studying his countenance, read there the silent suffering Dale had spoken of.

Her woman's heart longed to speak a word of sympathy and comfort; but how should she when she knew not what his sorrow was?

"I am glad," he said at length, "to hear that you are all well. I am going away, and could not feel satisfied to do so without learning that my services were not needed here."

"Going away?" she echoed. "We had not heard of it."

"No; it is scarcely an hour since I knew it myself."

"Where? how long?" she asked impetuously, with changed countenance; then blushing to think she had betrayed so much curiosity and interest—"Excuse me, but Percy and Clare will be anxious to know; some of us may be taken sick."

"Yes; but we will hope not," he said, in the same calm, even tone he had used all along, his gaze still fixed upon the fire. "I go out into the wilderness, Miss Nell, and the time of my return is uncertain."

"Now! in this most inclement season of the year?" she exclaimed. "Isn't it running a great risk? would it not be wiser to put off your journey till spring opens?"

"I think not," he answered slowly; "life is uncertain, and what my hand finds to do must be done with my might."

"But if you lose your life?"

"It will be in the path of duty; and there are some things worth even that risk, Miss Nell."

He turned his head, and his eyes looked full into hers.

"They must be of very great importance," she answered, returning his look with one as calm and quiet as his own, though her pulses quickened at the thought that he was perhaps about to appeal to her for sympathy in his mysterious sorrow.

But he did not.

"Do you not agree in my opinion?" he asked.

"Yes; if I had been in Percy's place when the war broke out, I would have done just as he did—periled my life and all I had for my country," she said with kindling eyes.

He smiled approval, then rising, "Good-by, Miss Nell," he said, taking her hand in his, "I must away."

"What! to-night? and do you go alone?"

"I start to-night, Wawillaway is to be my guide a part of the way," he said; "after that my horse and gun will be my sole companions."

"Oh, can't you get Wawillaway to go with you all the way? I should feel—so much more hopeful for your safe return!" she exclaimed; then blushing deeply, as she saw his face light up with pleasure while he asked,

"Do you really care for that?" she hastily withdrew her hand, saying almost pettishly:

"Of course I care to have you here in case any of the family should be taken sick. You understand our constitution, and are the only doctor in the town that we have the least confidence in."

His countenance fell, and she thought she heard a faint sigh as he turned sadly away, and with a silent bow left the house.

She dropped into a chair, hid her face in her hands, and burst into a passion of tears.

"Oh, how could I! how could I! when he has been so good and kind to me!" she sobbed. "It's just as if I had struck him a cruel blow, and oh! I could beat myself for it!"

Her words, and yet more her tone and manner in speaking them, had indeed wounded Kenneth. He had brought a care-burdened and sorrowful heart into her presence, and he carried it away with an added pang.

He was himself surprised to find that she had power to wound him so deeply. He had not known before how dear the wilful little maiden had become to him; but this pain opened his eyes.

"Ah, what have I been doing?" he cried, half aloud, as he strode onward toward his office, "and why am I regretting that for which I should be unutterably thankful—that I alone suffer, because of my imprudence? I must, I will be grateful that she has not given her young heart to such a one as I. And yet—and yet—but ah me, this is hoping even against hope! Yet will I not utterly despair, for with God all things are possible."

CHAPTER IX.

Nell cried till she brought on a slight headache, then made that an excuse for going to bed before the return of her brother and his wife. She did not want to face the keen scrutiny of Clare, who would be sure to detect the traces of tears and to make a shrewd guess at their cause.

The girl had ample space for repentance, overpowering anxiety and dread in the next two or three weeks; and though she continued to hide her feelings from those about her, seeming quite as light hearted and gay as was her wont, the darkness of night was witness to many sighs and tears.

Dale came in on the evening after her late interview with Kenneth, and seizing an opportunity for a few words in private, asked her what she thought of Dr. Clendenin's starting off upon such a journey at that inclement season of the year.

"Why should I trouble myself about it?" Nell asked, with a slight toss of her pretty head. "I presume the doctor knows his own business."

"Possibly," returned Dale, with gravity, "but can you conjecture what that business is?"

"Can you?" she asked. "Perhaps some Indian chief is ill, or has a sick wife or child, and wishes to test the skill of the medicine man of the whites."

"Your ingenuity does you credit, Miss Lamar," remarked Dale, poking the fire, "but I am satisfied that Clendenin has gone on the same errand that took him before; and that is a chase after a white woman living among the Indians."

"A relative?" queried Nell, with interest.

"No; he told me he had never had relative or friend taken by them; and that is what makes his evident anxiety to find her so puzzling, so utterly inexplicable to me."

"Neither relative nor friend," pondered Nell, as she lay awake that night, listening to the sough of the wind around the house, the creaking of the trees in its fierce blast, the rattle of sleet against the outer wall, and the distant howl of the prairie wolf, and thinking of Kenneth without shelter from storm or wild beast, "if it were his lady love he would never say that."

This was not a heavy or lasting storm, the morning sun rose in a clear sky, and several days of mild bright weather followed.

After that it grew bitterly cold, and for many hours a fierce tempest raged, and the snow fell fast, the wind whirling it furiously about till all the roads and paths were blocked up with it, and in places the drifts were many feet deep.

Kenneth was on his homeward way when this storm began, with, as he had said, no companion save his horse and his gun.

On the latter was his principal reliance for a supply of food, though he had in his saddle-bags sufficient coarse corn-bread to keep him from actual starvation.

And well was it for him that he had come so provided, as the whirling, blinding snow rendered the pursuit of game impossible for the time being.

Indeed he soon found it impossible to continue his journey, and coming upon a comparatively sheltered spot, at the foot of a rock, he dismounted, secured his horse, and with some difficulty collecting a supply of dry branches, twigs, bark and leaves, finally succeeded in kindling a fire with his flint and steel and a bit of burnt rag which he carried for the purpose in his tinder box.

His mission had not been successful and his heart was heavy with disappointment, care and grief, as he sat there over his fire listening to the howling of the storm as the wind swept through the forest, the giant trees bending and creaking in the blast, groaning, breaking, falling before it and beneath the weight of snow and sleet.

At length there was a slight lull in the tempest, and Kenneth crept out from his hiding place and wandered hither and thither in search of fuel with which to replenish his fire.

Plunging into a snowdrift his foot caught in something and he had nearly fallen over—what? was it a log? Surely not! His heart gave a wild throb, he stooped, and hastily brushing away the snow found an Indian lad sleeping that fatal sleep, that, undisturbed, ends in death.

Exerting all his strength, Kenneth took the boy in his arms, shook him roughly, shouted in his ears, and catching up a handful of snow, rubbed it briskly over the half frozen face.

He dragged him to the shelter of the rock, but not close to the fire, and continuing his efforts at length succeeded in rousing him, and finally in restoring circulation and warmth to his benumbed limbs.

Then he took him to the fire, fed him and made him share his blanket, taking him in his arms that it might cover them both: and so with their feet to the fire, and each hugged close to the other's breast, they slept through the dark, stormy night.

The morning broke bright, clear and cold, icicles depending from the trees, snow heaped high on every side, too high to admit of moving more than a few paces from their sheltered nook. It was as if they were shut up in prison together.

The lad knew that Kenneth had saved his life and he was very grateful. He was a Shawnee, and had been travelling from one Indian village to another, but blinded by the whirling sleet and snow had lost his way and at last, overcome with fatigue, hunger and cold, had lain down to rest and sleep.

He could speak but a few words of English; but Kenneth had gained considerable knowledge of the Shawnee tongue since making acquaintance with Wawillaway, and was able to converse with the boy to their mutual satisfaction.

They remained together for some days, keeping up their fire and feeding on some wild turkeys Kenneth fortunately succeeded in shooting; then parting with kindly adieus and a hearty shake of the hand, each went his way, Kenneth toward Chillicothe, the Indian lad in a nearly opposite direction.

While yet two or three miles from the town, Kenneth saw in the distance a white man and an Indian coming toward him from thence.

They were Dale and Wawillaway, and as they drew near the former uttered a joyous shout.

"Hello, doc! so here you are, safe and sound! We feared you were buried in the snowdrifts and we'd have to dig you out."

There was a hearty shaking of hands as they met.

"Did you come out in search of me?" asked Kenneth.

"We did," said Dale, "and are rejoiced to have found you so easily. Your friends have been exceedingly anxious in regard to your safety, fearing you could hardly have weathered the heavy storm of last week. How did you manage it?"

Dale and the Indian had wheeled about, and all three were ploughing their way through the snow in the direction of the town.

Kenneth answered the question as they went, with a brief account of his sojourn at the foot of the rock in the wilderness.

He said nothing of the object of his journey or whether it had been successful; but Dale's furtive yet searching glances read a fresh and bitter disappointment in the weary, haggard face, and drooping figure.

"And my friends have been anxious for my safety, you say?" Kenneth said inquiringly, and with a wistful look in his large gray eyes, thinking of a fair young face that had sometimes brightened at his coming.

"Yes," said Dale, "it has been for the last three days the most exciting theme of conversation with old and young. It's a fine thing to be a doctor, if you care to have high and low, rich and poor interested in your safety."

It was the middle of the afternoon. Mrs. and Miss Lamar plied the needle within doors while the children were engaged in winter sports without—sledding, sliding and snow-balling.

Suddenly they came tearing in, half wild with joy.

"Oh, mother and Aunt Nell, he's come! he's come!"

"Who?" and Nell's heart beat fast and loud. It had been well nigh breaking with the thought of a manly form lying still and cold out in the wilderness with a snow wreath for its winding sheet, yet she had given no sign, but seemed the gayest of the gay.

"Dr. Clendenin!" cried the children in chorus; "he didn't get lost in the snow or killed by the Indians, we just saw him ride by with Mr. Dale and Wawillaway."

Nell stitched away, apparently quite indifferent to the news, but her heart sang for joy, and all the rest of the day her ear was strained to catch the sound of his approaching footsteps.

The major brought him home to tea and though Mrs. Lamar welcomed him most cordially, and the children hailed his coming with delight, Nell's manner was reserved and quiet almost to coldness.

He took the limp, passive hand in his for an instant, as he gave one wistful glance into the unmoved face, then with the thought, "She does not care for me, and it is well," yet sighing inwardly, turned away and entered into conversation with the major and his wife.

"We have been very anxious about you, doctor, ever since that fearful storm set in," Mrs. Lamar was saying. "We feared you must perish if exposed to it. Did you not suffer terribly?"

"Oh no," he answered cheerily, "I fared very well," and went on to tell of the sheltered rock he had found, and that he had a fire, a good blanket and something to eat.

"Tell us all about it," the children begged, clustering round him and climbing upon his knees.

"Were you all alone?" asked Bess; "I do think it must be dreadful to be alone in the woods at night."

"No, I was not quite alone through it all," he said, stroking her hair.

"Oh, I know! you mean God was with you?"

"Yes; but I had a human companion, too, an Indian boy, who told me his name was Little Horn."

Nell asked no question, but she was not the least interested of those who listened to the story of the finding of the lad and the way in which the two passed their time while storm-stayed together in the wood.

She was furtively studying Kenneth's face while he talked, sorrowfully taking note of its worn, thin look, and the deepening of the lines of grief and care that made it seem older than his years warranted. Its expression at this moment was cheerful, as were the tones of his voice, but she had no need to be told that for him "Disappointment still tracked the steps of hope."

CHAPTER X.

Time passed on; a year, two years rolled away. Settlers had continued to move into the town and adjacent country, and Kenneth's practice had grown with the growth of the population.

This was, perhaps, one reason why there had been a great falling off in the frequency of his visits, other than professional, at Major Lamar's.

It was, at all events, the excuse he gave, for that and for absenting himself from nearly all the pleasure parties and merry-makings of the young people. Genial and pleasant in his intercourse with old and young, he yet was no ladies' man; seldom paid attention to any of the fair sex, except in the way of his calling; he had no time, he said, but always found abundance of it to bestow upon the sick and suffering. His whole heart and soul were in his work.

Some silly people began to call him an old bachelor, though he was still under thirty, and far from old looking.

Dale also was still single, and the two were as intimate and warm friends as ever.

Godfrey was attentive to business, but, unlike Kenneth, indulged a great fondness for ladies' society, and generally made one in every little social gathering and pleasure excursion, whether it were a moonlight row on river or creek, a picnic, or expedition in search of nuts or wild fruits, a visit to a sugar camp in the spring, or a gallop on horseback at almost any time of year.

He was very intimate at Major Lamar's, and never happier than when he could secure Miss Nell as his special partner in whatever festivity was going on.

She liked Dale, for he was gallant, courteous, well-informed, and a good talker of either sense or nonsense, but she took care not to receive too much attention from him, or to encourage hopes she never meant should be realized.

She was developing into a noble, lovable woman, fair and comely in more than ordinary degree.

She had a fine form, a queenly carriage, and Kenneth's eyes often followed her with a wistful, longing look as she passed, either riding or walking. Yet he stood quietly aside and left it to his fellows to strive for the prize he coveted above all other earthly good.

That strange, mysterious burden still rested on him, but was borne with a brave, cheerful resignation that was heroic.

There were times of deep depression, of bitter anguish of soul, of fierce conflict with himself, when the trial seemed more than mortal strength could bear; but these came at rare intervals, and faith and grace ever triumphed in the end.

Letters from home, where he had not visited since emigrating to Chillicothe, and his lonely journeys into the wilderness, of which he had made several in the interval we have passed over, seemed alike ever to bring him increased sadness of heart. Yet few but Dale knew this, Kenneth's mastery over himself enabling him to put aside his private griefs and cares when in the company of others.

Thus his heart was ever at leisure from itself and ready to sympathize in the interests, the joys and sorrows or physical sufferings of those about him.

As a natural consequence, there were many who cherished for him a very warm friendship.

The Nashes had removed to a farm a mile or more from town. Mrs. Nash was still the same cheery, genial soul she had shown herself on the journey to Ohio, and Nell Lamar, who had ever been a favorite with the good dame, loved to visit at the farm-house, and would sometimes tarry there for a week or a fortnight, when conscious of not being needed at home.

She and Mrs. Barbour were both there one sultry summer day, Nell expecting to make a prolonged stay, the other lady intending to return home in the cool of the evening. She had now two children younger than Flora, and had brought all three with her.

"It was a great deal of trouble," she complained in the old whining, querulous tones; "children were such a care! always in the way and making no end of trouble if you took them along, and if you left them at home you were worried to death lest something should happen to them."

This was repeated again and again, with slight variations, till her unwilling listeners would fain have stopped their ears to the doleful ditty, and Mrs. Nash, quite out of patience, at length exclaimed:

"Nancy, I should think you'd be afraid to fret so about your worry with the children, lest Providence should take them away! I don't deny that it is a good deal of work and care to nurse and provide for them; but they're worth it; at least, mine are to me, and there's nothing worth having in this world that we don't have to pay for in one way or another. And for my part, I'm willing to pay for my pleasures and treasures," she added, clasping her babe fondly to her breast.

The Nash family also had increased in numbers. Tom and Billy, now grown great hearty boys, were with their father in the field, and two little girls sat on the doorstep, each with a rag doll in her arms, which the busy mother had found time to make and Miss Nell's skilful fingers had just finished dressing. The baby boy on the mother's knee was the last arrival, six months old and the pet, darling and the treasure of the entire household, from father down to two-year-old Sallie.

"You never did have any sympathy for me, Sarah," whimpered Mrs. Barbour, lifting the corner of her apron to her eyes. "I wasn't born with such spirits as you have, and it ain't my fault that I wasn't, and I don't believe I'm half as stout and strong as you are; and it's just the same with the children, yours are a great deal healthier than mine, and that makes it easier for you in more ways than one. You and Nash don't have the big doctor bills to pay that we have, and you don't get all worn out with nursing."

"Well, Nancy," returned her sister-in-law, "maybe I'm not as sympathizing as I should be; but there is such a thing as cultivating good spirits and a habit of looking at the bright side, trusting in the Lord and being content with what He sends, and that has a good deal to do with health. Perhaps if your children had a cheerier mother, they'd have better spirits and better health."

"There it is! I'm always blamed for my misfortunes; that's just the way Dr. Clendenin talks to me, and Barbour too, and I think it's a burning shame," sobbed the abused woman. "I'm sure I wish I was dead and done with it! and so I shall be one o' these days; and then perhaps you and Tom will wish you'd treated me a little better."

"My brother Tom's a very good husband to you," remarked Mrs. Nash coolly," and I don't feel conscience smitten for any abuse I've given you either. It's Bible doctrine I've been urging on you. It bids us over and over again to be content, to be free from care, casting it all on the Lord, to rejoice in the Lord, to be glad in Him, to rejoice always, to shout for joy.

"And well we may, knowing that life here is short, and no matter how many troubles we may have they'll soon be done with and we shall be forever with the Lord; that is, if we're His children."

Here Nell broke in upon the conversation with a sudden exclamation. "That cat is acting very strangely!" and as she spoke the animal came rushing in from an adjoining wood-shed and dashed wildly about, gnashing its teeth furiously, its tongue hanging out and dripping with froth.

Both women sprang up with a scream. "It's mad! it's mad! it's frothing at the mouth!" Mrs. Nash clutching her babe in a death like grasp and springing toward the other children to save them, Mrs. Barbour snatching her youngest from the floor, while Nell caught up the next in age and sat it on top of a high old fashioned bureau, at the same time calling to Flora, who was outside, to "Run, run! climb a tree or the fence!"

Then seizing a broom she rushed at the cat and drove it under the bed.

"Oh what'll we do? what'll we do?" shrieked Mrs. Barbour, the children screaming in chorus. "Why didn't you drive it out of doors?"

"You run out yourself and take the children with you. I did the best I could," returned Nell, her voice trembling with agitation. "You, too, Mrs. Nash, save the children and I'll fight the cat. Where's your clothes line? quick, quick! Oh, I see it!" and snatching it from the nail where it hung, in a trice she had it opened out and a noose made in one end.

Then tearing off beds and bed clothes, tumbling them unceremoniously upon the floor, she mounted the bedstead, lifted a slat or two from the head, underneath which the cat crouched, snarling, spitting, foaming, biting in a frightful manner.

Nell shuddered and shrank back with a cry of terror as the infuriated animal made a spring at her, but gathering up all her courage, let down the noose and swung it slowly to and fro.

A moment of terrified, almost despairing effort, followed by success, the noose was drawn tight, the rabid creature lay strangled and dead, and the brave young girl dropped in a dead faint upon the pile of bedding on the floor.

The others had obeyed her behest and fled from the house, leaving her to battle single-handed with the enraged animal, while they filled the air with cries for help.

A horseman came at a swift gallop up the road, putting spurs to his steed as the sounds of distress greeted his ear.

"What is it?" he asked, drawing rein in front of the house and springing from the saddle.

"Oh, Dr. Clendenin, there's a mad cat in the house, and Miss Nell's trying to kill it!" cried the two women and Flora in chorus; but the words were scarcely uttered before he had dashed in at the open door.

His heart leaped into his throat at sight of the prostrate form on the confused heap of bedding, the body of the strangled cat so near that the toe of her slipper touched it.

"Oh, my darling!" he exclaimed in low, moved tones as he sprang to her side.

Then in almost frantic haste he searched for the marks of the creature's teeth on her hands and arms. There were none.

He tore off her shoes and stockings, his hands trembling, his face pale with a terrible fear.

"Thank God!" he said at last, drawing a long breath of relief.

He knelt down, loosened her dress, laid her more comfortably, her head lower, doing all with exceeding tenderness, and turning to Mrs. Nash, who had ventured in after him, leaving her little ones in Mrs. Barbour's care, said huskily: "Some cold water! quick! quick! She has fainted."

"Oh, doctor, is she hurt?" asked the woman in tremulous tones, as she hastily handed him a gourd filled with water from the well bucket.

He did not answer for a moment. He was sprinkling the water upon the still, white face, his own nearly as colorless. Would she never revive? those sweet eyes never open again?

Ah, the lids began to quiver, a faint tinge of rose stole into the fair, softly rounded cheek.

"I hope not," he said with an effort. "It was the fright probably. A fan, please."

Mrs. Nash brought one and gave it in silence.

Nell's eyes opened wide, gazing full into his. The faint tinge on her cheek deepened instantly to crimson, and starting up in confusion, she hastily stammered out some incoherent words, and burst into tears.

"Lie still for a little, Nell," Kenneth said, gently forcing her back.

Never were tones more musical with tenderness, never had eyes spoken a plainer language, and the girl's heart thrilled with a new, ecstatic joy. For years her hard but determined task had been to school it to indifference; but now, now she might let it have its way. He, so noble, so good, would never deceive her, never wrong her.

"Oh, Nell, you are not hurt? not bitten?" exclaimed Mrs. Nash almost imploringly.

"Hurt? bitten?" repeated Nell, in a half bewildered way. Then as her eye fell upon the dead cat and the whole scene came back to her with a rush, "No, no," she said, shuddering and hiding her face in her hands; "it sprang at me, but missed and fell back on the floor, and at last it ran its head into the noose, jerked away and strangled, and"—laughing hysterically—"I don't know what happened after that."

Mrs. Nash knelt down by her side and began putting on her stockings and shoes.

"The doctor pulled them off to see if you'd got a bite there," she explained. "Oh I'll never cease to thank the Lord that you escaped! I feel as if I'd been a mean coward to run off and leave you to fight the mad thing all alone. But it wasn't myself I was thinking of, but the children."

"I know it," murmured Nell, "and I told you to go."

Kenneth had moved away to the farther side of the room. His face, which was turned from them, was full of remorseful anguish. Alas! what had he done, won this dear heart that he dared not claim as his own? Oh, he had thought the grief, the pain, the loss all his own! but it was not so, she too must suffer and he could not save her from it, though for that he would freely lay down his life.

"Is it dead, have you killed it?" queried Mrs. Barbour timorously peering in at the open door.

"Yes," answered Mrs. Nash shortly, and stepping in, followed by the frightened but curious children, Mrs. Barbour dropped into a chair.

"Oh!" she cried, "it's just awful! I'm nearly dead, was most scared out o' my wits, and shan't get over it for a month!"

Then catching sight of the dead cat, "Ugh! the horrid thing! why don't you take it away, some of you? I feel ready to faint at the very sight of it. Doctor, you'll have to do something for me."

"There is nothing I can do for you, Mrs. Barbour," he said coldly. "You must help yourself, by determined self-control. After leaving Miss Lamar to face the living, furious animal alone, you may well bear the sight of it lying, dead, with all the rest of us here to share the danger, if there be any."

"There it is, just as usual," she sobbed, "I'm always blamed no matter what happens. I had my children to think of."

"Never mind," said Nell, sitting up; "it's all over and nobody hurt."

"Nobody hurt!" was the indignant rejoinder. "Maybe you ain't, but I am: I've got an awful headache with the fright, and feel as if I should just die this minute."

A loud hallo from the road without stopped the torrent of words for a space.

"Is Dr. Clendenin here?" shouted a man on horseback, reining in at the gate.

Kenneth stepped quickly to the door.

"What is it?" he asked.

"You're wanted in the greatest kind of a hurry, doctor; over there in the edge o' the woods, where they're felling trees, man crushed; not killed, but bad hurt—very."

Kenneth was in the saddle before the sentence was finished, and the two galloped rapidly away.

"People oughtn't to be so careless," commented Mrs. Barbour, as they all gathered about the door watching the horsemen till they disappeared in a cloud of dust. "Why don't they get out of the way when the tree's going to fall? How quick the doctor went off. He's ready enough to help a man, but wouldn't do anything for poor me!"

"He told you what to do for yourself," said her sister-in-law, a mixture of weariness and contempt in her tones.

"As if I could! There never was anybody that got so little sympathy as I do," she fretted, turning from the door and dropping into her chair again. "But I'll have another doctor. I'll send for Dr. Buell."

"Dr. Walter Buell; 'Dr. Water Gruel' they call him," laughed Flora, "because he won't let 'em have anything hardly to eat. He'll starve you, mother."

"Be quiet, Flora," was the angry rejoinder. "I'm not going to have you laughing at me. You ought to be ashamed of yourself, poor unfortunate creature that I am, and your mother too!

"To think that I should have happened here to-day of all days, when I don't stir from home once in a month! But that cat wouldn't have gone mad if I hadn't been here."

But her complaining fell upon inattentive ears. Mrs. Nash was busy ridding the house of the dead carcass and setting things in order, and Nell's thoughts were full of the new joy that had come to her, and of questionings as to when and where she should again meet him who had possessed himself of her heart's best affection. Would he return that evening? Verily she believed he would.

But no, he did not; and when she went home the following day, Clare greeted her with the news that Dr. Clendenin had gone East; he had been suddenly summoned to Glen Forest by a letter; some one was very ill, and as a pirogue was just leaving for Cincinnati, he had taken passage and gone down the river in it.

Nell's cheek paled a trifle and her eyes looked with mute questioning into those of her sister.

"He left good-by for you," said Clare.

And that was all—all! The girl's heart seemed to stand still with pain. What could it mean?

CHAPTER XI.

The tops of the Alleghanies loomed up darkly against the eastern sky as it flushed with the rosy hues of a new day; the delicate shades of rose pink and pale blue changed to crimson and gold, and anon the increasing light aroused old Vashti from the heavy slumber into which she had fallen some hours before.

She started up, rubbed her eyes, and glancing from the window, muttered, "'Bout time dis chile was wakin' up and lookin' after tings. Sun's jus' gwine to peep 'bove dose mountings. Wonder how ole marster is 'bout dis time?"

She had thrown herself down upon her bed without undressing. Finishing her remarks with something between a sigh and a groan, she slowly gathered herself up and went stumbling from the room, hardly more than half awake yet, having lost much sleep in the last two or three weeks.

But reaching the upper chamber where her mistress had kept solitary vigil through the night, she entered very quietly, extinguished the candle, drew aside the window curtains, letting in the morning light and air, then stepping to the foot of the bed, stood silently gazing upon its occupant, the big tears stealing down her sable cheeks.

The form lying there was attenuated, the face thin, haggard, deathly; the sunken eyes were closed, and the breath came fitfully from the ghastly, parted lips.

Mrs. Clendenin seemed unconscious of Vashti's entrance; her eyes were riveted upon that pallid face, the cold hand was clasped in hers, and her heart was sending up agonizing petitions.

They were granted; he stirred slightly, opened his eyes, looking full into hers with a clear, steady, loving gaze, while the cold fingers feebly responded to her tender clasp.

"My wife, my darling!" he whispered, and she bent eagerly to catch the low breathed words. "God bless you for your faithful love! I'm going—going home to be with Christ; and it's all peace—peace and light."

The eyelids drooped, the fingers fell away from her grasp, the breast heaved with one long-drawn sigh, and all was still.

She fell upon her knees at his side, still with his hand in hers, her face radiant with unutterable joy.

"Oh, thank God! thank God!" she cried. "My darling, my darling! at rest, at rest, and safe at last!"

"Dat he is, dat he is, bress de Lord!" ejaculated the old negress.

For many minutes the new-made widow knelt there gazing fixedly into the calm face of the dead; then rising she gently closed the eyes and composed the limbs of him who had been to her nearer and dearer than aught else on earth, not a tear dimming her eyes, but a light shining in them as in those of one on whom had been suddenly bestowed an intensely longed for and almost despaired of boon.

"No strange hands shall busy themselves about thee, my beloved," she murmured, "mine, only mine shall make you ready for your quiet, peaceful sleep, 'where the wicked cease from troubling and the weary are at rest.'"

Vashti looked on in wonder and surprise, silently giving such assistance as she might, without waiting for orders, bringing needed articles and making the room neat.

At length, the task completed, Vashti went down to her kitchen, but Mrs. Clendenin lingered still by the side of the beloved clay, gazing with hungry eyes upon the face that must soon be hidden from the sight beneath the clods of the valley.

A light step crossed the threshold and a slight girlish figure stood beside her. In an instant Marian's arms were round her mother's neck, her kisses and tears warm upon her cheek.

"Precious, precious mother! Oh, don't let your heart break!"

"No, darling!" she whispered, clasping the weeping girl in her arms; "it is full of joy and thankfulness for him, for he has laid down his heavy, heavy cross and received his crown, the crown of righteousness bought for him with the precious blood of Christ.

"Ah, my Angus, how blest, how blest art thou!" she cried, bending over the still form and pressing her lips to the cold brow.

They lingered over him for some minutes, the girl weeping and sobbing, the mother calm and placid; then together they went down-stairs and out into the shrubbery.

There were no curious eyes to watch them as they paced slowly up and down the walks, for the nearest neighbor was a full half mile away, on the farther side of the western hills.

The mother talked low and soothingly to her weeping child, speaking of the glories and bliss of heaven, and of the loving care of the Lord for His saints on earth.

"Mother, mother!" cried the girl, "I feared your heart would break; but instead you seem full of joy!"

"Ah, dear one, life has been a terror to him for many years; and shall I mourn that he has at last gotten the victory? That he is gone home to his Father's house, where there is perfect safety and fulness of joy forever more?"

"Mother," whispered the girl with a shudder, "what did he fear? Why have I never been told?"

"Dear child, do not ask! Oh, never ask that!" cried the mother in a startled tone, and turning a look of anguish upon her questioner.

The girl's face reflected it.

"Oh, why is it that I am not to be trusted?" she sobbed, almost wringing her hands in her bitter grief and distress; "why should I be deemed unworthy of confidence, even by my own mother? Would I—". But sobs choked her utterance.

"My darling, my precious child, it is not that, not that," faltered the mother, clasping her in her arms with tender caresses. "But let us speak of this no more, let us forget his sufferings, as he has forgotten them now. It is what he would have wished. Shall we not try, daughter?"

"Yes, yes, my poor, dear mother, I will for your sake," sobbed the girl. "Ah, if Kenneth were only here! When will he come?"

"I do not know," said Mrs. Clendenin, sighing slightly. "It is now several weeks since my letter went, but there are often delays, and it may not have reached him yet. I think he would start at once on receiving it, but the journey is long and tedious at the best, and there may be unlooked-for detentions consuming much time, so that we can hardly expect him for many days to come."

The letter she spoke of was the same that had caused Kenneth's sudden departure from Chillicothe only the previous day. A month later he reached Glen Forest.

Mrs. Clendenin, seated at the open window, saw him alight at the gate, and hastened out to meet him. There was a silent embrace, then an earnest scanning by each of the other's face, noting the changes wrought by time and the wear and tear of life.

Kenneth's eyes grew misty, for the dear face before him had aged very much since last he had looked upon it, and the dark hair had turned to silvery white.

She was regarding him with wistful tenderness. "Yes," she said, answering his unspoken thought in a half playful tone, yet smiling through gathering tears, "I am growing old, and you, my dear boy, are not quite so young as you were. Come in. Ah, it is good to have you here, at home again! You have heard, of course—"

"Yes, since arriving in the neighborhood, but I knew from your letter that all would be over long before I could reach you. It was a sore trial to think that even the small comfort and support of your boy's presence must be denied you."

"It was all right," she answered in low, sweet tones. "He was with me who has promised never to leave nor forsake those who trust in Him."

"I knew He would be, and that was my consolation," Kenneth returned in moved tones.

Then glancing about as they entered the house, "Where is Marian?" he asked.

The mother explained that she had gone on an errand to a neighbor's half a mile away, and would not probably be back for an hour or more.

Vashti was summoned, bade her young master welcome with tears of joy, and hastened to set refreshments before him.

But he did them scant justice. His heart was too full of contending emotions to allow of much appetite, though he had not tasted food for some hours.

Gazing upon the loved face he had not seen for years, listening to the well remembered tones of the dear voice that had been wont to soothe his childish griefs, to give the well earned meed of praise which was the highly prized reward of his boyish efforts to be and do all that was good, noble, and manly, he forgot to eat.

She had much to tell of all that had occurred in the family during his absence, but her principal theme was the sickness and death of her husband.

Kenneth listened with intense, sorrowful interest to her description of that last scene, and seemed to feel no surprise when she told of the joy and thankfulness with which she had parted from her heart's best treasure.

He had risen from the table and drawn a chair to her side. "Dear mother," he said in faltering accents, taking her hand in his, "what a life yours has been! What but the grace of God could have sustained you through it all!"

"Blessed be His holy name, it has always been sufficient for me!" she answered. "'Hitherto hath the Lord helped me,' and I am persuaded that He will help me to the end."

A moment's silence, which Kenneth was the first to break.

"Tell me of Marian, mother," he said. "She has grown? I shall doubtless find her greatly changed."

"More perhaps than you think; the dear child has shot up into a tall, graceful, blooming girl, very sweet and lovable, in her mother's eyes at least, with a beauty that oftentimes makes me tremble for her future. Kenneth, Kenneth, the child will surely be sought in marriage, and what shall we do?"

With the last words her voice took on a tone of keen distress and the eyes she lifted to his were full of anguish.

"It must not, must not be!" he answered hurriedly, his brow contracting in a spasm of pain. "Mother, keep her secluded here with you; let her have no communication with the other sex, old or young."

"Alas, I fear the utmost vigilance will not prevent it!" she cried, heaving a deep drawn sigh. "Oh, my darling, my darling, your mother's heart bleeds for you!"

"Dear mother," he said, again taking her hand and speaking low and tremulously, "can you not cast this burden also upon the Lord?"

"Sometimes," she said; "ah, I should die if I could not! But, Kenneth, what shall we do? Would it not be better to tell her all—to warn her in time?"

"Never!" he cried with energy, "it were too fearful a risk; it might cause the very calamity we so dread."

"Too true! too true!" she sighed, clasping her hands in her lap and closing her eyes, while her very lips grew white.

He bent over her, taking her cold hands in his, repeating low and tenderly the precious promise, "'When thou passest through the waters, I will be with thee: and through the rivers, they shall not overflow thee: when thou walkest through the fire, thou shalt not be burned; neither shall the flame kindle upon thee.'"

"Yes, yes, sweet words, sweet words!" she murmured. "Lord, increase my faith! But, Kenneth," opening her eyes and looking up earnestly, entreatingly, as it seemed, into his face, "you are sure, quite sure that this is the best, wisest, kindest course? not risking a greater danger than the one avoided?"

He answered her question with another.

"If we take the other course shall we not be running into a certain danger in the effort to avoid one that may never threaten us?"

"Perhaps. But ah, what a hard choice we must sometimes make! Yet He knows and will never send one unneeded pang; will cause all things to work together for good to them that love Him. May He in His tender mercy forgive my unbelieving fears!"

Oh, how Kenneth's heart yearned over her, as he gazed into the dear, patient, sorrowful face, how he felt that he would willingly give the best years of his life to remove every thorn from her path! And yet—and yet, was not the Love which permitted them to remain, infinitely greater than his?

Silence again fell between them for a short space. Then looking tenderly upon him she asked:

"But what of your quest, Kenneth?"

He shook his head sorrowfully. "Nothing yet, absolutely nothing. Hopes raised now and again but to be utterly disappointed."

"My poor boy," she sighed, "yours is a heavy cross! but if borne with steadfast patience your crown of righteousness will be all the brighter; for our light affliction, which is but for a moment, worketh for us a far more exceeding and eternal weight of glory."

He looked at her with glistening eyes. "Yes," he said, with a slight huskiness in his voice, "and even in this life it may be lightened."

"I fear not," she answered in gentle, pitying tones. "So many years have now passed there seems little hope that she yet lives, and even if she does, if she should be found, there may be nothing gained."

"I know, I know," he returned with emotion, and rising to pace the room, "and yet there are times when hope is still strong within me."

At that instant a slight, graceful, girlish figure came swiftly into the room, and with a glad cry, "Kenneth, Kenneth, you have come at last!" Marian threw herself into the manly arms joyfully opened to receive her.

She clung about his neck weeping from very excess of happiness. "Oh, I have wanted you so much, so much!" she cried. "I thought you would never come! I wish you would never go away again."

He folded her close to his heart with tenderest caresses, then held her off that he might gaze into her blooming face, drinking in its loveliness with feelings of mingled joy and anguish.

It was and yet was not the little pet sister he had left when he went away; she stood on the verge of womanhood now, innocent and fair, with a sweet blending of childish and womanly graces.

Ah, must that deadly curse fall on her? He shuddered at the thought, and almost groaned aloud.

She saw the pain in his face, and redoubling her caresses, "What is it, Kenneth?" she asked; "my poor Kenneth, you are not happy. Has some one been unkind to you? Ah, I know," she added quickly, in a lower tone, "it is for poor, dear father you are grieving; but you know he is so, so happy now, while here he was always sad and suffering."

He sat down and drew her to the old seat upon his knee. The mother had left the room and they were quite alone for the moment.

"How long since you sat here last!" he said, "and how glad I am to have you in the old place again."

And truly he was, yet peradventure not entirely for her own sake. To hold this sweet young creature close, to pet and caress her to his heart's content, was it not some slight relief to the longing desire to embrace that other one who was dearer still?

Had his thoughts some magnetic influence upon Marian's that led her, the next instant, to look up in his face and ask for news of "that pretty Miss Lamar"?

"What do you know of her, little one?" he asked gently smoothing the shining hair, conscious of the tell-tale blood mounting to his forehead, but avoiding the curious gaze of the soft, bright eyes.

"I saw her in church the Sunday before you left, and thought her very sweet and pretty. And do you know, Kenneth," giving him a hug and an arch, bewitching smile, "it's all my own notion and I never told anybody before, but I've had a sort of presentiment that some day you would make her my sister. Ah, I've always wanted a sister so much! But oh, Kenneth, I didn't mean to pain you!" she cried, noting the expression of his face. "Please forgive me and I'll never mention it again."

"Don't, darling!" he said hoarsely. "Marriage is not for me. I can not tell you why," as he read the question in her eyes; "but," with a strange, forced smile, "I want my little sister always to lay her plans to devote herself to the dear mother while she lives, and if it should please God to take her away first, then to come to be the light and joy of her bachelor brother's home."

She half withdrew herself from his arms, her features working with contending emotions.

"What is it, little sister? Do you not love me? do you not want to share my home?" he asked soothingly.

"Yes, yes, you know I love you; you know I'll be glad to be always near you," she cried, flinging her arms about his neck; then hiding her face on his breast in a burst of passionate weeping, "But why do you and mother have secrets from me, family secrets, as if I were not worthy to be trusted?"

"Ah, my little sister, be content with your ignorance!" he said in moved tones, drawing her closer to him. "Can you doubt that we love you well enough to tell you all if it would add to your happiness?"

"But I want to know," she sobbed. "If there is trouble or sorrow I ought to bear my share. Do you think I could be so selfish as not to prefer to do it?"

"No, dear sister, I believe you bear a very unselfish love to your mother and brother, and, therefore, I am sure you will not distress them by refusing to trust to their judgment of what is best in regard to those things. Believe me, the knowledge you crave could bring you nothing but grief and anguish. It is all it has brought me. The day may come when you must be told, but do not try to hasten it. I can be here but a short time to arrange matters for mother and you, and while I stay let us try to be happy."

"Oh yes, yes!" she cried, clinging to him and weeping afresh. "Kenneth, Kenneth, why can't we have you always? I'll try to be content not to know anything; but just tell me one thing: Why do you search for a white woman among the Indians? I've learned from some of your letters about your long journeys in the wilderness, why are you so anxious to find her, so grieved when you fail? Surely I may know that, may I not?"

He considered a moment. "Yes," he sighed, "if you insist upon it I will tell you, though I know you will regret having asked, for the knowledge can bring you only sorrow. Shall I tell you?"

She gave an eager assent; but at that moment the mother returned to the room, and he whispered in Marian's ear that they would defer it until another time.

Some days later, a fitting opportunity presenting itself, she hastened to claim the fulfilment of his promise; but when he answered the question she burst into bitter weeping, crying as she clung about his neck, "Oh, Kenneth, Kenneth, why did you tell me, why did I ask? I wish I had not!" and he had much ado to comfort her.

CHAPTER XII.

The episode of the mad cat had given a severer shock to Nell's nerves than she was at all aware of at the time. The joy and the new-born hope that sprang to life within her in meeting that look of ineffable tenderness in Kenneth's eyes buoyed her up at first, but the news of his sudden departure, leaving neither note nor message for her, was a heavy blow, and brought on the natural reaction from the excitement of her struggle with the rabid animal.

For days her prostration was so great that she could do little but lie on her bed, and when alone often bemoaned herself with bitter sighing and weeping, although in Clare's presence she constantly assumed a cheerfulness she was far from feeling, yet that deceived even that keen-eyed individual.

At length her woman's pride helped her to rally her failing energies. She rose from her bed and went about her accustomed duties and pleasures with a determined will to seem her old self; hiding her well-nigh breaking heart behind a smiling countenance.

She learned from Dale that Kenneth's summons had been to the dying bed of his father, and that though he could not hope to traverse the intervening distance in season to witness the closing scene, he yet felt it imperative upon him to make all haste to give his widowed mother the comfort and support of his presence at the earliest possible moment.

"Ah, he had no time to write before leaving!" thought Nell; and hope whispered that he would perhaps do so from some station on the way, or from Glen Forest immediately on his arrival there.

She waited and watched, now hopefully, now with feverish longing, and anon in almost utter despair, as weeks dragged on their weary round, bringing no word from him, no evidence that she was not completely forgotten.

She grew absent-minded, and would catch herself sitting in listless attitude, silent and abstracted, while others chatted and laughed gaily at her side; or moving about with a languor that attracted Clare's attention, and brought upon her vexatious questions and remarks.

"What was the matter? She was certainly not well, for it was not like her to be so dull. She was losing her appetite too. She should take more out-door exercise. Why did she stay in the house so constantly of late? Where would she like to go? What was there that she could eat? Really she must try to keep up, if only till Dr. Clendenin returned, for he was the only physician in the place in whom the major felt any confidence."

Nell answered, not always in the most amiable of tones, that she was perfectly well and did not know why people should persist in believing otherwise. She was in no haste for Dr. Clendenin's return, and hoped he would stay six months or a year if he felt inclined to do so.

Still, spite of her protestations, she continued to grow pale and thin, ate less and less, and at last was forced to take to her bed with a low, nervous fever.

It was now far on in October, but Kenneth had not returned, and Dr. Buell was called in by the major, much against the patient's will.

"I don't want him or his medicines," she said. "I'm not sick."

"Why, what nonsense!" said Clare; "why do you lie here if you are not ill?"

"Because I'm tired, tired!" sighed the girl, turning away her head. "I only need rest, and all I want is to be let alone."

"The fact is, you don't know what ails you or what you need; and you're not going to be let alone," remarked Clare, with the assumption of authority always so distasteful to her young sister-in-law.

The words, but especially the tone, brought the color to Nell's cheeks and an indignant light into her eyes.

She opened her lips to reply, but Clare had already left the room, and the next moment re-entered it, bringing Dr. Buell with her.

His remedies had no good effect. Nell drooped more and more. Major Lamar became extremely anxious and uneasy.

"I wish," he said to his wife again and again, "that Clendenin would come home. It is very unfortunate that he should be absent just now."

"Doesn't any body hear from him?" she asked, hearing the remark for perhaps the fiftieth time.

"I don't know. I'll go and ask Dale," he answered, taking up his hat and hurrying from the house.

He had not gone a hundred yards when he espied—welcome sight!—Kenneth himself walking briskly toward him.

They met with a hearty handshaking and words of cordial greeting.

"Come at last," said the major, "and just when you are sorely needed. I believe in my heart Nell's in a dangerous condition, and Buell's doing her no good. I must take you home with me at once."

"But—"

"No but about it," interrupted the major bluntly. "He was called in with the distinct understanding that the moment you returned the case would be put into your hands, you being the family physician."

Kenneth made no further objection, but went with his friend, asking a few hurried questions by the way in regard to the nature of the malady and the length of time that had elapsed since the patient's seizure.

Nell, lying alone on her bed, heard the well-known step and voice in the outer room. What a thrill the sounds sent through her whole frame, making every nerve tingle with excitement!

She half started up, flushing and trembling, then as step and voice drew nearer, fell back again, closed her eyes and hid her face in the bed clothes.

"Nell, are you ready to see the doctor?" asked Clare's voice at the door.

"No, nor ever shall be. I should think that you and Percy might be convinced by this time that his visits are doing me no good," answered the girl, in a tone of irritation.

"But it's Dr. Clendenin this time, Nell," said Clare, stepping aside and motioning him to enter.

Nell lay perfectly still and kept her eyes shut, resolved to appear utterly indifferent to his presence; but hers was a tell-tale face to him; he saw that the indifference was only assumed, yet failed to fully understand it.

"I grieve to find you so ill," he said, bending over her, and speaking in the tone of extreme gentleness and compassion that ever touched her heart to its inmost core.

She resented it, she did not want to have any kindly feeling toward him; she was determined she would not, so averting her face, answered, almost rudely, that she was not very ill, and would do well enough if she could only be left alone; then unable through weakness to maintain her self-control, burst into a fit of hysterical weeping.

"You see she's dreadfully nervous, doctor," remarked Clare, a little maliciously, for she knew that Nell could not endure the imputation.

"Tears will bring some relief; I will be in again in the course of an hour," said Kenneth, and was gone almost before he had finished his sentence.

When he came again he found his patient more composed, but the pale, sunken cheeks, and the great, hollow eyes filled him with remorse and anxiety; he could scarcely command his voice for a moment.

"Excuse my rudeness, doctor," she said, holding out a thin white hand. "I believe I'm just sick enough to be very cross."

She had resolved not to look at him, but, as she spoke, involuntarily raised her eyes to his and read there such yearning affection, such tender compassion as caused her to drop them instantly, while the hot blood dyed cheek and brow, but only to vanish again, leaving them paler than before.

And he? A wild impulse, scarcely to be restrained, seized him to catch her in his arms, fold her to his heart, and pour out the story of his love.

The desire was so overpowering that it may be he would have yielded to it had not the major's entrance at that instant prevented.

But Nell had read the look, and the sweet story it told was as a cordial to her fainting spirit.

She rallied from that moment, the next day he found her sitting up, and in a week she was able to drive out.

After that his visits, which had been but few and brief from the first, were rarer and shorter still, and soon they ceased entirely.

She seldom saw him now, except at church or on the street, when they would exchange a passing bow and smile, and yet he had not told the story of his love, save with his eloquent eyes.

But she blamed herself for that; for with the strange inconsistency of human nature, she had shrunk from being left alone with him, studiously avoiding giving him an opportunity to speak the words for which her very soul was hungering and thirsting.

During all this time Wawillaway had been a frequent visitor at the house of Major Lamar, coming often to Chillicothe with baskets of his own weaving for sale, and never failing to call upon these friends who had made much of him ever since his signal service to Nell.

When he remained over night in the town it was usually as their guest, sleeping on the kitchen floor, wrapped in his blanket, and with his feet to the fire.

He was an especial favorite with Nell, and the liking was mutual, he having a great admiration for the "white squaw" whom he had saved from the panther's teeth and claws, while she felt that she owed him a debt of lasting gratitude; a debt that was doubled by an occurrence that took place some months subsequent to her recovery from her late illness.

Mounting Fairy one bright spring morning, she sallied forth with the intention of paying a visit to her friend Mrs. Nash.

Wild animals were now seldom seen in the vicinity of the town, and she felt secure in taking a short ride without escort; but on the way found herself confronted by danger of another kind which she had not taken into account.

She was passing through a bit of woods, when a man suddenly sprang from behind a tree, seized her bridle, bringing her pony to an abrupt halt that had nearly thrown her from the saddle, and with a lecherous, impudent stare into her face, and a demoniacal grin, said:

"I'm powerful glad o' this meetin'; ben a wantin' to scrape acquaintance this long while; fur you're a mighty purty gal."

Nell's cheek blanched and an involuntary shiver of fear crept over her.

The man was a tall, broad shouldered, powerfully built fellow, of the border ruffian class, whom she had seen about the streets and in the stores of the town a number of times in the last few months.

She knew little of him except his name, which seemed to her strangely appropriate, such was the ferocious and animal expression of his bronzed and bearded face.

She had felt instinctive loathing of the man from the first casual glance at him, had seen his evil eyes more than once following her furtively with a look that filled her with a nameless terror; and it may well be imagined that she was now filled with affright at this unexpected encounter in the lonely wood.

A conciliatory course seemed wisest, and with a heroic effort to hide her alarm, she addressed him politely.

"I am in haste, Mr. Wolf; please be good enough not to detain me."

"Not yet, my beauty, can't let you go just yet; we'll have a little chat first.

Come, I'll help you to 'light, and we'll go and sit together a spell on that log yonder," he said, taking hold of her left arm.

"Unhand me! how dare you?" she cried, her cheeks crimson, her eyes flashing with indignation, and bringing her riding whip down on his hand with all the force she could muster.

The stinging blow made him release her for an instant, but he kept his hold on the bridle, and an attempt on her part to urge her pony forward only made the creature rear and plunge in a dangerous manner.

"No, you don't!" cried the ruffian with a derisive laugh; and uttering a fearful oath, he threw his arm about her waist and had nearly lifted her from the saddle.

"Help! help!" she shrieked wildly till the woods rang again with the sound, and striking madly at him with the whip.

She was answered instantly by the Indian warwhoop close at hand, and half a dozen savages, armed with rifles and tomahawks, sprang out from the wood, not a hundred yards away.

Wolf, having left his gun leaning up against a tree at some little distance, was unarmed except the hunting knife in his belt, and seeing himself about to be overpowered by numbers, fled with the utmost precipitation, plunging into the forest and instantly disappearing in its depths.

Nell, not knowing whether to look upon the red men as friends or foes, felt her heart leap into her mouth, expecting to be tomahawked and scalped on the spot; but the next moment, recognizing in the foremost warrior her friend Wawillaway, she uttered a cry of joy.

"Very bad white man," he said coming up to her, "want killee you."

"No, I hope not," she said carefully steadying her voice, "but I am so glad, so glad you came and drove him away, Wawillaway. Oh, you have done me a greater service to-day than even the killing of the panther!" she added with an irrepressible shudder.

It was long before Nell ventured again beyond the limits of the town without a protector; but fearing Wolf's vengeance upon her brother, should he bring the ruffian to punishment, as he undoubtedly would should he hear of this day's peril to her, she carefully concealed the occurrence, exacting a promise from her Indian friend to do the same.

CHAPTER XIII.

At about the same time that Nell Lamar met with her adventure with Wolf, important events were transpiring at Glen Forest.

Mrs. Clendenin was summoned away to a distance from home by the serious illness of a sister of her late husband. Ignorant of the precise nature of the disease, she was unwilling to expose Marian to it, and though almost equally reluctant to leave her behind, decided upon that as the safer course.

So with much tender, motherly counsel bestowed upon this child of her love, and many an injunction to Vashti to watch over her darling, she took her departure.

The young girl felt inexpressibly lonely without the mother who had been to her friend, teacher and almost sole companion, everything in one, for they had led a very secluded life, paying and receiving few visits; indeed, seldom going anywhere but to church, except that Marian took many a ramble and many a ride on her pony through the adjacent woods and over the nearer hills, usually unaccompanied save by Caius, a huge mastiff who had hitherto proved a most efficient protector.

Mrs. Clendenin had indeed never been neglectful of the Christian duty of ministering to the sick and suffering so far as lay in her power, and Marian was in this regard following in her mother's footsteps.

A mile away over the eastern hills lived two elderly maiden ladies, Esther and Janet Burns, the one a paralytic, the other feeble and nearly blind from cataract.

They had a farm, the rent of which yielded them a support, but their lives were lonely, and Marian's visits were a great boon.

She had fallen into the habit of going over almost daily to Woodland, as their place was called, and spending an hour in reading to them from the works of one or another of her favorite authors.

The Clendenins had been for generations great lovers of books, and the library at Glen Forest, though what would be considered small and of little value in these days, was large and select compared with those of their neighbors.

Marian continued her visits to Woodland after her mother had gone, and, because she found it so much less lonely there than at home, sometimes lingered half the day, to the great content of the Misses Burns.

They would gladly have induced her to take up her abode with them during her mother's absence, but to that she would by no means consent; home was home after all, and though it might be pleasant to spend a part of the day elsewhere, when night came she wanted to be in her own familiar room, with old Vashti within call.

On Sunday Marian always attended service in the little country church spoken of in a former chapter.

The neighborhood was a very quiet one, few coming or going, the same faces showing themselves in the sanctuary Sunday after Sunday, and the sight of a new one was always a source of no little interest; it may therefore be supposed that the advent among them, a week after Mrs. Clendenin set out on her journey, of a fine looking young man, a total stranger, well dressed, and of serious and gentlemanly deportment, created some little stir and excitement; especially among the younger portion of the congregation.

He sat in the pew of Mr. George Grimes, who kept the nearest inn, the sign of the Stag and Hounds, and the services had not been over many minutes before every one knew that he had engaged board there for a month, and that he was an Englishman, apparently wealthy, having brought a valet with him.

The congregation had passed out into the churchyard, and a subdued hum of voices exchanging neighborly greetings and inquiries after each other's health, mingled pleasantly with the twittering of birds, the sighing of the wind through the forest, and the low murmur of the stream on the farther side of the road.

The stranger stood aside, looking on and listening with a well bred air of kindly interest.

"Who is that, Grimes?" he asked, his eye following admiringly a graceful girlish figure as it tripped past them down the path that led out to the road where the horses were tied, and, with the assistance of one of the young men, who stepped eagerly forward to give it, sprang lightly into the saddle.

"Miss Marian Clendenin, of Glen Forest, Mr. Lyttleton: one of the prettiest young ladies in the county, if I'm a judge o' beauty," replied Grimes, lifting his hat to the fair girl.

"She sits her horse well," remarked the stranger, still following her with his eyes as she cantered away in the direction of her home, Caius bounding nimbly on by the pony's side. "But she seems quite alone, is there no more of the family?"

"Most of 'em lie yonder," replied Grimes, pointing to a row of graves not far from the spot where they stood. "Children all died young but this girl and an older brother who went West years ago. Father died within the last year, and the mother's away nursing a sick sister, I hear."

Lyttleton seemed interested, asked several more questions, walked over to the graves and carefully read the inscriptions on the tombstones; Grimes standing by his side and going on with much garrulity to tell all he knew or had ever heard of the family, and that was not a little, for he was a great gatherer and retailer of news, for which few had better opportunities.

He spoke of the late Mr. Clendenin as a man of singularly secluded habits, upright and honest in all his dealings, but strangely averse to the society of his kind.

"And I suppose," he added, "that's what has kept his wife and daughter pretty much shut up at home: at any rate the girl's never seen at a cornhusking or quilting, or any sort o' merry making, and the young fellows never get a chance to wait on her. About the only place she does go to is Woodland, to read to those poor sickly old ladies; but she's there every day I'm told."

"She is then of a literary turn, this young heroine of yours?" sneered the stranger interrogatively.

"That's just what she is, sir, so I've heard on good authority, they're a bookish family." And as they rode homeward Grimes went on to expatiate at length upon Marian's reputed literary tastes and acquirements.

"You are a good trumpeter," remarked Lyttleton. "Pray tell me, are the Clendenins wealthy?"

"Glen Forest's a valuable place, and there's only the two of them, as I told you, after the mother dies."

"And the son doesn't get it all, as is usually the way with us?"

"No: and I dare say there's money laid by, too."

The next afternoon Marian, reading to her friends in the wide, cool porch that ran along the front of the house at Woodland, saw a horseman coming leisurely along the road, as, looking up from her book, she sent a casual glance in that direction.

"It is the English gentleman," she said in a low tone, as he drew rein at the gate.

It was long since either Esther or Janet Burns had been able to go to church, and Monday's visit from Marian was anticipated with even more than ordinary eagerness because of the detailed account she would bring of all she had seen and heard the previous day. Of course she had not, on this occasion, omitted to mention the stranger in Grimes's pew.

"Where, my dear?" asked purblind Janet, straining her eyes in a vain effort to see him. "Is he riding? I surely heard horse's hoofs."

"Yes, and he is alighting at the gate," said her sister. "What can he want here? Marian, child, will you call Kitty to see what he wishes?"

"I'se here, missus," the girl answered for herself, coming round the corner of the house. "What do you want, sah?" hurrying down the path to meet the approaching stranger.

"I am very thirsty and would be thankful for a glass of milk or cold water, my good woman," he answered, lifting his hat to the ladies.

At that Miss Janet stepped forward and hospitably invited him to come in and rest himself for a little, remarking that the day was very sultry and he must have found the heat of the sun very oppressive.

"I have indeed, madame," he said, accepting the offered kindness with alacrity, and stealing a glance of mingled curiosity and admiration at the fresh, blooming face of the young girl guest. "I think the sun shines with a fiercer heat here than in Europe, and if I do not intrude shall be very glad to rest in this shady nook until he approaches somewhat nearer his setting."

Both the sisters assured him he was welcome, and Kitty was directed to bring a glass of morning's milk and some home-made cake for his refreshment.

The Misses Burns were good, simple-minded, unsuspicious women, Lyttleton an accomplished man of the world, thoroughly unscrupulous and selfish, but able, when it suited his purpose, as it did on this occasion, to conceal his true character by polished manners and a most pleasing and insinuating address.

He was a fluent talker and knew how to adapt his conversation to those with whom he was thrown, in whatever station in life.

He addressed the older ladies almost exclusively, but his eyes continually sought Marian's face, which glowed with interest and intelligence.

He stayed for more than an hour, and made himself so entertaining that they were sorry to see him go, and gave him a pressing invitation to come again, which he readily promised to do.

With thanks for their hospitality and a courteous adieu, he at last took his departure.

"A very fine-looking, intelligent and well-bred gentleman," remarked Miss Esther, as man and horse disappeared down the road.

"He has evidently been accustomed to good society," added her sister, "has travelled a great deal and knows how to describe what he has seen; but while he talked to us, his eyes sought Marian's face for the most part."

"Surely that was but natural, seeing how much younger and fairer than ours it is," Miss Esther said, with a pleased smile and an affectionate, admiring glance at the now blushing maiden. "I am sure she makes a pretty picture sitting there under the drooping vines, with Caius crouching at her feet."

"How did you like him Marian, dear?" asked Miss Janet; "my dim eyes cannot judge whether he is as comely as Esther says."

"I do not think him quite so handsome as Kenneth," Marian answered with some hesitation, "he doesn't look so good and noble and true. But," she added quickly, the color deepening on her cheek, "I do not know him well enough yet to judge of his character, and he talks very well. Now shall we go on with our reading? I can only stay to finish the chapter, for you see the sun is getting low."

Lyttleton, as he rode briskly on toward his temporary home, was saying to himself, with an evil smile, "A pretty girl, very young, hardly sixteen I should say, and as innocent as a child; I flatter myself 'twill be no difficult task to win her confidence and learn all she knows. How much that may be I have yet to discover."

Determined to make diligent use of his opportunities, he became from that time a daily visitor at Woodland, and so conducted himself as to win the entire confidence of all three ladies, and cause them to look upon his visits as a great treat.

He had travelled much and had many adventures to relate, and stores of information to impart in regard to the strange lands he had seen. He had spent some weeks in Paris during the late Revolution, had witnessed the execution of Marie Antoinette and of many of the nobility, and had had some narrow escapes of his own; all of which he described to his little audience with thrilling effect.

Often, too, he brought a book in his pocket, usually Shakespeare's works, Milton's Paradise Lost, or some other poem, from which he would read passages in a rich, mellow voice so exquisitely modulated that it seemed to double the beauty of the author's words.

Marian's soul was full of poetry, and she would listen like one enchanted, her eyes shining, her lips slightly apart, her breathing almost suspended lest she should lose a single word or tone.

Lyttleton, without seeming to do so, noted it all with secret delight.

After a little he fell into the habit of accompanying her on her homeward ride or walk, whichever it might be, and of meeting her in her rambles, thus gradually placing himself on a footing of intimacy.

And Marian had forgotten her first intuitive perception of his character; his charms of person and manner had come to exert a strange fascination over her; she thought of neither the past nor the future when he was by her side, but lived only in the blissful present, while he saw and exulted in his power.

He made no open declaration of love, but when they were alone in the silent woods it breathed in every look and tone, filling the innocent girlish heart with a strange, exquisite, tremulous happiness.

Caius, always by her side, or crouching at her feet, was the sole witness of these interviews, and Marian could not bring herself to speak of them even to her two old friends, who, in their guilelessness, had no thought of harm to her from the daily intercourse of which they were cognizant.

Sometimes Lyttleton drew her on to talk of herself, her home, her absent brother, and asked many questions in regard to him, which Marian answered readily because it was a pleasure to speak of Kenneth.

She was eager in his praise, she would have delighted to show him to her new friend.

"You and he were both born at Glen Forest?" Lyttleton one day remarked, inquiringly.

"No; only I," Marian said, a slightly troubled look coming into her eyes; "I and the brothers and sisters who died very young. Kenneth is many years older, and it was when he was a babe that my parents came here to live."

"Ah? and where did they live before that? where was Kenneth born?"

"Somewhere in eastern Tennessee; I cannot tell you exactly, for there was no town, no settlement, just my father's cabin in a little clearing he had made in the forest, and another, a neighbor's, half a mile away."

Marian spoke hastily, with half-averted face and a perceptible shudder.

"Why that shudder, my sweet girl?" he asked, gently pressing her hand, which he had taken in his.

"I was thinking of the terrible occurrence that led my father and mother to abandon the spot," she said in low, tremulous tones; "an attack by the Indians in which several were killed. It is scarcely ever alluded to in the family and I never heard the full particulars."

"Then we will speak no more of it," he said, and began to talk of other things.

Some days later they were again alone together; they had been climbing the hills till quite weary, and were now resting, seated side by side upon a fallen tree, within sight of Glen Forest, the pretty mountain stream that flowed past it singing and dancing almost at their very feet.

Marian had her lap full of wild flowers which she was arranging in a bouquet, Lyttleton watching her with a curious smile on his lips, glancing now at the deft-fingers, now at the glowing cheeks.

She looked very pretty, very sweet and innocent; she had thrown off her hat and the dark brown curls fell in rich masses over neck and shoulders.

Caius, upon her other side, seemed to be keeping jealous watch over her, regarding Lyttleton with something of a distrust she did not share; she had perhaps never been so happy before in all her short life.

Neither had spoken for several minutes, when Lyttleton, leaning over, said softly, "Do you know, pretty one, that I leave you to-day?"

Marian dropped her flowers and looked up with a start, her cheek paling, and her eyes filling with tears.

"Shall you be sorry to see me go?" he asked tenderly, taking her hand and pressing it to his lips.

Her eyes fell, her lip quivered, one bright drop rolled quickly down her cheek. It was a rude awaking from her blissful dream.

"Oh, why did you come at all," she sobbed, "if you must go away again? and so soon!"

She did not see his exultant smile.

"Why you know I must go," he said, "since my home is not here; but I am very glad I came, as otherwise I should never have known you, my pretty darling, the very sweetest, the dearest little girl I ever saw;" he bent fondly over her and touched his lips to her forehead.

But she shrank from the caress, her cheek crimsoning.

"No, no; you must not do that. I—I cannot allow it."

"But why not? Why should we not be kind and affectionate to each other? Ah, don't move away from me, don't avert your sweet face, or I shall think you quite hate me, and I am going away to-day."

She covered her face with her hands to hide the tears that would come, and struggled with the sobs that were half choking her.

All the brightness seemed to have suddenly gone out of her life. "Why had she let herself care for him when he was going away and would never, never come again?"

"Don't weep, sweet girl, dear Marian; it breaks my heart to see your tears, my own darling," he murmured low and tenderly, moving nearer and venturing to steal an arm about her waist; "and yet there is a strange pleasure in the pain, because they show that you are not wholly indifferent to me, that you have yielded to me at least one small corner of your precious little heart. Is it not so, dearest?"

Surely this was the language of love, and her heart leaped up with joy in the midst of her pain. She did not repulse him now, but let him draw her head to a resting place on his shoulder and kiss away her tears.

"Don't shed any more, vein of my heart!" he whispered, "for I will return to you, perhaps in a few months, certainly within a year."

"Oh, will you?" she cried, smiling through the tears, lifting her eyes for an instant to his to meet a gaze so ardent that she dropped them again, while a crimson tide swept over face and neck.

The sun had touched the western hilltops, and the trees cast long shadows at their feet, when at last they rose and moved slowly on in the direction of Glen Forest.

He would not go in, and they parted at the gate with a long tender embrace.

"Do not forget me, sweet Marian; I will come again," he repeated.

"No, no, never! I shall never forget!" she sobbed, "but, you, you will forget me when you are far away and meet other and prettier girls."

"I have seen thousands, but never one half so lovely or half so sweet," he whispered, as for the last time he snatched a kiss from the rich red lips.

He was gone, hidden from her by the windings of the road, and Marian hurried up the path to the house, sat down on the porch step, and with her arms round the neck of her faithful dog, her cheek resting on his head, wept as if her heart would break.

Old Vashti found her thus.

"What de mattah, chile?" she asked, "you didn't hear no bad news?"

Marian shook her head. "I'm so lonely!" she sobbed.

"Well dat's bad nuff, chile, but don't fret yo' heart out dat way; de missus come back soon, please de Lawd; so cheer up, honey, and come and eat yo' suppah. I'se cooked a chicken and made some o' dose muffins you's so fond of."

But Marian was destined to be more lonely still. Sad news reached Glen Forest the next morning just as she was preparing to pay her usual visit to Woodland. Miss Janet, in her blindness, had missed her footing at the top of the stairs and fallen down the whole flight, striking her head with such force that she was taken up insensible, and in a few minutes had ceased to breathe.

The shock of the terrible accident brought a second stroke of paralysis upon the bereaved sister, and in a few days they were lying side by side in the little churchyard. They had been lovely and pleasant in their lives, and in death were not divided.

CHAPTER XIV.

One beautiful October day two well-mounted gentlemen, each followed by a servant, came galloping into Chillicothe, and halted at Major Lamar's door.

In the one the major instantly recognized an old friend and companion in arms, Captain Bernard, now a wealthy Virginia planter; the other was introduced as an English gentleman, Mr. Lysander Lyttleton, his guest for some weeks, whom he had persuaded to accompany him on a visit to this new state, of whose beauty and fertility they had heard the most flattering accounts.

The major gave them a hearty welcome, and proffered the hospitalities of his house, a larger and more commodious dwelling than the one he had occupied at the beginning of our story. Tig was summoned to take charge of the servants and horses, and the major himself conducted his guests to the parlor and introduced them to his wife and sister.

Dinner was already on the table; two more plates were added and they sat down to partake of the meal, but while in the act of taking their places their number was augmented by a new arrival, a very plainly dressed, sober looking man, who came in with the air of one who felt quite at home, giving and receiving a cordial greeting.

"Ah, Tommy," said the major, shaking hands with him, "you are just in time. Tig, set up a chair and bring another plate for Mr. Dill."

Having been introduced in due form to the other guests, and requested to ask a blessing, the new comer bowed his head over his plate, each one present copying his example, and with outspread hands and closed eyes, poured out a long prayer of fervent thanksgiving for the food set before them, and all other blessings temporal and spiritual, mingled with much humble confession of sin, and very many petitions; winding up with this remarkable one: "O Lord, we beseech thee to go into the highways and byways and hedges of our hearts and drive out the Canaanites, and the Hittites, and the Hivites, and the Perizzites, and the Girgashites, and the Amorites, and the Jebusites."

The elders of the family preserved a grave and decorous silence to the end, which the guests and the children had some difficulty in doing; the latter, especially the little boys, being almost convulsed with suppressed laughter.

At length the Amen was pronounced, Mrs. Lamar hearing it with an involuntary sigh of relief, for she had been very uncomfortably conscious that her dinner was growing cold, and she particularly prided herself on always having her meats and vegetables served up hot.

She mentally resolved to enjoin it upon the major never again to call upon Tommy Dill to ask a blessing when other guests were present.

But the guests showed no lack of appreciation of the fare, partaking of it with keen appetites and praising the viands without stint.

"Such game as this would be considered a rarity in my country," remarked Lyttleton, as the major heaped his plate for the second or third time; "but I presume it is abundant here?"

"Plenty of it to be had for the shooting," was the reply; "our woods are full of wild fowl, deer, bears, rabbits, squirrels and coons; and the rivers abound in fish. And such crops of corn as are raised in this Scioto valley you never saw, I venture to say. I'm glad you've come out here, Bernard; I shall take delight in showing you the land."

"Ah, the major is riding his hobby now," laughed Mrs. Lamar; "he is quite convinced that Ohio, you know we have just been admitted into the Union, Mr. Lyttleton, is the finest of all the states."

The Englishman bowed an assent, a half mocking smile playing about his lips.

Nell saw it and her eyes flashed. She thought he despised her country.

"How long since you left England?" asked the major, addressing Lyttleton; and then began an animated discussion of the political situation in Europe, the attitude of France and England toward each other, the career of Bonaparte, then the French revolution, particularly the Reign of Terror, Mr. Lyttleton greatly interesting the company by a graphic description of those of its scenes of which he had been an eye-witness.

He turned frequently to Nell as he spoke, for he read intense interest in her bated breath, changing color, the kindling of her eye when he told of some heroic deed, the tears that suffused it and the tumultuous heaving of her breast when the anguish of the wretched victims was his theme.

A connoisseur in female beauty, he was struck with admiration at the first sight of Nell, the delicacy of her complexion, the perfect symmetry of form and features, the queenly grace of every movement, and the abundant wealth of beautiful hair that crowned her shapely head. There was no little display of artistic taste in its arrangement, and in the simple elegance of her attire.

Lyttleton mentally pronounced Clare also a fine-looking and intelligent woman. She bore a prominent part in the conversation, while Nell contented herself almost entirely with silent listening, though from neither lack of ideas nor bashfulness, as her speaking countenance and quiet ease of manner fully attested.

Lyttleton wanted to draw her out, to hear her opinion on some of the controverted points, so seated himself at her side, when the dining-room had been forsaken for the parlor, and asked what she thought of the sentiments expressed by himself and others.

He found she had an opinion and was able to maintain it with spirit and ability.

They were still talking earnestly when Kenneth came in; so earnestly, that they were not aware of his entrance until the major pronounced his name in introducing Captain Bernard.

"Dr. Clendenin."

Lyttleton turned hastily at the sound and scanned the tall, manly figure and noble face with ill concealed eagerness and curiosity; then as the major named him, "Mr. Lyttleton, lately from England," rose with a slight bow, and accepted Kenneth's offered hand with a show of cordiality and a "Most happy to meet you, sir."

But neither then nor afterward did he give the smallest hint of his acquaintance with Marian, or his visit to the neighborhood of Glen Forest. He had read Marian's nature, delicate, sensitive, reserved, and felt sure that she would confide to no one the secret of their solitary rambles, their stolen interviews, much less of the wooing of his looks and tones, scarcely put into plain words by his wily tongue.

"I have not committed myself, did not ask her to be my wife, or even say 'I love you,'" was his inward thought; "and she would die rather than own that she had been so lightly won."

Kenneth declined an invitation to be seated.

"I am summoned in haste to a very sick patient," he said, "and merely stepped in, in passing, to ask Mrs. Lamar's kind offices for another who is suffering from the lack of proper nursing."

"Those poor devils of country doctors have a hard life of it," remarked Lyttleton superciliously, when Kenneth had gone.

"It is a noble, self-sacrificing life," replied Nell, with some hauteur, "I know of none that is more so than Dr. Clendenin's."

She would not have Kenneth pitied or patronized by this insolent stranger, and she glanced with scorn at the white hands, delicate and shapely almost as a woman's, one of which was toying with the seals of a heavy gold watch chain in a way to display to advantage a brilliant gem that glittered on the little finger.

They were alone at the moment, the major and his friend having followed Mrs. Lamar and Kenneth to the outer door.

Lyttleton lifted his eyebrows meaningly, and with a slight expressive shrug of the shoulders:

"Ah, I beg pardon, Miss Lamar! an intimate and particular friend of yours? I was not aware of it; and in fact was merely speaking of the class in general."

"And I was defending the whole profession," remarked Nell, "of which Dr. Clendenin, our family physician, is the representative to us. We owe him much for his kind and faithful services in more than one dangerous illness among us."

Lyttleton remarked that her sentiments did her honor; then with a desire to introduce a fresh topic, "You have an odd character in that Mr. Dill," he said, "or is that the sort of grace usual at meals in this part of the world?"

"I never heard such from any one else," Nell answered with gravity. "He is an excellent man, but slightly deranged. There was a meeting of one of our church courts in town yesterday, and he always attends. But he has gone now to his home and we shall probably see no more of him for some time."

"I'm going with the major to take a look at the town; will you go along, Mr. Lyttleton?"

Captain Bernard spoke from the open door.

"Thank you, yes;" and with a courteous "Good-afternoon" to Nell, Lyttleton followed the others into the street.

He had come to Chillicothe with the undivulged intention of taking up his residence there for some months, and having made the tour of the town he called at the General Anthony Wayne and engaged board and lodging for himself and servant; his choice secretly influenced by the discovery that it was there that Dr. Clendenin took his meals; for Lyttleton had his own private reasons for wishing to see and hear all he could of Kenneth and his manner of life.

Captain Bernard made a like arrangement, though for a shorter period of time; then having seen their luggage bestowed in their rooms and refreshed themselves by a change of linen, they returned to the major's for the rest of the day and evening, in accordance with his urgent invitation.

Mrs. Lamar being still absent on her errand of mercy, it fell to Nell's lot to do the honors of the tea-table; a duty of which she acquitted herself with an ease and grace that increased the admiration Lyttleton had already conceived for her.

Primitive customs still prevailed in Chillicothe; the tea hour was so early that when they rose from the table the sun had scarcely set behind the western hills. And the hunter's moon shone full-orbed over the tree tops.

The captain proposed a walk, remarking that the evening was much too fine to be spent within doors, and he and the major set off together, strolling along in leisurely fashion, smoking and talking of "the days of auld lang syne."

They had invited Nell and Lyttleton to accompany them, but both had declined; the one pleading the necessity of attending to some domestic duty devolving upon her in her sister's absence, the other that he found himself already sufficiently fatigued with riding and walking.

"Never mind me, major," he said, seating himself in the porch, and coaxing little three year old Bertie to his knee; "I'll amuse myself with these little folks till you return."

He soon had the whole flock about him, telling them stories and singing them songs, and they were having a merry time when Aunt Nell came to the door to say that it was their bed time and Maria was waiting.

Daylight had quite faded out of the sky and the air grown so chill that the warmth of the blazing wood fire in the parlor was far from unpleasant to Lyttleton as he followed the children into the house.

Begging the guest to excuse her for a moment, and to make himself entirely at home, Nell went away with Maria and the children.

Lyttleton stood by the fire musing.

"What a handsome girl! and her manners would not disgrace a court. She's some years older, and more formed than Clendenin's sister; quite as fine looking too, though an entirely different style of beauty; not over twenty I should say. The other I take to be fifteen. Clendenin admires her vastly; I saw that in his glance, and that he saw in me a possible rival. Well, I shall enjoy getting into her good graces none the less for that."

Two candles were burning on the table, and beside them a piece of delicate embroidery which Nell took up on her return to the room.

Lyttleton drew a chair to her side and exerted his conversational powers to the utmost for her entertainment; evidently not without success; her low musical laugh rang out again and again, she gave him many a bright glance from her liquid eyes, and many a quick word of repartee.

He grew more and more interested in her and congratulated himself on his good fortune in having come upon such a gem "here in the wilderness."

Suddenly he started, turned pale, and half rose from his chair with a low exclamation of fear or dismay. His eyes seemed fixed upon some object behind Nell, whose back was toward the hall door, and she turned her head hastily to see what it was.

A tall Indian, dressed in native costume, tomahawk and scalping knife in his belt, and feathers in his hair, stood there regarding the Englishman with a contemptuous smile.

"Ugh! big baby!" he grunted.

"Wawillaway!" cried Nell, springing up and shaking hands with the chief in the most cordial manner; "you are welcome, always welcome to my brother's wigwam! Mr. Lyttleton, you need not be alarmed; Wawillaway is my very good friend, and has always been a brother to the white man."

The major coming in at that moment with Captain Bernard, echoed his sister's words of welcome, as he grasped the chief's hand and shook it heartily.

The captain did likewise, gazing with admiration upon the tall sinewy form and well developed limbs of this untutored son of the forest.

Leaving the gentlemen to entertain each other, Nell led the way to the dining-room, and with her own fair hands set before the chief an abundant supply of the best food the house afforded.

He ate heartily, then wrapping his blanket about him, stretched himself upon the kitchen floor with his feet to the fire.

"Pray do not deem me a coward," Lyttleton said in a low aside to Nell on her return to the parlor. "It was my first sight of an Indian, I unarmed, and I expected to see that tomahawk go crashing through your brain."

"I shall endeavor to make all due allowance," Nell answered courteously; but he fancied that he read contempt in the smile that accompanied her words.

It nettled him, and he mentally resolved to seize the first opportunity of proving to her that he was not lacking in courage.

CHAPTER XV.

"What do you think of this Englishman?"

Dale was pacing Kenneth's office with his hands in his pockets, while the latter, seated before his table, where were arranged various bottles, gallipots, and a delicate pair of scales, was busily engaged in weighing out medicines and putting them in powders.

He smiled slightly, then answered in a grave, somewhat preoccupied tone:

"Handsome, intelligent, travelled, apparently wealthy! can be very interesting in conversation, but haunts my office a little more than is perfectly agreeable to a man whose time is often more than money."

"No insinuation I hope?" returned Dale, laughing and shrugging his shoulders.

"Not at all, Godfrey, I feel at liberty to invite you to retire when I wish to be rid of you."

"Thank you; I regard that as an incontrovertible proof of friendship. But to return; I don't fancy the fellow; he's too highly polished; his extreme suavity of manner fills me with a desire to knock him down. There's nothing like an air of patronage to make my angry passions rise."

"And then he's forever at Miss Lamar's side, robbing every other fellow of the least chance to bask in her smiles. I haven't been able to exchange a dozen sentences with her in the week that he's been in our town. I vote that he be sent back to his own country."

Dale did not see the half spasm of pain that contracted Kenneth's brow for an instant.

"I must go now, have to ride ten miles into the country," he said, folding the last powder; then bestowing them, along with such other medical and surgical appliances as he might have need of, in his saddle-bags, he summoned Zeb to put them on his horse, ready saddled, at the door, and donning overcoat and hat, hurried out, mounted and away at a rapid gallop.

The principal streets had now been cleared of trees and Indians wigwams alike; they were very wide and straight, giving an extended view and plenty of room for the passage of equestrians and vehicles.

Far ahead of him Kenneth could see a lady and gentleman on horseback cantering briskly along; he overtook them, and in passing caught, and returned, a smile and bow from Nell Lamar and the Englishman.

They were out for a ride through the gay, beautiful woods this delicious October morning.

Something akin to envy of Lyttleton stirred for a moment in Kenneth's breast; but he struggled against it.

"Why should I grudge to him the prize that can never be mine?" he asked himself. "And am I so utterly, so abominably selfish, that I cannot rejoice in her happiness, though it be with another? Faster, faster, good Romeo," he continued aloud, patting the neck of his noble steed; "let us bestir ourselves, my boy, for we are needed yonder, and jealousy and envy must be left behind."

The intelligent creature seemed to understand, and urged by neither whip nor spur, flew over the ground with almost the speed of the wind.

Far in the distance a farm-house loomed up into sight, and as they drew rapidly nearer Kenneth could descry a horseman galloping furiously toward it from the opposite direction.

His first thought was that it might be another messenger from the house to which he was bound, some miles farther on, and where a patient lay very ill.

But no; the man drew rein at the gate of the dwelling already in sight, and as Kenneth came dashing up, was in earnest colloquy with the farmer.

They hailed him.

"Hollo, doctor! stop a bit. Have you heard the news?"

"No," he answered, coming to a sudden halt alongside of the other horseman, whom he now recognized as a farmer living some distance down the prairie. "Are you the bearer of evil tidings, Coe, an accident, some one hurt? I have hardly time to stop unless my services are needed."

"Worse than that, doctor; he's beyond your help, poor fellow; but you'd best listen, for all that!"

"Yes," put in the other man, with an oath, "it's the doin's o' those cussed red skins, an' if ye don't look out doc, they'll be takin' your scalp afore ye know it."

"What! you don't mean that the Indians have begun hostilities again, Wolf?"

"Yes, sir; I do!" he cried with a yet fiercer oath, and bringing his fist down heavily upon the palm of the other hand; "here's Coe brings news that Captain Herrod's found lyin' in the woods murdered and scalped; Captain Herrod, a man greatly loved by his neighbors, as ye must know, and of course it's their work; and the next thing they'll be burning down our houses about our ears, and butcherin' and scalpin' men, women and children, as they did afore Mad Anthony Wayne whipped 'em into good behavior. The dirty, sneakin', treacherous rascals!" he went on, "I hate 'em like pizen."

"Is there any positive proof that Herrod met his death at their hands?" Kenneth asked, turning to Coe.

"No; but it looks likely; and I'm out to warn the settlers in the valley that we'd best be moving close together and building block-houses for protection."

"That we had," exclaimed Wolf, again cursing the savages as cruel and treacherous.

"They have often proved so in past times," said Kenneth; "yet there have been some noble exceptions, and certainly we have not been guiltless in our treatment of them."

"We've paid 'em back in their own coin," Wolf answered with a savage grin; "and we'll do it again; I'd as lief shoot a red skin as a dog any day."

"Yet it is as truly murder as to kill a white man," said Kenneth, "for God hath made of one blood all nations of men. But we have no time to talk, Coe. You go on to Chillicothe?"

"Yes, and beyond, warning everybody to be getting ready for the worst. I must be off. Good day to ye both, gentlemen."

He put spurs to his horse, but Kenneth called after him:

"Stay a moment; I passed a lady and gentleman riding out from the town. Be on the lookout for them and warn them to hurry back, will you?"

"All right, doc!" and each sped on his way, Kenneth's thoughts divided between grief for the violent death of a friend and neighbor, and anxiety for his patient, and for sweet Nell Lamar, who might be even now in danger from the savages.

Alas, to have to trust her to the Englishman's care, and he in all probability entirely unarmed!

It was sorely against his will that Kenneth continued to increase the distance between her and himself.

Nor did he tarry unnecessarily in the sick room or snatch even a moment to refresh himself with food, though in need of it and urgently pressed to sit down to a well spread board.

"Do now, doctor, stop and take a bite," entreated the lady of the house, following him to the door; "why it'll be the middle of the afternoon or even later before you can get back to Chillicothe."

"Thank you kindly, Mrs. Bray," he said, tightening his saddle girth as he spoke, "but I really do not feel hungry, and am in very great haste to return."

"Excited over this news of poor Captain Herrod?" she said. "Well, it's just as likely to have been the work of some white man as of the Indians, I think; somebody that's had a grudge against him."

"He was much beloved, Mrs. Bray."

"That's true too, and yet I've heard he had an enemy."

"I do not know, but hope it may not prove the beginning of hostilities," Kenneth returned as he sprang into the saddle. "Good afternoon, madame. Now, Romeo, good fellow, on at the top of your speed."

He glanced warily from side to side, alert but courageous, as he skimmed over the prairies and plunged through the forests; yet no sign of lurking savage rewarded his vigilance.

He did not halt or slacken his pace till fairly within the limits of the town; then allowing his panting steed to fall into a walk, he looked up and down the streets.

People were hurrying along in unusual haste, or standing in groups talking earnestly, with grave, sad, anxious faces.

Major Lamar, detaching himself from one of these knots of talkers, called to Kenneth to stop, then coming to his side asked if he had heard the news.

"Of poor Captain Herrod? Yes. What is thought of it, that it's the doing of the Indians?"

"There are various opinions. We have held a town meeting, resolved to prepare for the worst, discovered that there is no ammunition in town, and started a party down the river in a pirogue, to bring a supply from Cincinnati."

"No ammunition in town, is it possible, and we may be attacked at any moment!"

"True: but we do not hear of any Indians being seen on the war path. We will hope for the best."

"Miss Nell?" inquired Kenneth, "I passed her and Lyttleton as I left town this morning."

"Yes; they met Coe and came back in something of a panic. Nell hardly the more alarmed of the two, I fancy;" and there was a sly twinkle in the major's eye, an almost imperceptible smile lurking about the corners of his mouth.

"She is safe then? I was a little uneasy, not knowing how far they meant to go."

By this time quite a little crowd had collected about Romeo, and Kenneth was plied with eager queries as to the road he had been travelling, and whether he had seen any signs of hostile Indians.

His replies negativing the last question, seemed to afford some slight satisfaction, some hope that there was less occasion for alarm than had been feared.

Still all were in favor of proceeding with the work, already resolved upon in the public meeting, of fortifying the town. Kenneth was dismounting at his office door when Barbour hailed him, with a request that he would come at once to his house, as his wife seemed in a very bad way.

"What is the matter?" asked the doctor, hurrying along by Barbour's side.

"I hardly know, doc; she's a good deal alarmed with this story of Captain Herrod's murder, and really seems hardly able to breathe."

"Hysteria, doubtless."

"Dangerous?"

"No, not particularly so," returned the doctor dryly.

But Mrs. Barbour managed to detain him in attendance upon her for a couple of hours, insisting that she should certainly die if he left her, till at last he was compelled to tell her that he could not stay another moment, nor was it at all necessary that he should.

Returning to his office he found Major Lamar waiting for him, with an invitation to tea. Kenneth demurred, though beginning to be most uncomfortably sensible that he had not tasted food since an early breakfast, but the major would take no denial.

"I have some very fine game, and have set my heart upon sharing the enjoyment of it with you," he said; "and I shall be quite in disgrace with my wife if I fail to bring you according to promise. Bernard and Lyttleton are to sup with us too; so that you may feel assured of a feast of reason and a flow of soul," he added, jocosely; "the Englishman is a good talker, you know."

"Yes, his conversational powers are enviable," Kenneth answered in a tone of hearty good will. "And since you are so kindly urgent, major, I will go with you."

A vision of Lyttleton basking in Nell's sunny smiles, calling forth her silvery laughter with his mirth-provoking sallies, thrilling her with his stories of wild adventure, or moving her to tears with the pathos of his description of human suffering or heroism in times of danger, had brought about this decision, erroneously ascribed by the major to the attractiveness of the picture he had drawn.

Kenneth made a hasty toilet and they walked over to the major's together.

Full half of Lyttleton's time during this week in Chillicothe had been spent there, as Kenneth knew to his no small disturbance. In vain he reminded himself that he could never claim Nell as his own, therefore had not the shadow of a right to stand in the way of another; he could not school his heart into a willingness to utterly resign the faint hope that would linger there, spite of reason's mighty arguments against it.

CHAPTER XVI.

Lyttleton and Nell were in the gayest spirits that morning as they sped briskly onward through forest and over prairie, talking cheerily of the sweetness of the air, the beauty of the woods, and exchanging many a little harmless jest, no thought of danger troubling them.

They were several miles out from the town when they espied a small cloud of dust far ahead which seemed to be rapidly drawing nearer.

"What is it?" cried Nell, reining in her pony, while she sent an anxious gaze in the direction of the approaching cloud. "Ah, I see, it is a man riding as if for life."

"After a doctor, I suspect," observed Lyttleton; "some one hurt, perhaps."

"But he must have passed Dr. Clendenin," returned Nell, "so it can hardly be that." And as the man at that moment came dashing up she turned her pony aside to let him pass.

Instead he halted close beside them with a suddenness that nearly threw his horse upon his haunches.

"Go back," he panted; "turn right around and go back to the town as fast as you can make your beasts move; don't spare whip nor spur, for there's no tellin' but the woods may be full of Injuns this minute. They've found Captain Herrod lyin' dead and scalped in the woods, and I'm out to rouse the neighborhood; for of course it's altogether likely to have been the doin's o' the redskins."

"Captain Herrod!" exclaimed Nell, tears starting to her eyes; "can it be? It is not more than a week since he dined at my brother's table, and we all liked him so much."

"Yes, miss, he was a fine man, liked by a'most everybody," said Coe. "But we'd best be moving on. We'll put the lady in between us, sir, for her better protection. And now for Chillicothe!"

As the three came galloping furiously into the town, people rushed to their doors and windows, and Coe, checking his horse, and calling aloud that he was the bearer of important tidings, an eager, questioning crowd quickly gathered about him, and the news spread like wildfire through the place.

Lyttleton dashed up to the major's door, and only waiting to assist Nell to alight, he remounted and hurried back to the spot where they had left Coe; then giving his horse into his servant's care, he followed the crowd and was present at the town meeting.

"What a precious pack of fools, to be caught so!" he muttered on hearing the announcement that there was no ammunition in the place. "I say, captain," to his friend Bernard, who stood by his side, "I wish we were well out of this, I've no mind to stay here and be butchered by the wild Indians."

"Better go at once, then," sneered the captain.

"Go? through the woods where they are probably swarming? Thank you, no; 'twould be a greater risk than to stay where I am."

"Suppose then you go with the party in the pirogue, down the river to Cincinnati?"

"Nonsense! that would be scarcely safer; the savages might easily pursue it in a canoe, or fire on us from the shore."

"Then my advice to you is to stay and meet the danger like a man."

"Of course, of course," stammered Lyttleton; "but I wish I'd never come. I shouldn't, if I hadn't understood that all danger of hostilities was entirely past. I've no mind to go home to old England without my scalp."

"If that's your only concern," returned the captain dryly, "you may set your mind at rest; there's no danger that you will go back without your scalp."

"You mean that they'll finish me if they get the chance," muttered Lyttleton, turning away with a look of intense disgust.

"He's a coward!" said the captain to himself; and Nell Lamar was at that very moment expressing the same opinion to Clare at the conclusion of a breathless narration of the events of the last hour.

"Perhaps not, don't be too ready to judge him hardly," returned Clara, who was partial to the Englishman's handsome person, winning address, and apparently full purse, and would have been more than willing to bestow Nell's hand upon him.

"I have no wish to be unjust or uncharitable," said Nell, "but he was so pale and so agitated from the moment he heard the news till he left me here at the door that I was even forced to the conclusion that he was afraid."

The afternoon was full of excitement. Dale ran in for a moment to say good-by. He was one of the party detailed to go for ammunition.

"You will be in danger?" Nell said inquiringly, as they shook hands.

"Yes, probably: yet perhaps not more so than those who stay behind. I'm not specially uneasy on that score, in fact, have but one objection to going upon the errand, that in case of an attack during our absence I shall not be here to help defend you."

He seemed excited but full of a cheerful courage. "Don't be too anxious, ladies, I cannot help hoping the whole thing will blow over," were his last words as he hurried away.

An unspoken fear lay heavy at Nell's heart, Dr. Clendenin, where was he? Coe had told of his warning to him, but that he had gone on his way all the same as if no danger lay in it, and Nell reflected with a feeling of exultant admiration, that he would never desert the post of duty through fear of consequences to himself.

But should she ever see him again? He might be even now lying dead and scalped by the roadside or in the woods, as Captain Herrod had been found, or perchance wounded and bleeding, dying for lack of help.

How she shuddered and turned pale at the very thought, while now and again a wild impulse seized her to mount her pony and away in search of him.

At length the suspense and anxiety were unendurable, and hastily tying on her garden hat, she hurried out into the street.

She had gone scarcely a square when at no great distance she descried, glad sight, Romeo and his master surrounded by a little crowd of eager, excited men, and with a sigh of intense relief she turned a corner and walked briskly on, her heart full of joy and thankfulness.

But Kenneth could never have guessed her feelings from her quiet, almost indifferent greeting that evening, and indeed was sorely pained by the contrast of her manner to him and to Lyttleton, whom in her heart she despised.

The latter hovered about her all the evening, admiring the delicate embroidery growing beneath her white, taper fingers, paying her graceful compliments and indulging in witticisms that now and then provoked a saucy reply or a ripple of silvery laughter.

Apparently they were full of careless mirth, while the others, sitting together about the fire, discussed with grave and anxious faces the present threatening posture of affairs. Kenneth bore his share in the conversation, being frequently appealed to by the major, as one whose opinion was worthy of all consideration, yet furtively watched Nell and her vis-a-vis; the seeming favor in which Lyttleton was held pained him, yet Nell was not consciously coquetting.

Both the major and the captain had seen something of Indian warfare, and the transition was natural and easy from the threatened danger of the present to the perils and exploits of the past, each having something to tell of the daring and bravery of the other.

At first the stories were of encounters with the red men of the woods, then revolutionary scenes were recalled.

"Major," exclaimed the captain, "do you remember your big Hessian?"

"Yes, perfectly: that is, his general appearance; he was not near enough for his features to be very strongly impressed upon my memory."

"And he has never appeared to you?" queried the captain with a laugh.

"No," returned the major, gazing meditatively into the fire; "what right would he have to haunt me, captain, seeing he was killed in battle?"

"None, of course; and he shows his sense of justice in refraining."

"What were the circumstances?" inquired Kenneth, with interest which seemed to be shared by all present.

"It was on one occasion when our forces and those of the British were drawn up in line of battle in full view of each other," said the captain, "that a big Hessian officer stepped out in front of his men and with a good deal of angry, excited gesticulation and loud vociferation in his barbarous tongue, seemed to be defying the American army much as Goliath defied the armies of Israel.

"The impudence and effrontery of the thing roused my ire; I turned with an indignant remark to the major here, he was only captain then, by the way, but before the words had left my lips he had taken a gun from a soldier and shot the fellow down where he stood."

"Some of those Hessians were very brutal," remarked Kenneth.

"Yes," said the captain, "war was their trade, and what better could one expect from men who fought, not for country or for principle, but simply for hire; the more shame to the government that employed them against freemen battling for their liberties!"

"Yet preferable, I should say, to the wily and treacherous savages the Americans have been accustomed to fighting." Lyttleton's tone was flippant. "I'd sooner encounter an infuriated Hessian, Frenchman, any kind of white man, or even ghost, than a whooping, yelling painted savage on the war path, as they call it."

"That's an acknowledgment," remarked the captain dryly; "especially in view of the fact that they, too, were employed against us by the mother country, as

Americans once delighted to call her."

"However, that is all past, and certainly we owe no grudge to you, Lyttleton," he added turning toward the latter with a genial smile.

"All Indians are not cruel and treacherous," observed Nell, her fair cheek flushing and her violet eyes kindling; "Tecumseh is a noble exception; Wawillaway also; I would trust my life in his hands without the slightest hesitation."

"Yes, Wawillaway is a good Indian," assented her brother; "has always been friendly to the whites. Nor shall I ever forget his good service to you, Nell."

The major referred to the adventure with the panther, which he had related to his guests on a former occasion; of the more recent and greater service rendered her by her Indian friend, he knew nothing.

But Nell was thinking of it, recalling with a slight shudder Wolf's lecherous stare; her eyes were on her needle-work.

Kenneth could not see their expression, but he wondered at the trembling of her slender fingers as she drew the needle in and out, and the varying color on her cheek.

A moment of silence following the major's last remark, was suddenly broken by a thundering rap upon the outer door.

All started to their feet, with the common thought that the threatened danger had come, and Kenneth turned with a quick, protecting gesture toward Nell, while Lyttleton glanced hurriedly around, as if in search of some hiding place.

Neither movement was lost upon the young girl; she saw and appreciated both; more afterward than at the moment.

But their alarm was groundless. Tig had gone to the door and a voice was heard asking for Dr. Clendenin. "What is it, Gotlieb?" he asked, stepping out to the hall, and recognizing in the messenger a German lad whose parents lived next door to the Barbours.

"Mine mudder she send me for you, doctor, to goame right quick to Meeses Barbour; she pees ferry seeck."

Kenneth had his doubts about the correctness of the report, yet nevertheless, bidding a hasty good-night to his friends, hurried away with the messenger.

He found the patient again in violent hysterics, which Gotlieb's mother was vainly trying to relieve.

"O doctor," she cried, "it is goot you haf come. I know not what to do for dis womans. She schream and she laf and she gry, and I can't do notings mit her."

"What caused this attack, Mrs. Hedwig?" he asked.

"Vell, doctor, I prings mine work to sit mit her, and I zay 'I must make dese flannel tings for mine childer pefore de Injuns comes; pecause it pees very cold in de woods for mine Lena, and mine Gotlieb, and mine Karl, when dose Injuns take 'em.' And just so soon I say dat, she pegins to schream and to laf and to gry lige—lige von grazy womans."

She seemed much disturbed, and alarmed, inquiring anxiously, "Do you dinks she fery bad sick, doctor? vil she die?"

"Oh no," he said, "she'll be over it directly."

"She might have known better than to talk about the Indians coming. It frightens me to death," sobbed the invalid; "and Tom was shamefully thoughtless to send such a person in to sit with me. He ought to have stayed himself; there are plenty of other men to work at fortifying the town. But nobody ever thinks of poor me."

"It would be far better for you if you could forget yourself, Mrs. Barbour," said Kenneth. "Drink this, if you please, and then go to sleep."

"Go to sleep, indeed, and she sitting there working on those flannel garments, just as if the Indians would let her children live to wear them, if they come."

It was late when Kenneth returned to his office, and he was weary in mind and body; yet hours passed before he retired to rest. His thoughts were full of Nell, going over and over each scene in his life in which she had borne a part, recalling every look she had given him in which he had read the sweet secret of her love, his features now lighted up with joy, now distorted with pain, cold drops of agony standing on his brow.

"What a heartless wretch must I appear to her!" he groaned, pacing his office with folded arms and head bowed upon his breast. "Oh my darling! I would die to save you a single pang, and yet I dare not tell you that I love you. I must stand by in silence and see another win you. Perhaps even now your love is turned to hate, and if it be so I cannot blame you."

CHAPTER XVII.

It was long past noon: the sun shone, but as through a veil, a soft October haze mellowing the brightness of the beautiful woods where a solitary figure, that of a tall Indian, was following the trail with long, rapid strides.

It was the Shawnee chief Wawillaway; not on the war path, for though armed as usual with gun, tomahawk and scalping knife, no war club was in his hand, no paint on his face.

He had been on a peaceful errand to Old Town, to dispose of his baskets, game and peltries, and was now quietly wending his homeward way.

No report of Herrod's death, and the consequent excitement and alarm among the settlers in the Scioto valley, had reached Wawillaway, and when he saw three white men, Wolf and two men whom he had hired to assist him on his farm, coming toward him, no thought of hostile intention on their part or his own was in his heart.

They met him in the trail and he shook hands cordially with them, inquiring about their health and that of their families.

A little talk followed and Wolf proposed to the chief to exchange guns, took Wawillaway's on a pretence of examining it with a view to purchase, slyly blew out the priming, and handing it back, said he did not care to swap.

Wawillaway had seen his treacherous act, but still unsuspicious, took his own gun handing back the other.

"Have the Indians begun war?" asked one of Wolf's companions.

"No, no," said the chief, "the Indians and white men are all one; all brothers now."

"Why, haven't you heard that the Indians have killed Captain Herrod?" asked Wolf.

Wawillaway looked astonished, and incredulous.

"No, no! Indian not kill Captain Herrod," he said. "Captain Herrod not dead?"

"Yes, he is; it's certain that he was found dead and scalped in the woods a few days ago," said Wolf.

"Maybe fire water; too much drink make fight."

"No, Herrod hadn't any quarrel with the Indians; and we don't know which of them killed him."

"Maybe some bad white man killed Captain Herrod," suggested Wawillaway; then shaking hands all round again, he turned to go on his way, when the dastardly Wolf shot him in the back, mortally wounding him.

The brave chieftain, wounded as he was, and deprived of the use of his gun, turned upon his cowardly assailants with his tomahawk, and spite of the superiority of numbers, killed one, and severely wounded Wolf and the others.

A distant sound of horses' hoofs sent them flying into the woods, leaving the lifeless body of their comrade, and the bleeding, dying chief lying in the trail.

Nearer and nearer came the sounds, and in another moment two farmers returning from Chillicothe to their homes, had come to a sudden halt beside the prostrate forms and were gazing with grief, horror and dismay upon the bloody scene.

"It's Wawillaway!" cried one, hastily dismounting and stooping over the chief. "Who can have done this cruel, wicked deed, for he has always been the white man's friend! Ah, he's not dead, thank God! Come, Miller, help me to raise him up."

They did so as gently as possible, but life was ebbing fast; they saw it in his glazing eye and the clammy sweat upon his brow.

Another horseman came galloping up and drew rein close at hand, then leaping to the ground came hurriedly toward the little group.

"Dr. Clendenin," cried Miller, "you have come in the nick of time!"

"No," sighed Kenneth, taking the cold hand of the chief, "he is beyond human help. Wawillaway, my poor friend, whose fiendish work is this?"

With a great effort the chief rallied his expiring energies sufficiently to tell in a few broken sentences, of Wolf's perfidious and cruel deed, then gasped and died.

"He is gone," Kenneth said in a voice tremulous and husky with emotion, "and this foul deed of a blood-thirsty, conscienceless wretch, will in all probability be visited upon our infant settlements in a tempest of fire and blood."

"Wolf! the scoundrel is rightly named," muttered Miller between his clenched teeth. "Andrews," to his comrade, "we should be scouring the woods in search of him at this moment. If we could catch and deliver him up to justice, it might go far toward averting the threatened storm."

"Yes, and there's no time to be lost; but the first thing is to hurry home and secure the safety of our families."

"The alarm should be given at once in Chillicothe," said Kenneth, hastily mounting as he spoke; "that shall be my task, and doubtless a party will be sent out at once in search of this cowardly villain, Wolf."

In another moment all three had left the scene of blood and death, and were galloping furiously through the woods; the farmers toward their homes, Kenneth in the direction of the town.

The sun had set some time before, it was already growing dark, and when he reached Chillicothe many of the people had retired for the night.

Coming in at the end of the town farthest from Major Lamar's house, and stopping to call up and consult with several of the other influential citizens, whose dwellings lay between, he was late in reaching it.

Nell was roused from her first nap by a loud knocking on the outer door, and a familiar voice calling, "Major!"

She sprang to the window and opened it.

"What is it, doctor?" she asked, her voice trembling a little with excitement and alarm in spite of herself.

"I am very sorry to disturb you," he answered, something in his low, earnest tones sending a strange thrill through her whole being, "but there is not an instant to be lost. Dear Miss Nell, rouse the household and dress yourself with all haste, not forgetting a shawl and bonnet, for the night air is chill in—"

The door opened at that moment and the major's voice was heard.

"What's wrong? Ah, is it you, doctor?"

"Yes, major, Wawillaway lies dead out yonder on the trail to Old Town, slain treacherously in cold blood, by that scoundrel Wolf, and of course we may expect an attack from the Indians as soon as they can get here after the news reaches them. It has been decided that the women and children shall be collected in Ferguson's house; that being the largest in town. Can I be of any assistance in getting yours there?"

"No, no, thank you. I'll have them there directly, and you will be wanting to warn others."

The doctor rode rapidly away, while the major shut the door and called to his wife and children.

"Up! dress yourself as fast as you can! Nell!"

"Yes," she answered. "I'll be there in amoment."

She had heard all and was hurrying on her clothes with trembling fingers, the tears rolling down her cheeks.

"O Wawillaway, Wawillaway, you have died for me!" she sobbed. "O that cruel, cruel wretch! worse than the wild beast that shares his name!"

Sounds of commotion came from below, the little ones crying, Clare calling in frightened tones, "Nell, Nell, do come help with the children, if you can! I shall never get them dressed." The servants added their terrified clamor, as they rushed hither and thither in obedience to the orders of master or mistress, collecting such articles of value or necessity as could be thought of and found in the hurry and alarm of the moment.

The major alone preserved his calmness and presence of mind, and thus was able to control and direct the others.

At Clare's call Nell dashed away her tears, snatched up hat and shawl and ran down-stairs.

"Dressed!" said Clare. "You've been very quick. Now help with the children. They're too frightened or too sleepy to get into their clothes, and Maria's so scared she's of no use whatever."

"Calm yourselves, wife and sister," said the major, coming from an adjoining room. "We must put our trust in God, who we know will not suffer any real evil to befall His people; and the Indians can hardly reach the town under an hour or two at the very earliest."

His words and the quiet composure with which they were uttered had a soothing effect upon the ladies, calming their agitation and reviving their courage.

In a very short time the whole family were in the street rapidly winding their way to Mr. Ferguson's, toward which terrified women and children were now hurrying from every quarter.

The town was thoroughly awake; lights gleamed in all the houses, and every possible preparation was being made to receive and repel the expected attack. Sentinels were posted, and an old man who had served as drummer in the Revolutionary war was appointed to give the signal, the roll of the drum, should the enemy be seen approaching.

As the major and his family neared the place of rendezvous, they fell in with Captain Bernard and Lyttleton, who followed them into the house inquiring if there were anything they could do to make the ladies more comfortable.

As the light of a candle burning in the hall fell on Nell's face, Lyttleton saw the traces of tears on her cheeks and bright drops still shining in her eyes.

"Do not be too greatly alarmed; doubtless we shall succeed in keeping the savages at bay," he whispered protectingly. "I have a brace of pistols here, and you may rest assured will make your safety my special charge."

"I am not afraid," she said, drawing herself up slightly, while the color deepened on her cheek—"no, I believe I am; but it is not that that causes my tears;" and they burst forth afresh as she spoke.

"What then?" he asked in surprise.

"I weep for my friend, my poor murdered friend, lying stiff and stark yonder in the woods," and the tears fell like rain.

"What, the Indian!" he exclaimed in utter amazement.

"Yes, for Wawillaway. Did he not save my life? Yes, twice he has rescued me from a wild beast, first a panther, then a Wolf," she said with a shudder.

"Aunt Nell, Aunt Nell, I so sleepy, I so tired," sobbed little Bertie, her three year old nephew and especial pet; "please sit down and take me in your lap."

She had the child by the hand; the crowd was pushing them on; was between them and the rest of the family, and now separated her from Lyttleton.

"Oh, here you are! come this way," the major said, appearing in an open doorway at the end of the hall; and snatching up Bertie, he hurried back into the large living room, Nell following.

Tig had brought a great armful of buffalo robes, deer and bearskins, of which he was making a very comfortable couch in one corner, under the direction of his mistress.

Clare soon had the children laid upon it, and snugly covered up with shawls. She then sat down beside them with her babe in her arms.

"Can't you lie down too, Nell?" she said. "There's room enough, and you'd better sleep while you can."

"That is not now," Nell answered with a sigh, "but I will sit down here beside Bertie."

She seated herself on the farther side from Clare, where her face was in shadow, and little Bertie laid his head in her lap.

She bent over him, softly stroking his hair and dropping silent tears upon it. She could not forget Wawillaway.

The room; the house; was full of terrified women and children—many of the latter crying violently from discomfort and fright, while the tearful, trembling mothers vainly strove to soothe and comfort them.

Mrs. Barbour, occupying a distant part of the same room with the Lamars, paid small attention to hers; being too much taken up with her own feelings, too busy bewailing her hard fate, somehow much more to be commiserated than that of any other person present, and now and then going off into a violent fit of hysterics.

Mrs. Nash was there, quiet, patient, cheerful, doing the best to allay her sister-in-law's excitement and alarm, and that of her own and her brother's children; nor were her kind ministrations entirely confined to them; she contrived to speak words of hope and cheer to others also.

The room was dimly lighted by a candle burning on a table which had been pushed into a corner to be out of the way of the numerous beds spread upon the floor.

Mrs. Hedwig placed her two younger children under this table, bidding them "Go to shleep and nefer fear dose Inguns; your mutter vil pe right here and take care off you;" then getting possession of a chair, she sat down close beside them, drew the candle near her, snuffed it carefully, opened a bundle she had brought with her, and began sewing most industriously.

"How can you, Mrs. Hedwig?" cried Mrs. Barbour: "you're the most cold-blooded creature I ever saw!"

"Dish ish flannel to keeps mine childer warm; mine childer must haf dese flannel tings to wear in de woods mit de Inguns," explained the German woman, dashing away a tear. "But I hopes dose Inguns nefer gets here to shteal mine leetle dears."

"If they do come, they'll kill a good many more than they steal," sobbed another woman. "Oh, dear, oh, dear! if our men only had plenty of ammunition it wouldn't seem half so bad!"

"Do stop such doleful talk, all of you," said Mrs. Nash. "You'll frighten the poor children to death."

"Where are the men? what's become of my Tom?" fretted Mrs. Barbour.

"The men are doing their duty," answered Mrs. Nash; "some are guarding this house, some posted as sentinels on the outskirts of the town, others collecting bows and arrows, clubs, knives, tomahawks, anything they can fight with, or putting their valuables in some place of safety."

"And they have sent out a party in search of Wolf," added Mrs. Lamar. "I heard the major and Captain Bernard speaking of it; and if they can catch the wretch they will hang him, or give him up to the Indians and let them wreak their vengeance on him, as in justice they should, instead of on the innocent."

"Let us trust in the Lord and try to sleep," said a pious old lady who had laid herself calmly down beside her grandchildren. "We need rest to strengthen us for the morrow's duties and trials; most of us profess to be Christians, and why should we not be able to feel that we are safe in our Father's hands?

"'Not walls nor hills could guard so well

    Old Salem's happy ground;

  As those eternal arms of love

    That every saint surround.'"

A silence fell upon the room as the sweet old voice ceased, even Mrs. Barbour being shamed into momentary quiet.

Clare laid her babe down, stretched herself beside it and the older children, and her regular breathing soon told that she slept.

But Nell still sat with Bertie's head in her lap, her face hidden in her hands, while tears trickled between the white slender fingers, for her thoughts had gone back to her murdered friend.

"I shall never see him again in this world," she was saying to herself, "and oh, shall I meet him in another? Why, why did I never speak to him of Jesus? Now it is too late, too late!"

Some one sat down beside her and a voice said in low, rich tones, "I will not be afraid of ten thousands of people, that have set themselves against me round about! Dear Miss Nell, some trust in chariots and some in horses; but we will remember the name of the Lord our God."

"Thank you," she said, uncovering her face and hastily wiping away her tears, "but oh, it is not that, not fear of the Indians," she sobbed, the tears bursting forth afresh. "Dr. Clendenin, you have not forgotten what I owe to Wawillaway, and you know but the half!"

"I know that he saved you from the panther," he said with a look of surprise.

"Yes; and from I know not what at the hands of this very ruffian, Wolf." And in a brief sentence or two she told of her danger and her escape, adding with a low cry of pain, "And oh, I fear that it was in revenge for this that poor Wawillaway was slain. He has died for me!"

Kenneth was much moved, indignation against Wolf, gratitude for the fair girl's rescue, admiration of the brave chieftain, grief for his sad end, contending for the mastery in his breast.

"The wretch!" he said, "he is not worthy to live! He has killed a better man than himself. I too, grieve for Wawillaway. But, Miss Nell, you are looking sorely in need of rest; as your physician I prescribe a few hours of sleep."

He gently lifted the curly head from her lap to the couch, and bade her lie down beside the child.

"The major is with the party who are in pursuit of the assassin, and has left you and the rest of the family in my care; so that his authority is vested in me for to-night, in addition to that which I may lawfully claim as medical adviser," he said with one of his rare sweet smiles, "so do not venture to disobey my order, fair lady, and," he added in a still lower whisper, "let me give you this for a pillow to rest your weary head upon: 'I will both lay me down in peace and sleep: for thou, Lord, only makest me dwell in safety.'"

CHAPTER XVIII.

Overcome with grief and weariness Nell unconsciously obeyed orders ere many minutes had passed, and as the hours dragged on bringing no new cause of alarm, very many followed her example, even Mrs. Barbour at length succumbing to the spell of tired Nature's sweet restorer.

They had a rude awaking. With the first streak of dawn in the east, the sudden, loud roll of the drum burst upon the startled air;—the appointed signal of the near approach of their savage foe.

Women and children sprang up with wild shrieks and cries of terror and despair. Kenneth, who had been pacing the hall, a self-appointed sentry, stepped hastily in at the door of the room where the Lamars were, his eyes turning anxiously toward their corner of it.

Mrs. Lamar sat on the side of the couch, trembling with agitation, clasping her babe close to her breast and trying to soothe the older ones, who were clinging about her, with the exception of Bertie whom Nell, deathly pale, but calm and quiet, was sheltering in her arms.

Watching her with tell-tale eyes, Kenneth essayed to speak; but could not make his voice heard amid the weeping and wailing.

"O doctor, save me, save me!" shrieked Mrs. Barbour, rushing toward him with outstretched arms and streaming eyes. "I'll be the first they'll attack; I know I will, and Tom isn't here to take care of me."

"Yes, he is," shouted Mr. Barbour hurrying in, "yes, he is, Nancy; though there's no great occasion, for it's a false alarm, all a mistake. The Indians are as much scared as we are, and are running the other way."

The excitement toned down rapidly while he spoke, and now the room was nearly quiet, all who were old enough to understand being eager to catch every word.

"God be praised," ejaculated Kenneth fervently. "But the signal, why was it given?"

"Ah," said Barbour, smiling, "our old friend had gone back, in feeling at least, to old revolutionary times and could not refrain from sounding the reveille."

"'Twas just good sport for him, no doubt, to frighten a parcel of poor women and children nearly out of their wits!" was Mrs. Barbour's indignant comment.

"Not at all," said her husband; "he thought every body would understand it."

Mothers caressed their little ones with murmured words of joy and thankfulness, feeling as if they had been suddenly rescued from impending horrible death, or captivity hardly less to be feared; neighbors and friends shook hands or embraced with mingled smiles and tears, congratulating each other that they were, after all, in no immediate danger.

The party sent in search of Wolf returned without him; he had made good his escape from that part of the country.

There was a large body of Indians at that time near Greenville, and to them Chillicothe presently sent a deputation of her prominent citizens.

The Indians, among whom was the celebrated chief, Tecumseh, gathered in their council house, received the white men and listened to their account of the late unfortunate occurrence, their detestation of Wolf's bloody deed, their ineffectual efforts to catch him, and determination to put him to death if ever they could secure his person.

The Indians replied that they knew nothing of these matters and desired to remain at peace with the whites, and finally Tecumseh and some others of the chiefs were persuaded to return with the deputation, and repeat these assurances to the people of Chillicothe and its vicinity.

A day was appointed, and the people gathered, an immense throng, to look upon and listen to the great Shawnee chief.

Major Lamar, his wife and sister were there; the older children too, for the major said it would be something for them to remember all their lives.

Captain Bernard and Lyttleton contrived to be near the Lamars, the latter close at Nell's side, leaning over her now and then, with an air of devotion and proprietorship exceedingly distasteful to Kenneth, who furtively watched them from afar.

But when Tecumseh's tall, commanding figure stood before them, and he began to speak, every eye turned toward him, every ear was intent to listen to his voice and that of his interpreter, a white man who had been a prisoner among the Indians.

Even as translated the speech was full of eloquent passages. He spoke in the strongest terms of the friendly relations existing between the whites and the Indians; said they were brothers, and that the Indians would never violate their treaty. He hoped both parties would abide by it forever, and the peace and brotherly love between them be as lasting as time. A shaking of hands followed the speech, and the throng quietly dispersed.

CHAPTER XIX.

The Indian sachems departed, and life in Chillicothe fell back into its accustomed grooves.

Captain Bernard left for his Virginia home, but Lyttleton remained a boarder at the General Anthony Wayne, a self-appointed spy upon Kenneth's movements, and very frequent visitor to the hospitable dwelling of Major Lamar.

He continued to be a favorite with Clare, but found scant favor with Nell, whose politeness was sometimes freezing, while at others she would be only tolerably gracious. She was constantly comparing him, and always to his disadvantage, with Dr. Clendenin.

Lyttleton was handsome, polished, and an accomplished conversationalist, but Kenneth was fully his equal in these respects, and oh, how much more noble, brave and true; what an earnest, unselfish, useful life he led; how different from that of this gay idler who seemed to have no thought of anything but his own ease and pleasure!

She had about made up her mind that Lyttleton was a coward, too, remembering how pale he had turned on his first sight of Wawillaway, and having heard that he showed great agitation at the roll of the drum which so frightened the women and children with its false alarm that the Indians were almost upon them.

And nothing else so excited Nell's scorn and contempt as cowardice in a man.

Besides he now and then indulged in some remark disparaging to Kenneth, insinuating that he was of low birth and connections, less highly educated than himself, unskillful in his profession, pharisaical in his religion, and wanting in ease and refinement of manner.

All utterly false, as Nell knew; and she never failed to retort with cutting sarcasm, stinging rebuke, or a panegyric upon Dr. Clendenin so warm and earnest that she recalled it afterward with burning blushes.

What if her words should reach Dr. Clendenin's ears! What would he think of her, for with a sore heart she was compelled to acknowledge to herself that eloquently as his eyes had spoken once and again, his lips had never yet breathed one word of love to her; and not for worlds would she have him think she cared for him.

But there was no danger that Lyttleton would report their conversation; he would be loth indeed to give Kenneth the pleasure of knowing how high he stood in Miss Lamar's estimation, nor would he dare repeat his own base innuendoes. It dawned upon him at length that depreciation of his rival was not the best means of ingratiating himself into the fair girl's favor, and he changed his tactics, avoiding as far as possible all mention of Dr. Clendenin's name in her presence.

But she neither forgot nor forgave what he had already said, and in revenge threw out an occasional hint that she had grave doubts of his own bravery, while at the same time she lauded that of Dr. Clendenin to the skies.

Lyttleton was deeply mortified and cast about in his mind for some way of proving to her that he was not wanting in the manly attribute of courage.

"You seem to have an unbounded confidence in Dr. Clendenin's valor," he said one day in a tone of pique; "pray tell me what he has ever done to prove it?"

"With pleasure," she answered in grave, sweet accents, but with kindling eyes and a slight smile hovering about the lips, "I have seen it tried, or known it to be so, in many ways during the several years of our acquaintance;—in unhesitating exposure to contagious disease, in encounters with the fierce wild beasts of our hills and forests, in long lonely journeys out into the wilderness, all endured without flinching.

"So much for his physical courage. His moral courage is fully equal to it. He is not afraid or ashamed to show his colors, to stand by his principles, to acknowledge his allegiance to his divine Master by work or act, in whatever company he finds himself. He is not afraid of ridicule, of taunts or jeers, and I am sure would never hesitate to espouse the cause of the downtrodden and oppressed."

"I hate cant," said Lyttleton, coloring, "and never could abide these people who set themselves up as so much better than their neighbors."

"I entirely agree in those sentiments," replied Nell, "and so would Dr. Clendenin. He never obtrudes his sentiments or talks cant; and has a very humble opinion of himself; yet his life is such, so pure, earnest, self-denying and useful, that no one is left in doubt as to whose servant he is: and oh, he knows how to speak words of comfort and hope to the weak and weary, the sin-burdened and sorrowing!"

"And permit me to add, is most fortunate in having secured so fair and eloquent an advocate," returned Lyttleton with a bow and a mocking smile; "yet I must beg to be excused for my inability to see in him the paragon of perfection your rose-colored glasses would make him."

"If my glasses are rose-colored, permit me to say, yours are evidently begrimed with London smoke," retorted Nell.

"You hate me because I am an Englishman," he said gloomily; "and it is most unjust, since I had personally nothing whatever to do with what you Americans are pleased to style the oppressions of the mother country."

"No, I don't think I absolutely hate you, Mr. Lyttleton," she said meditatively, staying her needle in mid air for an instant; "on the contrary I have occasionally found your society not at all disagreeable; but," and the needle again went swiftly in and out, while her eyes were fixed upon her work, "I think if I were in need of a protector from—any great immediate danger—an expected attack by hostile Indians for instance, I should prefer one of my countrymen by my side."

"Now, Nell, that was really too bad," remarked Clare, after Lyttleton had gone. "The English are hardly less brave as a nation than ourselves."

"Of course, I don't deny that, but he's an exception, and deserving of all and more than I gave him for his mean way of depreciating a—"

"An absent rival," put in Clare with a laugh, as Nell paused for an appellation suited to Kenneth's worth. "Really I think you might forgive his evident jealousy, which is certainly flattering to you."

"No, not a rival but a far better and nobler man than himself," said the girl, the rose deepening on her cheek.

Lyttleton went away full of anger and chagrin, and lay awake half the night trying to contrive some means of convincing Miss Lamar that no more valiant man than himself was anywhere to be found.

He summoned his German valet at an unusually early hour the next morning.

"Hans," said he, while the man was busied about his person, "you are from Hesse, I think, and were over here during the war?"

"Yass, mynheer, that ish so; but I dells it not to dese peobles."

"No; of course not; and you need not fear that I shall betray you. But your experience may enable you to be of use to me in a new capacity."

"Vat ish dot, mynheer?"

"Have patience, Hans, and I will explain all in good time. Were you an officer?"

"Nine, nine, mynheer; not so goot as dot; vat you galls a brivateer?"

"A private, you blockhead," corrected Lyttleton, with a laugh. "Well, I wish you had been higher, though," he added meditatively. "If I could but get hold of the uniform of a Hessian officer, it would not matter now."

"Vell, mynheer, an' you gan keep von leedle segret, I dinks dot gan be found?"

"What! here in this little out of the way village?"

Hans nodded wisely. "Yaas, I finds him pootyquick."

"If you will do so and will make use of it as I direct," said Lyttleton, "you shall be handsomely paid for your trouble. And may rest assured that I will never betray your secret."

"Vell den, mynheer, I dell you, and I porrows de gloes, and does de work. Karl Hedwig was in de war, an—vat you call it?"

"Officer?"

"Yaas, and he's got de soldier gloes."

"Now? Here?"

Hans answered in the affirmative, going on to explain that Hedwig, whom he recognized as an old acquaintance, and his former superior in the army, had begged of him not to divulge the fact that he had served against the Americans: fearing that it would render him unpopular; but doubtless if it could be done without incurring that risk, he would lend his uniform for a consideration.

Lyttleton authorized Hans to hire it for the winter, naming a liberal sum and enjoining secrecy.

"I expect to find use for it one of these days or nights, which is all you need to know at present," he concluded.

Hans promised to attend to the commission promptly, and with due care that none should know of it save Hedwig and himself.

Godfrey Dale ran in to Major Lamar's that morning, directly after breakfast, to say that the young people were getting up a riding party for that afternoon, and to ask Nell if he might be her escort.

"You must please excuse my coming at so early an hour," he said, with a mischievous smile; "it was in order to forestall the Englishman, who almost monopolizes you of late, it seems to me."

"No, he does not," said Nell, looking but ill pleased. "He is here a great deal, I know, but I cannot forbid him the house."

"I left him in Clendenin's office," remarked Dale. "He is generally to be found there when he is not here; seems to admire the doctor prodigiously, tells me he has conceived a very warm friendship for him."

"Then he is an arrant hypocrite!" exclaimed Nell, her eyes flashing with indignation. "He is always saying or hinting disparaging things of him to me."

Dale looked surprised, then angry, then laughed lightly.

"To you, Miss Nell? Well, I suppose he dreads Clendenin's rivalry, and thinks all is fair in love."

"I shall think but ill of you, Mr. Dale, if you uphold him on any such plea as that," Nell said with vexation.

"Uphold him? No, indeed, Miss Nell. I only wish to be as charitable as the case will allow."

CHAPTER XX.

Night was closing in dark and stormy after a day of clouds and incessant rain, mingled with sleet and snow; the wild November wind swept madly through the streets, whistled, shrieked and roared in the wide chimneys and through the forests, bending the trees with its furious blast, and causing a solitary horseman to bow his head almost to the saddle bow in the vain effort to shield his face from the fierceness of its wrath.

"Courage, my brave Romeo, this has been a hard day for you and me, but rest and shelter and food are not far off now," he said, patting the neck of his steed with gentle, caressing hand, as a temporary lull succeeded a more than ordinarily fierce onset. They had crossed the last prairie, threaded the mazes of the last forest, and were close upon the outskirts of the town.

It had, indeed, been a hard day, and the doctor was cold, wet and hungry; icicles had gathered on hair and beard, and the heavy overcoat he threw off on entering his office was stiff with frozen rain.

Zeb had a bright fire blazing, and on his master's entrance hastily lighted a candle and set it on the table.

"Ah, this looks comfortable," said Kenneth, shaking off the icicles and drawing near the fire. "Hurry, Zeb, and attend to Romeo. But first, has any one called?"

"Yes, sah; de major lef' word you please step roun' dar; one ob de chillen sick."

"Much the matter, Zeb?"

"Dunno, massa doctah; 'spec' you kin tell best 'bout dat when you gets dar; yah, yah," and Zeb vanished.

I think Kenneth sighed a little inwardly, and cast a somewhat regretful look upon the comforts he was leaving behind, as he made ready again to face the storm, donning a fur cap and a camelot cloak which he took down from a nail in the wall.

As he threw it off in the hall at Major Lamar's, the parlor door opened and a sweet voice said, "Come in, doctor. It was really almost too bad to ask you to come through this storm, and I think my brother regrets having done so; for little Bertie does not seem to be seriously ill now, though some hours ago he had quite a fever."

"Ah, I am glad to hear so good a report," Kenneth said, taking the soft white hand held out to him, and smiling down into the violet eyes. "But what sort of doctor should you think me if I were afraid to face wind, rain and sleet at the call of sickness?"

"Come to the fire and warm your hands," she said lightly, ignoring his query; "they are much too cold for the handling of my pet boy."

"You are right," he returned, holding them over the blaze.

They stood there side by side for several minutes, chatting on indifferent topics, the weather, the state of the roads, cases of sickness in the town.

He thought he had never seen her look so lovely, the beautiful, abundant hair gleaming like gold in the glancing firelight, the full, red lips, the large liquid eyes, so intensely blue, that now looked half shyly into his, now drooped till the heavy silken fringes swept the fair cheek whereon the soft color came and went with every breath.

Her dress was simple, but extremely becoming, plain gray in color, made with a long full skirt that fell in soft folds about her graceful figure, and neatly-fitting bodice, edged at neck and wrists with ruffles of delicate lace.

Her only ornaments were a knot of pale blue ribbon in her hair and another at her throat.

She was in one of her gentlest, most lovable moods, and he could scarce control the impulse to catch her in his arms, hold her to his heart, and cover the sweet face with kisses.

But he must not, he dare not, and at that instant the door opened and the major came in, carrying the sick child, and followed by his wife.

"Ah, doctor, glad to see you; though, since this little chap has suddenly changed so much for the better, I'm more than half ashamed of having called you out in such weather."

"No matter for that, major, it is no new thing for me to face a storm," returned Kenneth, shaking hands with Mrs. Lamar, then turning to examine his little patient.

Nell slipped away to the privacy of her own room for a moment. Her cheeks were burning, her heart throbbed wildly; she had read Kenneth's impulse in his speaking countenance.

"He loves me, he does love me!" she murmured, pacing hurriedly to and fro;

128

"his eyes have said it over and over again, but why does he always force back the words that I can see are sometimes trembling on his very lips, as though it were a sin to speak them? O Kenneth, Kenneth, what, what is this separating wall between us," she cried, leaning her burning brow against the window frame and looking out into the storm and night.

A fierce gust of wind sent the sleet with a furious dash against the window pane and she shivered with a sudden cold.

The room was fireless, for in those days it was not thought necessary to heat any but the living rooms, and the air was damp and chill.

But she could not go down again, not yet; and wrapping herself in a thick shawl, she again paced silently to and fro schooling her heart into calmness.

The summons to supper found her so far successful that a slightly heightened color was the only remaining trace of excitement.

Dr. Clendenin had accepted an urgent invitation to remain and there was one other guest, a lady friend of Mrs. Lamar, from one of the neighboring settlements. She had been in Chillicothe a day or two and now found herself storm-stayed.

They were a cheerful party, enjoying the light and warmth and savory viands all the more for the cold, darkness, and fierce warring of the elements without.

Nell seemed the gayest of the gay, full of mirth and jest and brilliant repartee: but she avoided meeting Kenneth's eye, while he saw every look, every movement of hers, and when in passing an empty cup to be refilled, their hands touched, it sent a sudden thrill through both.

Kenneth was very weary and could not prevail upon himself to decline a seat for the evening beside the major's warm, hospitable hearth, nor refuse his eyes the privilege of feasting upon Nell's beauty, his ears that of drinking in each low sweet tone of her voice and the silvery sound of her rippling laughter.

"Where's your master?" asked Dale, looking into Kenneth's office, where Zeb was luxuriating in front of a blazing, roaring fire, seated in the doctor's arm-chair, hands in pockets, pipe in mouth and heels on the mantelpiece.

"Gone to de major's, sah," answered the boy, bringing his feet and the forelegs of the chair to the floor with a loud thump, and removing the pipe, as he turned to look at his interlocutor.

"He has, eh? and you're having a good time in his absence?"

"Yes, sah, massa doctah neber grudge dat when de work's done."

"No, I daresay not," and Dale drew back his head and shut the door.

"Gone to the major's, eh!" he soliloquized as he stepped back into his own den; "well I reckon I'm about as storm proof as he, so I'll follow, not being in the mood to appreciate solitude, and feeling that my hard day's work merits the reward of a little rest and recreation."

Lyttleton had come to a like resolve and was at that moment closeted in his own room with his valet, to whom he seemed to have been giving some directions; his last words as he wrapped himself in his cloak and went out, were, "Come towards midnight, for though these people accustom themselves to such confoundedly early hours, I'll manage to keep them up for once, and follow my orders implicitly. We could not have a more favorable time, the darkness, the storm, why if spirits ever walk abroad one would expect it to be on such a night as this," he concluded with a mocking laugh.

"Dat ish so, mynheer, and I dinks von vill valk dese shtreets pefore morning goomes," returned Hans, echoing the laugh.

Arrived at the major's, Dale found the family and guests seated around the fire, the ladies on one side, the gentlemen on the other.

The circle widened to admit him, Nell laughingly expressing great surprise at seeing him on such a night.

"Well I don't know," he said, "why I should be supposed less storm proof than the doctor here, and to tell the truth, fair ladies, I couldn't endure the thought of his basking in your smiles, while I sat alone in my dingy office."

"You forget," said Kenneth, "how often the case has been reversed, Godfrey. If you follow me up in this fashion I shall never be even with you."

"Not at all necessary that you should, my good fellow," remarked Dale, toying with Nell's ball of yarn, for she, as well as the other ladies, was knitting, and he had drawn his chair close to hers, with a familiarity Kenneth regarded with a jealous pang.

"Alas that he could not have forestalled Dale in this! And did she care for Dale," he asked himself, watching them without appearing to do so. How could he bear it if she did? Yet better that by far, than seeing her in the possession of Lyttleton.

His absence would be at least one advantage reaped from the increasing fury of the storm. Lyttleton was not a rugged pioneer like themselves, and would surely remain closely housed until it had spent its wrath.

He was mistaken; scarcely had the thought passed through his mind, when there came a loud rap upon the outer door, quickly followed by the

Englishman's entrance.

"What you, too, sir, out in this terrific storm!" exclaimed Dale, not too well pleased, as the circle again widened to admit the new comer.

"Why, yes," said Lyttleton, "I'm not a milk-sop, my dear sir, and finding both the bar-room at the tavern and my own apartment extremely dull, I ventured out, trusting to a heavy cloak for protection from wind and rain, and to the kind hospitality of these friends for a welcome here."

"You are heartily welcome, sir," said the major; "but draw up closer to the fire, for I am sorry to see that the cloak has not proved a perfect protection from the wet."

"Thanks—no; I found I had miscalculated, to some extent, the force of the wind," laughed Lyttleton, with a downward glance at his nether limbs, as he accepted the invitation.

It was unworthy of Nell, but seized with a sudden impulse to vex Kenneth, and excite his jealousy, by way of revenge for his strange, his unaccountable silence toward her, she seemed for the next hour scarcely conscious of his presence, while at the same time she lavished smiles, sweet looks, and pleasant words upon his two rivals.

It did pain him sorely, though he gave no sign by word or look, and the sharpest pang was the thought that she was less noble and true, less worthy of the exalted place she had hitherto held in his esteem, than he could have believed.

But the storm grew wilder, the air was full of weird and eerie sounds, and an awed, half fearful silence fell upon the little company.

They drew their chairs nearer together, and Lyttleton, breaking the silence, began telling legendary tales of storm and flood in his own and other lands, following them up with stories of second sight, of murder, suicide and ghostly visitants, fit to curdle the blood with horror.

The lady guest and Mrs. Lamar, too, had some to match these last, and though the major, the captain, Kenneth and Dale, listened with incredulous looks and smiles, it was with an interest that made them, as well as the others, unconscious of the lapse of time till Dale, glancing casually at the tall old clock ticking in a corner, exclaimed that it was half past eleven.

Lyttleton had just finished one of his most thrilling and horrible ghost stories, which had wrought up the female portion of his audience, at least, into a state of extreme nervous excitement; and at that instant there came a blast that seemed to shake the house to its very foundations, the door flew open, and in stalked a tall Hessian in officer's uniform, drawing his sword and vociferating loudly in his native tongue.

The ladies shrieked, the Hessian advanced toward the major, brandishing his weapon, gesticulating wildly, and yelling with a fury that drowned the noise of the raging tempest!

The gentlemen seemed stunned with astonishment. Lyttleton was the first to recover himself.

"Begone!" he cried, hastily placing himself so as to shield Nell from the approach of the enraged foreigner, and drawing a pistol from his pocket, "begone, sirrah, or I will shoot you through the heart."

With that the Hessian turned about and beat a hasty retreat, grumbling and swearing as he went.

Lyttleton stepped quickly to the door and secured it after him, then returned to Nell's side to whisper with triumphant air, "Ghost or mortal, I have driven the wretch away, and you are safe, fair lady."

The other two ladies, pale, trembling, half-fainting with terror, hailed him gratefully as their deliverer; but Nell had recovered from her fright in the very instant of uttering the shriek called forth by the sudden apparition.

Was there not something familiar in the face, the form, the stride with which he crossed the room?

She looked Lyttleton keenly in the eye, then returned his whisper with another.

"Did it require any great stretch of courage to order your valet out of the house?"

She had drawn her bow at a venture and was surprised to see by his air of overwhelming confusion and chagrin, that her arrow had sped straight to the mark.

"Your Hessian as sure as I stand here, sir!" cried Captain Bernard, recovering himself and clapping the major on the shoulder. "Well, well, I'll believe in ghosts hereafter. I never was more astonished or taken aback in my life. Lyttleton, you showed yourself the most quick-witted and self-possessed of any of us. Allow me to congratulate you on the laurels you have won."

"I—I—" stammered Lyttleton with a deprecating glance at Nell, whose lips were curling with scorn.

"We will spare your modesty," said the major, grasping the Englishman's hand warmly, "but let me tender you the thanks of the company."

Lyttleton was strangely confused and embarrassed; the ease and perfect self-possession on which he so prided himself, had on a sudden entirely forsaken him; he darted a quick, imploring glance at Nell, and half in pity, half in contempt she returned an answering look that told him his secret was safe.

The others saw this by-play with varied feelings of wonder, curiosity and surprise, but no one understood it.

Captain Bernard was the first to speak.

"Well, gentlemen, it is growing very late and no prospect of abatement of the storm. I move that we adjourn *sine die*. Mr. Lyttleton, shall I have the pleasure of your good company to our hotel?"

CHAPTER XXI.

Never had scheme more signal failure than that of Lyttleton for convincing pretty Nell Lamar of his dauntless bravery; he went away from the major's that night crestfallen and angry, cursing his ill-luck and her quickness of perception.

Nor was fair Nell herself in a much more enviable state of mind; there was a sad, reproachful look in Kenneth's eyes as he bade her a courteous good-night, which haunted her for days and weeks like a nightmare.

She purposely avoided him when he called the next morning to enquire about

Bertie, and when the weather permitted her to resume her walks and rides, was careful to select those in which she was least likely to meet him.

He was not slow to perceive this and it wounded him deeply; particularly as Lyttleton was very frequently her companion and his society seemed not unpleasant to her, if one might judge from her bright looks and smiles.

Yet Nell despised Lyttleton heartily, and at times herself scarcely less.

"Nell Lamar, you are becoming an arrant and shameless coquette!" she would exclaim almost fiercely to herself in the privacy of her own room. "I'm ashamed of you! no wonder Dr. Clendenin looks at you as if he despaired of you and pitied you for your depravity. Well, whose fault is it but his; why do his lips refuse to speak what his eyes have said over and over again? Oh, it is mean and shameful! I will not care for him or his reproving looks! He is no better than I, and yet—and yet—O Kenneth, Kenneth, you are good and noble and true, though I cannot understand it!"

Thus she was by turns angry and repentant, now reproaching him, and now herself.

She did not, however, give Lyttleton much encouragement. As she had said to Dale, she could not forbid him the house, neither could she avoid being in the same room with him when there, as no other, the kitchen excepted, was warm enough for comfort at that inclement season, nor could she prevent his joining her in the street.

She usually declined his attentions when it could be done without positive rudeness, yet he persevered, the prize seeming to him all the more valuable because of its difficulty of acquisition.

Dale looked on with vexation and a growing dislike to Lyttleton; but Clare gave the latter her countenance, making him always welcome to the house, saying little things that flattered his vanity, and vaguely hinting that Nell was capricious and might be won in time by clever courting.

The major was apparently oblivious of the whole matter, while the gossips of the town compared notes and speculated as to the probability that the Englishman's suit would eventually prosper.

These queries and conjectures now and then reached Kenneth's ears, inflicting a sharp pang all unsuspected by the talkers; for it had come to be the popular opinion that Dr. Clendenin was a confirmed bachelor, utterly indifferent to the charms of the softer sex; and not by word or tone, or so much as a change in the calm gravity of his demeanor, did he let them into the secret of his silent suffering.

And it was not slight; many a night of sleepless anguish it cost him to think how "his darling, his own precious little Nell," as he must call her, was being wiled away from him by one who could never, he was sure, half appreciate her worth, and was far from deserving so rich a prize.

But could it be possible that she would throw herself away thus, that she would give her hand without her heart? For was not that all his own, had not those beautiful, eloquent eyes betrayed her secret to him spite of herself? And yet, and yet—had he, beyond a doubt or peradventure, read that look aright? Oh, if he might but go to her, pour out the story of his love and sue for hers? But alas, alas, he dare not, 'twould be a more grievous wrong than to keep silent and let her think what she would of him.

And though he longed continually for her sweet society, though he felt as if shut out of a heaven on earth while staying away from her dear presence, he must constrain himself to do so, always have some excuse ready when the major urged upon him the hospitalities of his house.

And what right had he to accuse the dear girl in his heart of fickleness and coquetry? He, and he alone, was to blame for her conduct, because his looks had told the story of his love and his lips failed to confirm it.

There was, perhaps, more than usual sociability among the young people of Chillicothe that winter, and Lyttleton was invited everywhere, generally accepting; always when he knew that Miss Lamar would be one of the guests; and not unfrequently she was much vexed by the marked attention he was pleased to bestow upon her.

Some of the other young ladies would have received them with far more complacency, deeming the handsome, fascinating, and apparently wealthy Englishman no mean prize in the matrimonial lottery.

Of course Nell was teased and jested with about her adorer, but to the surprise of the well-meaning jokers, their witticisms were received with hauteur, and sometimes positive anger, leaving no room for doubt that the subject was an unpleasant one.

Still most of them made up their minds that it was only their remarks that were so distasteful to her, and not the man himself, or his evident predilection.

Nell usually enjoyed the sleigh rides, the quiltings, the social tea-drinkings, and evening parties which constituted the winter festivities of the town, and was the life of them all; but this season she was glad to get away from them, or rather from Lyttleton's society, to the quiet and seclusion of Mr. Nash's farm-house, to which she was carried off by its mistress one bright December morning, for a fortnight's visit.

Mrs. Nash had come into town to exchange butter and eggs for dry goods and groceries. That done she called at the major's, proposed to Nell to take a vacant seat in her sleigh, and return with her, and was delighted by a prompt acceptance of the invitation.

"I don't know how Mr. Lyttleton will be able to endure so long a separation," remarked Clare demurely.

"And I don't care!" returned Nell, with spirit. "I shall enjoy it extremely, and selfish as it may seem, that is all I am concerned about."

"How about Dr. Clendenin?" queried Mrs. Nash with a roguish smile.

The girl's face flushed, then paled.

"He is seldom here and will not miss me," she said in a quiet tone as she left the room to make the necessary preparations for the trip.

"Your English friend will be sure to follow you," said Clare as they bade good-bye.

"He would not dare!" cried Nell. "But don't you let him know where I am, for there is no saying how far his audacity may carry him."

"Quite as far as you travel to-day, I've no doubt," laughed Clare.

"Nell," said Mrs. Nash, as they glided swiftly over the snow, leaving the town behind. "I hear that Englishman is very attentive to you; but I can tell you Dr. Clendenin is worth a dozen of him."

"What has that to do with it?" asked Nell dryly, screening her face from view in the folds of a thick veil. "They are not rivals."

"I don't know what you mean, my dear child. I do know that Dr. Clendenin loves you."

"He has made you his confidante?"

Nell's tone was a mixture of inquiry, pain, incredulity, anger and pique.

"Not intentionally; but words could not have told it more plainly than his looks, tones and actions when he found you lying insensible beside the carcass of that mad cat, and thought you had been bitten."

"All your imagination, *mon ami*, Dr. Clendenin and I are nothing to each other."

Nell strove to speak lightly, but there was an undertone of bitterness which did not escape her friend.

Mrs. Nash mused silently for a moment, saying to herself there had probably been a lovers' quarrel, but she hoped it would all come right in the end, and she would be on the lookout to do anything in her power to bring about a reconciliation.

She was not one of the prying kind, however, and knew that Nell would be quick to resent any attempt to worm her secrets from her, so when she presently spoke again, it was upon a widely different topic.

They had a pleasant sociable time together for several days, Nell finding positive pleasure in helping her friend to make up winter garments for the children.

Then came a heavy snow storm followed by bright weather, clear and cold, making excellent sleighing.

Mrs. Nash had carefully avoided broaching the subject of Nell's love affairs, but they had, nevertheless, been seldom absent from her thoughts, which had busied themselves with projects for restoring harmony between the two, whom she supposed to have had a misunderstanding.

She had cast about in her mind for an excuse for sending for the doctor, that so they might be brought together and given an opportunity for mutual explanation. So anxious for this was she that it seemed hardly a matter for regret when she found she had taken cold with the change of weather, and had a slight sore throat.

Mr. Nash was going into town and she requested him to call at the doctor's office and ask him to come out and see her.

Nell heard, and it sent the blood to her cheek and made her heart beat quickly. She had not exchanged a word with Dr. Clendenin since that evening when she had read, or fancied she did, reproof in his eye and voice because of her flirtation with Lyttleton; and she both longed and dreaded to meet him.

The latter feeling increased as the time drew near when he might be expected; the merry jingle of sleigh bells, and the sight of a cutter with a gentleman in it wrapped in furs, dashing up to the gate, had almost sent her flying from the room, so strong was the impulse at that moment to avoid him.

But a second glance told her that was not Kenneth's noble figure which sprang from the vehicle and came hurrying up the path to the house.

She sat still and in another moment Lyttleton stood smiling and bowing before her, hat in hand.

"Excuse this intrusion, fair lady," he said, "I have felt like a Peri shut out of heaven since your withdrawal from the major's house, and I come as bearer of a letter which I must even hope may secure me a welcome."

He tendered it gracefully as he spoke.

"Ah, thank you!" she cried, her face flushing with pleasure, for letters were a rare thing in those days.

He bade her read it while he sat by the fire and chatted with Mrs. Nash, to whom, with his usual tact and skill, he soon managed to make himself extremely entertaining.

"Now, fair lady," he said, turning to Nell as she refolded her letter, "may I not claim a reward for the slight service I have had the happiness to render you?"

"Of what kind, sir?" she answered with a saucy smile.

"The privilege of taking you out for a short drive. The sleighing is superb."

Nell was in a most gracious mood, and then here was the wished for chance to escape the dreaded meeting with Dr. Clendenin. She consented at once and hastily donned cloak and hood.

"I'm afraid you will find it very cold," objected Mrs. Nash, more anxious to detain the young girl for Kenneth's coming, and to prevent any acceptance of attentions from his rival, than she would have liked to acknowledge.

"Oh no, madame," hastily interposed Lyttleton, "I have a foot-stove and plenty of robes, and there is no wind; indeed I assure you it is quite delightful out to-day, the air is so pure and bracing."

"And I am warmly dressed, and have a thick veil," added Nell.

Lyttleton tucked the robes snugly about her, saying, "I trust you will not suffer from cold, Miss Lamar."

"Oh, no!" she answered with a gay laugh.

"Now which way shall we travel?" he asked, gathering up the reins.

With the thought that Dr. Clendenin would be coming from the town, and the desire to avoid a meeting, Nell named the opposite direction.

But they had not gone half a mile when that very thing occurred.

Dr. Clendenin had a patient some miles farther out from town, had called there first, and was intending to take Mr. Nash's in his way home.

He bowed with grave courtesy to Nell and her companion, in passing, recognizing the latter with a jealous pang that was like the stab of a sharp knife.

Nell's cheeks flushed and her eyes fell; she was thankful that her veil hid her agitation from Dr. Clendenin; but then and many times through the succeeding weeks and months, she would have given much to deny to him the knowledge that she had accepted this attention from Lyttleton.

In vain she asked herself what concern was it of his, what right he had to object? She could not shake off the feeling that she was in some way, to some extent, accountable to him.

From that day she was as ready with excuses as Kenneth himself when the only alternative was to permit Lyttleton to be her escort.

CHAPTER XXII.

Lyttleton cordially hated Clendenin, but endeavored to conceal his dislike and ill-will under the mask of friendship, haunting the doctor's office all through the winter and spring with nearly as great persistency as during the first week of his sojourn in Chillicothe.

He indulged a like feeling toward Dale, though to a less degree; hating him as a rival in love, Kenneth as that and something more.

Spring opened early. Bright, warm days with hard frosts at night made the sap in the sugar maples run freely, and many farmers in the vicinity of the town were busied in catching and boiling it down. Then visits to the sugar camps became one of the popular amusements of the young people.

Dale got up a party to go on horseback to one five or six miles away, inviting Lyttleton, but taking care first to secure to himself the honor of playing escort to Miss Lamar.

Lyttleton was very angry when he learned this, but having promised to go, tried to console himself with the young lady he considered next to Nell in beauty and fascination.

He managed to conceal his ill humor, the others seemed in high spirits, and they had a merry time.

In returning they made a circuit through the woods. They were following the course of a little stream when Dale, who was taking the lead, suddenly gave a loud "Hurrah!"

"What is it? what is it?" cried the others, hurrying up.

"A bear's stepping place," he answered gleefully, pointing to some deep indentations in the soft, spongy ground; evidently the tracks of some large wild animal, and leading off from the water's edge into the woods.

"A bear!" cried Lyttleton, horrified, "then let us hurry these ladies home with all speed."

"Not much danger, sir," remarked a young fellow named Bell; "bears are lazy at this time of year, and we all have our guns. If the ladies are not afraid, I'd like very much to follow up the track and see where his bearship lodges."

"So should I," said Dale. "However, we can note the spot and return to it to-morrow."

"No, lead on; I'm not afraid," cried Nell. "He's likely to be in his hole any how, isn't he?"

"Yes; unless he's on his way to the water here, for a drink. They come after that about once in two or three days."

A consultation was held, and a majority being in favor of following up the track, they did so, finding it led them to a large hollow tree distant some few hundred yards in the depths of the wood.

Nothing was seen of the bear himself, but the young men, familiar with his habits, made no doubt that he was inside the tree, and promised themselves fine sport in hunting him out, and a grand feast upon his flesh; the fat part of which is said to make a very luxurious repast when boiled or roasted with turkey or venison.

Bell proposed to climb the tree, which was rough and knotted, and look into the hole; but to that the ladies objected.

So they turned about and went home, the young men arranging on the way for the proposed hunt.

The next day, their number augmented by the addition of Major Lamar and Dr. Clendenin, they returned to the spot.

Bell, armed with a long pole sharpened at one end, climbed the tree, the others looking on near by, each with his gun loaded and ready for instant use.

"Here he is," cried Bell, peeping in at the hole in the tree. "Out o' this, Sir Bruin! out I say!" prodding the creature with his stick as he spoke.

The beast uttered a low growl, but did not move. But Bell continued to punch, prick and order him out, until finally he obeyed, moving heavily to the hole and slowly dragging himself out.

As soon as he was fairly clear of the hole, Dale and the major, who had been selected for the duty, fired; taking aim so accurately that the animal fell dead instantly.

Tig, Zeb and Hans were directed to take care of the carcass.

Bell, who upon starting the bear had slipped out on to a large limb and nonchalantly awaited the shooting, dropped to the ground and with the rest of the hunters moved on in search of other game.

"You are a daring fellow," observed Lyttleton admiringly, to Bell. "I was really alarmed for your safety."

"Oh, I didn't feel myself in much danger," returned Bell, with a light laugh; "for you see I had time to slip aside, after starting him, before he could get clear of the hole, and I knew Dale and the major would not miss their mark."

The party had traversed some miles of forest, shooting several deer and a number of wild turkeys, when they came upon the "stepping place" of another bear, and then upon bruin himself returning from the stream where he had been slaking his thirst.

This one was of less amiable disposition, or wider awake than the first, and when Lyttleton, who happened to be nearest, fired at it, aiming so carelessly in his haste and excitement that he only wounded without disabling it, the creature turned, rushed at him in fury and rose on its hind legs prepared to give him a hug which would have left no breath in his body.

But there was a sharp report, a bullet whizzed past him, almost grazing his cheek, entered the creature's eye, penetrating to the brain, and it dropped dead at his feet.

He staggered back pale and trembling.

"You are not hurt?" asked Kenneth's voice close at his side.

"Yes; no—I—I can hardly tell."

"Well done, doc!" cried the major, running up to them; "he's a big, powerful fellow," looking down at the bear, "and could have given a tremendous squeeze, such as would crush a man's bones to bits. Lyttleton, I think Dr. Clendenin has saved your life."

Lyttleton stammered out some words of thanks, then moved away muttering to himself, "Confound the thing, he's the last man I'd willingly owe such a debt to!"

CHAPTER XXIII.

Spring deepened into summer and still Lyttleton lingered in Chillicothe, though with no apparent object unless it might be the hope of winning Miss Lamar. He continued to be a constant visitor at the major's, welcomed by him and Clare, but seeing little of Nell, who took particular pains to avoid him, by going out at such times as he was likely to call, or busying herself in another part of the house when he was in the parlor.

He noticed this with anger and chagrin, yet as we have said, difficulty of attainment only increased his estimate of the value of the prize he sought; and suspecting, in his egregious self-conceit and egoism, her conduct to he merely an affectation of coyness with the purpose to bring him to a formal declaration of love, for how could any woman resist such fascination as his of person, manner and fortune, he determined to seize the first opportunity to make her an offer of heart and hand.

With that end in view he dropped in one day at the major's just at tea time;

ostensibly for the purpose of inquiring if they had heard a piece of news that was creating some little excitement in the town, and sure of an invitation to stay and partake with them of the evening meal.

The news was concerning Wawillaway's assassin, the dastardly ruffian Wolf. He had fled to Kentucky to escape the merited punishment of his crime at the hands of the two sons of the murdered chief, who, in accordance with the Indian code, making it the right and duty of the nearest of kin to kill the slayer of their relative, had vowed vengeance upon him.

The murderer may, however, purchase his life at a price agreed upon by the family of his victim, and Wolf had employed an agent to make terms with the two young men.

It was now announced that these terms had been agreed upon, and the business would be concluded by an interesting ceremony at Old Town, to take place the following day.

Lyttleton had heard several gentlemen say they meant to be present and to take their wives or sweethearts with them, and had determined that he too would go, if possible as Miss Lamar's escort.

But Dale had the start of him this time, as on several former occasions, and was already in the major's parlor, discussing the news with the family, and engaged to conduct Miss Nell to see the ceremony, when Lyttleton came in; as the latter presently learned from the conversation.

He was disappointed and angry, but so sure of success in his more important errand that he comforted himself with the thought that this was Dale's last chance to serve him such a trick.

Dale, for his part, had no idea that any such calamity awaited Nell or himself, and having a little urgent business matter to attend to, went away shortly after tea to which both callers had been hospitably invited, in a very cheerful frame of mind, leaving the field to Lyttleton.

He knew the Englishman to be a rival, but did not consider him a dangerous one; and at all events Nell was secured to himself for the coming day.

Clare, though at one time quite sure that Dr. Clendenin and Nell cared for each other, had now entirely given up the idea of ever seeing them united. She could not worm out the facts from Nell, but concluded that there must have been an irreconcilable quarrel.

"Well, she was not sorry, for this Englishman was certainly very much in love, and would make a better match, from a worldly point of view at least." So she did what lay in her power to favor and advance his suit.

Something in his look or manner told her of his purpose to-night, and she contrived that the two should be left alone in the parlor soon after Dale's departure.

Lyttleton seized the opportunity at once, poured out passionate expressions of love, and in plain words asked Nell to become his wife.

She tried in vain to stop him, he would be heard to the end.

"Mr. Lyttleton," she said, rising with flushed cheeks and sparkling eyes, "I thank you for the honor you have done me, but I cannot entertain such a proposition for a moment. Nay, hear me out," as he seemed about to enter a protest, "even as you have compelled me to hear you. I would have spared you the pain of a rejection, but you would not let me."

"My dear Miss Nell—Miss Lamar," he stammered, "it cannot be that I hear aright! or if I do that you understand what it is that you are rejecting. I will say nothing"—with an affectation of humility—"of any charms of person or address that some may attribute to your humble servant, but an honored and ancient name, an assured position among the English gentry, fine estate, large fortune—"

She interrupted him, drawing herself up to her full height, while her eyes flashed and her cheek crimsoned with indignation.

"If I ever marry, Mr. Lyttleton, it shall be neither position nor estate—least of all money."

"What more can you ask, pray?" he inquired, folding his arms and throwing back his head with an air of hauteur.

"Something of infinitely greater worth," she replied, her eyes kindling, "infinitely better and higher; the love and confidence of a true and noble heart, the heart of a man who lives not for himself, but for others, who is not content to pass his days in inglorious ease and idleness, but does with his might what his hands find to do to glorify God and benefit his fellow men."

"Clendenin, curse him!" he muttered between his clinched teeth.

Her quick ear caught the words not meant for it.

"Yes," she said, with a peculiar smile, "Dr. Clendenin answers the description very well, but not he alone; I am thankful to say there are others among my countrymen who do."

"Your countrymen! always your countrymen," he blazed out growing very red and angry; "a set of clodhoppers who are obliged to earn their bread by the sweat of their brows. Mark my words, miss, you'll see the day when you would be very glad to share the inglorious ease of a member of the favored class denominated the English gentry."

"No, sir," she answered with spirit, "I am heart and soul an American, and our differing nationalities would be an insuperable objection to the acceptance of your offer were there none other."

At which, boiling with rage and disappointment, he hastily caught up his hat and left the house.

Nell's conscience pricked her with the reminder that those last words were untrue; since, had Lyttleton been an American, and Kenneth an Englishman, it would have made no difference in her feelings toward either.

Lyttleton hurried on through the streets and out into the country beyond, neither knowing nor caring in his rage and disappointment what direction he took. All he wanted was to avoid observation until he could recover his accustomed self-control; lest otherwise the story of his rejection should be bruited about and himself treated to scorn and ridicule in consequence.

Unconsciously he struck into the trail that led to Old Town.

The sun had set, but there was yet sufficient light to show him the stalwart figure of a huntsman with his gun on his shoulder and a string of birds in his hand, coming to meet him.

Lyttleton stood still for a moment, debating in his own mind whether to go on or to retrace his steps, when the other called out in a well-known voice,

"Dat you, mynheer? It ish goot you haf come. I have some dings der dell you."

"What things, Hans?" asked Lyttleton moving on to meet his valet, to whom he had given permission for a day's sport in the woods.

"I dells you pooty quick, mynheer," returned Hans close at his side; then went on to relate how he had fallen in with a party of Indians on their way to Old Town to take part in the coming ceremony, and that they had among them a white woman who seemed, from her looks and actions, to have been with them a long while.

Lyttleton listened eagerly, and when Hans had finished his story, tried to elicit further information by asking questions in regard to the height, complexion, demeanor, and apparent age of the woman.

When these had all been answered. "It may be she," he said musingly as if thinking aloud; then in a quick, determined way, "Hans, you must take me at once to see this woman. It may prove of the greatest importance that I should see and talk with her this very night."

Hans, already weary and footsore with his day's tramp, would have greatly preferred to move on to Chillicothe and get a warm supper at the General Anthony Wayne, followed by a lounge on the bench before the bar-room door. Accordingly he showed some unwillingness to obey the order.

It was, however, speedily overcome by the offer of double wages for that week. He turned about at once and by the light of the moon, just rising over the tree tops, the two followed the trail till it brought them to the Indian town, where after some search they found the object of their quest seated alone at the door of her wigwam, smoking a pipe and seemingly wrapped in meditation, enjoying the moonlight and the cool evening breeze which was particularly refreshing after the day.

Lyttleton accosted her courteously in English, and she answered in the same tongue, inviting him to take a seat on the bearskin by her side.

"Thank you, I do not wish to crowd you, I will sit here," he said, appropriating a stump close at hand.

Hans, by his master's direction, had refrained from approaching very near, and was resting himself on a fallen tree a few hundred yards distant.

He saw that Lyttleton and the woman were soon in earnest conversation, but could not hear the words spoken.

Some of the Indians were nearer, but few of them had any knowledge of English, the language used by both speakers during the interview, most of them none at all, and only from looks, tones and gestures, could they gather any hint of the subject of the conference.

It lasted for a full hour; then Lyttleton rose and stood before the woman, talking and gesticulating with great earnestness. He seemed to be vehemently urging some request which she was inclined to deny; at length he drew out a silken purse full of broad gold pieces which glittered in the moonlight as he held it up.

"Promise me," he said, "and this is yours; keep your promise till I see you again and it shall be doubled."

"Give it me then," she cried, stretching out an eager hand.

"You promise?"

"Yes, yes; why not?"

He dropped it into her open palm, saying impressively, "Remember. Now, good-bye," and turned exultingly to go on his way.

"Stay," she cried.

"Well, what more?" he asked facing her again, "is it not enough?"

"Yes; but you have not told me who you are, or why you—"

"It does not matter; all you have to do is to follow my directions," he interrupted somewhat haughtily, and strode rapidly away.

"Your errand shpeed so petter as goot, mynheer?" queried Hans as they struck into the trail again.

"I flatter myself it will all come out right in the end, Hans," was the reply; then there was a muttered word or two that sounded like an imprecation upon some absent person, with a threat of vengeance for some real or fancied injury.

Chillicothe seemed sleeping when they re-entered it; the streets were silent and deserted, the houses closed and dark; only from the bar-room window of the General Anthony Wayne gleamed the light of a single tallow candle. Master and man entered there without noise or bustle and presently slipped quietly away to the room of the former.

CHAPTER XXIV.

Curiosity was rife in Chillicothe and its vicinity in regard to the ceremony about to take place at Old Town, and as the set time drew near very many whites of both sexes might have been seen approaching the spot, singly or in parties.

Clendenin, hindered by the demands of his profession, was one of the last to arrive on the ground.

He found the Indians drawn up in a hollow square, outside of which was the concourse of white spectators, inside Wolf with his promised bribe,—a horse, a new saddle and bridle, and a new rifle for each of the sons of his victim.

Kenneth had come alone. He knew that Dale had preceded him, and whom he was to escort thither, and there they were on the opposite side of the square; Nell in a becoming riding hat and habit, sitting her horse with accustomed ease and grace; Dale by her side, the picture of content and good humor.

Kenneth sighed involuntarily; what would he not have given to be in Dale's place, yet he was glad to see his friend so favored rather than the Englishman.

The next moment he perceived that Lyttleton also was one of the assembled throng; at some little distance from those two, but in a position to get a good view of their faces, and that he was watching them closely, with a look of jealous rage.

Kenneth's eyes turned to Nell again to see hers fixed for an instant upon the burly form and ruffianly face of Wolf, with an expression of disgust and horror.

But the ceremony was beginning, and for a little claimed the attention of all present.

The two young men came forward into the hollow square, Wolf presented his horses and trappings, they lifted their hands toward heaven invoking the Great Spirit, and declaring that to Him alone they transferred the blood and life of Wolf forfeited by the death of their father.

They then shook hands with Wolf in token of their forgiveness, saluted him as a brother, and lighting the calumet of peace, smoked with him in the presence of the Great Spirit.

The scene was one of deep solemnity and many eyes filled with tears as they gazed upon it.

But it was over and the crowd began to disperse, tongues were loosed, and Kenneth, silently threading his way among the talkers, casually overheard the remark, "There is a white woman here, they say, who has been a great many years with the Indians."

He almost caught his breath for an instant as he suddenly reined in his horse, his heart beating like a hammer, a wild hope springing up within his breast, a rush of mingled emotions surging through his brain.

Strange that he had not thought of such a possibility.

He turned back, dismounted and secured his horse to a sapling; doing it all mechanically. Then he strolled about among the Indians, shaking hands with them and kindly inquiring after their health and that of their families, patting the heads of the papooses, nodding smilingly to the older children, and scanning with furtive, but keen scrutiny, the face of each elderly squaw.

At length he came upon the object of his search, a woman past middle age, whose features were unmistakably those of the white race.

She sat on the grass in the shade of a tree, near the door of a wigwam, her fingers busily employed in embroidering a moccasin.

She seemed scarcely aware of his presence as he stood before her vainly striving to still the tumultuous beating of his heart.

Controlling his voice by a great effort, he addressed her in English, in a quiet tone.

"How do you do, mother?"

She looked up for an instant, shook her head slowly, and dropped her eyes upon her work again.

"You understand me?" he said inquiringly, "you have not forgotten your native tongue?"

"Me squaw," was the laconic answer, unaccompanied by so much as a glance.

He sat down on a stump near at hand, the very same on which Lyttleton had seated himself the previous night, and watched her silently for a moment, while he considered the best manner of approaching her so as to win her confidence and learn whether she could indeed tell him aught of that which all these years he had been trying to discover.

"You are a white woman, why should you wish to conceal the fact?" he said at length in a soft, persuasive tone. "I have no design against you, but on the contrary would gladly do you any service in my power."

Again she raised her head, this time giving him a steady look, and was it fancy that for a single instant there was something like a gleam of recognition in her eye.

If so it was gone again before he could be sure it had been there; while she answered indifferently in the Shawnee tongue, that she did not understand what he had just said, and that she was not a pale face but an Indian woman, the wife of a Shawnee brave.

Kenneth sat for a moment in perplexed silence; her assertion that she did not belong to the white race was evidently false, yet what could be her motive for making it? If she preferred to remain with the tribe no one could force her away, or would be likely to care to do so.

As he watched her again busied with her work, apparently wholly careless of his presence, and studied her face, recalling the description that had been given him, calculating what her age might be, and the changes produced by the hardships and exposure of her wild life, the conviction grew upon him that it was possible, even probable, she was the very woman for whom he had so long and vainly searched.

He determined upon a bold course.

Leaning toward her and gazing full into her face, "Reumah Clark," he said, "have you quite forgotten the old life in the little valley among the mountains of Eastern Tennessee, the husband and children you then loved so dearly, the kind neighbors at whose house you were when the Indians swooped down so suddenly upon you all?"

She had not been able to repress a slight start at the unexpected sound of that name, or to entirely preserve the stolidity of countenance with which she had begun the interview.

She rose hastily and disappeared from view within the wigwam.

The action left in Kenneth's mind little room for doubt of her identity, but alas, of what avail that he had found her, if she could not be induced to speak of those long past occurrences and to reveal the secret which, if known to any mortal, was possessed by her alone?

His heart beat almost to suffocation while he forced himself to sit waiting quietly there at the door of her wigwam in the forlorn hope that she might return in a truthful and communicative mood.

He was alone, no one near, though at the distance of a few hundred yards, the young Indians were engaged in active sports and their shouts and laughter occasionally broke the stillness of the woodland scene.

He waited what seemed an age to his tortured nerves, perceiving neither sound nor motion within the tent, then rose and moved slowly toward the spot where he had left his faithful steed.

He had not quite reached it when a hand was laid lightly upon his arm, and turning he found a tall young brave standing by his side.

"Does the pale face forget?" he asked in good English, holding out his hand.

"Have we ever met before?" asked Kenneth, earnestly scanning the lad's face, while he took the hand in a cordial grasp and shook it heartily.

"Indians never forget good white men," continued the lad, "white man find Little Horn in the snow, take him in his arms, carry him to his fire, wrap him in his blanket, feed him. White man very good. Indian boy love good white man."

"Oh I remember you now!" cried Kenneth, joyfully, shaking hands with increased cordiality, while his face lighted up with his rare, beautiful smile. "I am glad to meet you again. Tell me, can I do anything more for you?"

"Little Horn's turn now. What would my friend with White Swan, the warrior Black Eagle's squaw?"

"I wish to talk with her about my mother and father, whom she once knew," said Kenneth. "But she refuses to listen or to speak."

"Has my friend heap money?"

"I have some. Will money open her lips?"

The Indian gave an expressive grunt, then went on to tell of Lyttleton's visit to their camp and interview with the woman, of which he had been an unnoticed witness.

He had not heard or understood all the talk between them, but enough to enable him to gather by the assistance of their tones and gestures, the holding up of the purse, and the eager hand outstretched to receive it, that a bribe had been offered and accepted, and her conduct of to-day, which also he had closely watched, had convinced him that her promise had been to maintain silence toward Kenneth, of whose intended visit Lyttleton must have known.

Clendenin listened in great surprise. Who could it have been? He did not know that he had an enemy in the whole world, and this visit was entirely unexpected even to himself.

But Little Horn's communication gave him fresh hope. "Would he be his messenger to the white squaw," he asked earnestly; "would he go to her and say that if she would talk with the pale face, and answer his questions as well as she could he would give her as much money as the pale face visitor of the previous night had promised her if she kept silence?"

The Indian accepted the commission, went at once to the wigwam, Kenneth slowly following, passed in, and a few moments after reappeared in company with the woman.

A change had come over her face; it no longer wore the stolid look Kenneth had seen upon it during their earlier interview, the features were agitated and there were traces of tears on the cheeks. His words had recalled half forgotten scenes of bitter sorrow, terror and despair.

"Speak! I listen," she said in the English tongue, seating herself and motioning to him to do the same, then burying her face in her hands.

He dropped upon the grass by her side and began at once in low, quiet, almost mournful tones.

"Many years ago, before I was born, there stood two log cabins, some half mile apart, in a little valley among the mountains of Tennessee. A young couple named Clark, with a family of several small children, lived in one; the other was occupied by two couples bearing the same family name, Clendenin; the men were distantly related; one older by twenty years or more than the other; he had married a widow with one child, a daughter, and she had shortly after become the wife of his younger kinsman."

Kenneth paused.

"Go on," said his hearer, in smothered tones.

Little Horn, with native delicacy, had withdrawn and thrown himself upon the grass just out of earshot.

Kenneth went on.

"These two families were the sole residents of the little valley; the nearest white neighbor lived miles away on the other side of the mountains, and between lay forests filled with wild beasts and hostile Indians.

"One lovely summer day Mr. Clark was helping his neighbors in the field, his wife visiting theirs. She had taken her children with her and they were at play in the door-yard.

"In the course of the day both mother and daughter were taken sick, and two babes were born within half an hour of each other.

"Mrs. Clark had her hands more than full in attending upon the women, and the children, both boys, hastily wrapped in a blanket and laid in the same cradle, had received no further attention, when a scream from her own little ones, 'Mother, mother! the Injuns! the Injuns!' sent her flying to their rescue."

"Yes, yes," sobbed his listener. "Oh, my darlings, tomahawked and scalped before my very eyes! I see their bleeding corpses now! Their father's too, shot down as he came running from the field to try to save us. And then I was dragged away never to see home or relations again!"

"Then you are indeed Reumah Clark?"

Kenneth's voice trembled with agitation as he asked the question.

She bowed assent, her face still hidden in her hands. But suddenly dropping them she gazed eagerly, searchingly, into his face.

"And you, you who look so like the dead, who are you?"

"One of those babes born on that terrible day," he answered with emotion; "which, I do not know; and that is what I have hoped even against hope, that you could tell me. You laid us down together, you remember, and to this day the question remains unsolved which was the uncle and which the nephew. Did you observe any mark upon either, anything at all to distinguish him from the other?"

Clendenin was greatly agitated as he put this question, and his breathing was almost suspended as he waited for the reply.

"Yes," she said; "one had a very peculiar mark on his breast. I was sort o' expecting it, and looked for it right away."

"What was it, and on which child?" he asked with the tone and manner of one to whom the answer must bring life or death.

"Wait," she said, "let me tell it in my own way. Clark he'd been a cabin boy aboard a ship, and an old sailor had tattooed an anchor on his arm. 'Twas fur up above his elbow, and didn't show except he took pains to roll his sleeve up a-purpose."

She spoke hesitatingly, as one who had half forgotten the use of her mother tongue, and to Clendenin the suspense was agony well nigh unendurable; but by a strong effort he kept himself quiet.

"Well," she continued, "the oldest Mrs. Clendenin was over to our house not a week afore that awful day, and Clark he showed her that mark on to his arm, and I saw that she turned kind o' sick and faint at the sight, and then quick as thought she slipped her hand into the bosom of her dress.

"Clark, he'd turned away with a laugh, and gone out o' the door; and I asked her what she did that for, and she said she was afraid her child would be marked, and if 'twas to be she wanted it where it wouldn't show.

"Then she got up to go home, and says she, 'We'll not speak of this, Reumah, and I'll try not to think of it, so there'll be less likelihood of mischief coming of it.'"

"And it was her child, the older woman's?" cried Kenneth, breathlessly; "and is this what you speak of?" tearing open his shirt bosom as he spoke.

"Yes, that's it, as sure as I'm a living woman!" she answered, gazing curiously at the deep red mark in the form of an anchor on the left breast. "And now you know which o' the two you are."

He drew a long, sighing breath of relief, as one who feels a heavy weight fall from his shoulders, clasped his hands, and lifted his eyes to heaven, his face radiant with unutterable joy and thankfulness, his lips moving, though no sound came from them.

She watched him in wonder and amazement.

"What's the difference," she asked, as he resumed his former attitude, "and how comes it that your mother didn't know by that very mark that you were hers?"

"She died within the hour," he said with emotion; "raising herself in the bed, and looking through the open door, she saw her husband slain, his reeking scalp held aloft by a savage, and with a wild scream she fell back and expired."

"And the rest?"

"The younger Clendenin gained the house barely in time to secure the door before the Indians reached it, and keeping up a vigorous fire through a chink in the wall, his wife, ill as she was, loading for him, there happening to be two guns in the house, he at length succeeded in driving off the enemy.

"A few weeks later they left forever the scene of the terrible tragedy, taking the two babes with them."

The interview lasted some time longer, Kenneth expressing his gratitude to the woman with much warmth and earnestness, and urging her to return to civilized life.

This she steadily declined to do, saying that she did not know of a living relative among the whites, had an Indian husband, children and grandchildren, and had learned to like her wild life.

Hearing that, he ceased his importunity, gave her all the money he had with him and a written promise of more, tearing a leaf from his note book for the purpose; then with a cordial shake of the hand, and an invitation to visit him the next day in Chillicothe, that he might redeem his promise, bade her good-bye.

As he turned to go Little Horn rose from the grass and came toward him, asking of his success.

In reply Kenneth told him he had learned all he wished to know from the white squaw, and was greatly indebted to him for his timely assistance.

He would have added a reward, but the lad utterly refused to accept it, saying it was very little he had done in return for what he owed to the saviour of his life. And then he added that his influence with the white squaw was due to the fact that he was her son, and that he had informed her of the great service Kenneth had done him years ago.

CHAPTER XXV.

Never since early boyhood had Clendenin borne in his bosom so light and glad a heart as that with which he left Old Town upon the close of his interview with Reumah Clark.

One thought—that there was now no barrier between him and his sweet and beautiful Nell, unless indeed, she herself had created one, filled him with a joy and thankfulness beyond the power of words to express.

But an enemy lay in wait to rob him of it.

Lyttleton, closely watching Clendenin, had noticed that he tarried behind in the Indian camp while others were leaving it; but carefully abstaining from any allusion to the fact, he conducted the young lady whose escort he was to her home, then leaving the town by the opposite side, made a circuit through the woods that brought him back to a hill overlooking the trail to Old Town, ascending which he waited and watched for Kenneth's return.

Very impatient he grew toward the last, but not to be baulked of his prey by hunger or weariness, he remained at his post of observation until his eyes were gladdened by the sight of the manly form of Clendenin mounted on his gallant steed and following the trail at a brisk canter that was bringing him rapidly nearer.

Lyttleton now hastily descended the hill, galloped across a bit of prairie and struck into the trail just in time to meet the man whom he cordially hated in his heart while in outward seeming he was the warmest friend.

"So here you are at last, doctor," he said with a genial smile, "I declare I was actually growing uneasy about you."

"How so?" returned Kenneth in surprise, "it is nothing unusual for me to be out scouring the country at any or all hours of the day and night."

"Yes, but among the savages you know. I saw that you lingered behind as the rest of us set out on our return to the town, and I thought it not at all impossible that the wild creatures might be moved to do you a mischief."

He looked keenly at Kenneth as he spoke, thinking to read in his countenance how his errand had sped. He had never seen it half so bright and joyous.

"Ah, he has won," he said to himself with a pang of mingled disappointment and envy. "He has learned all, and it is in his favor. Curse him, he shan't have her too if I can prevent it!

"You seem to have had a pleasant time," he said aloud, "I think I never saw you look quite so cheery."

Kenneth only smiled, he felt so free and happy, as light and joyous as a bird on the wing.

"I congratulate you on your good luck, whatever it may have been," continued Lyttleton, still eyeing him curiously; "and I must ask a return in kind from you, for I too have been made a happy, yes, the very happiest of men to-day."

Clendenin turned upon him a startled, questioning look, his very lips growing white; he tried to speak, but could not find his voice.

"Yes," Lyttleton went on with a cruel delight in the pain he saw he was giving; "I am sure you will think so when I tell you that Miss Lamar is my promised wife and I shall soon be the husband of the finest woman in America."

Kenneth answered not a word, the blow was so sudden, so terrible, so stunning; for it never occurred to him that those words which sounded the death knell of his fondest hopes were a falsehood, and, ah! he had thought it impossible that Nell could ever give herself to one so utterly devoid of noble qualities as this stranger who was now boasting of having won her.

Lyttleton perceived with savage exultation how he had wrung the heart of the man whom he hated;—hated all the more bitterly because he owed him his life and because of his own ill-desert as a trifler with sweet Marian's affections: whose sworn foe he was even before leaving England for America; his very errand to this country being one of wrong to him, an errand which he now foresaw was likely to miscarry through the information gleaned from the white squaw of the Shawnee brave.

They were passing a farm-house; some one standing at its gate hailed the doctor, and with a slight parting inclination of the head to Lyttleton, Kenneth turned aside and obeyed the call.

The sun was touching the top of the hill which bounds Chillicothe on the west, as he resumed his homeward way, a different man from the one who had left Old Town so full of joy and glad anticipation; the very dropping of his figure, as he moved slowly along with the bridle lying loosely upon Romeo's neck, spoke of utter dejection.

What was life worth without his love, his darling? Oh, why had not this knowledge come to him a little sooner, this that unsealed his lips. Why had he not yielded to his impulse that stormy night as they stood alone together by the fire, and poured out the story of his love? How much wiser and kinder to have done it, even though he had to tell her, too, that an impassable barrier stood between them!

He could see it so plainly now, but then, his eyes were blinded.

And she, how could he blame her if her love had at last turned to aversion and she had given herself to another?

But alas, alas, how ill she had chosen, a man devoid of principle and utterly selfish; for so far had Kenneth succeeded in reading Lyttleton's true character.

But these were vain regrets; he must school himself to bear bravely his grief and disappointment; trouble did not spring out of the ground, and the loving Father above never sent to His children one unneeded pang.

And was life indeed all dark to him? Was it nothing that a terrible dread had been taken away? That he had reason, intellect, education, health and strength, that God had given him skill to relieve pain and suffering?

Ah, his mercies were far beyond his deserts, and life could not be a desolate waste while power was granted him to minister to the comfort and happiness of others; and while there remained to him, not only the love of the two dear ones at Glen Forest, but also the sweeter, dearer love of Him who saith to His children:

"Lo, I am with you always even unto the end of the world." "I have loved thee with an everlasting love." "I will never leave thee nor forsake thee."

The precious comforting words came to him almost as if spoken by an audible voice, and were as balm and healing to his wounded spirit.

There were business matters claiming his immediate attention, and he now resolutely turned his thoughts upon them.

He decided upon an early visit to his old home; he must see her whom he had always called mother, but who, as he had learned from Reumah Clark, was in reality his sister; sweet Marian, too. Ah, she must never know that he was less nearly related to her than she fondly believed. It would but give her unnecessary pain.

But first of all steps should be taken to get Reumah Clark's evidence in a form that would make it available legal proof of his identity, for there was much dependent upon that.

On reaching the town he at once sought Godfrey Dale, and they were closeted together for an hour or more.

In this interview Dale learned what had been his friend's secret grief, that it had in a measure passed away with the knowledge of his true parentage, though it was sorrow of heart to him that it proved the tie of kinship with the dear ones at home less close than he had once believed, and the importance, for certain grave reasons, of his being able to bring forward indisputable proof of his identity.

Dale understood the management of the business; the first step in which was to get the woman into the town and have her deposition taken before a magistrate.

It was probable that she would come in the next morning of her own accord, in order to receive the money for which she held Clendenin's note; if she did not Dale was to go in search of her.

"It is to be hoped that secret foe of yours will not get hold of her again in the meantime," he remarked. "Who can he be? I know of no one who has cause for enmity toward you, unless, indeed, as a rival in the good graces of a certain fair damsel," he added jocosely, "and, why Kenneth, man, that would be Lyttleton! And he's mean enough to serve you such a scurvy trick, too. But then, on second thought, how would he know anything about the woman or your interest in her? No; I confess I am nonplussed."

"Beside," said Kenneth sadly, "he tells me he is a successful rival, so he might well afford to refrain from any interference with my welfare."

"He successful with Miss Nell?" cried Dale with scornful incredulity. "Don't you believe it! And yet," with a sudden change of tone, "women are strange, unaccountable creatures, and it is possible her seeming contempt and dislike were only assumed to hide her real feelings. Heighho! I really thought your chances better than mine; those last by no means so poor as Lyttleton's."

A party of the merchants of the town were to start three days from this time for the East, to buy goods. Their custom was to go in companies, as, a great portion of the country being still in wild state, much of it was covered with immense forests, containing but a few widely scattered dwellings. They must, perforce, carry a good deal of money with them and it was unsafe for one to travel alone.

Kenneth had announced his intention to join this party, but that evening's mail brought a letter from Glen Forest which so filled him with anxiety and alarm, made his presence at home so urgently necessary, that he at once decided to risk going with no companion but Zeb, and to set off at dawn of the coming day, leaving to Dale the whole care and responsibility of getting Reumah Clark's evidence into proper shape.

Dale used every argument and persuasion to induce his friend to wait for company; two days he thought would make so little difference, and the risk to a solitary traveller was so great; but all to no purpose; Clendenin would hardly stay to hear him out, there was so much to be attended to in the few hours that remained before he should leave for an absence that might extend to months.

Several patients must be visited and recommended to the charge of a brother physician, some purchases made, and some friends called upon for a word of farewell.

It would seem a strange, unkind, ungrateful thing to go without saying good-bye to Major Lamar and his family, who had always made him so entirely one of themselves.

And Nell? Ah, he could not, would not go away without learning from her own lips if Lyttleton's story were true.

And if it were not? But ah, he dare not think any further.

His heart beat almost audibly as he opened the gate and hurried up the path to the house.

The bright moonlight showed him the major sitting alone in the porch.

"Ah, good evening, doctor," he said, rising to shake hands and set a chair for his guest. "I am especially glad to see you to-night, as I am just in the mood for a friendly chat."

"Thank you, major, but I am in unusual haste," Kenneth answered. "Can I see the ladies?"

"Sorry to say I cannot give you that pleasure to-night, doctor," was the laughing reply. "Mrs. Lamar has gone to bed tired out with the exertion and excitement of the day, and Nell is not at home; won't be for a week or two, at least; has gone home with a friend living fifteen miles from town."

Kenneth almost staggered under the blow. Then a wild impulse seized him to follow her and know his fate from her own mouth, though it would delay his journey for one day, if not for two. But recalling some words of the letter just received, words that made him feel that every moment's delay on his part was hazardous to sweet Marian, he put it from him with heroic self-denial, briefly explained his errand, parried some remonstrances such as Dale had already wasted upon him, and with a cordial parting shake of the hand and a farewell message for the family, turned and went away.

Lyttleton's heart that afternoon was like a cage of unclean birds full of malice, envy, anger and hate. Kenneth having left him in answer to the summons to the farm-house, he pursued his way to the town muttering imprecations upon the head of his late companion and mentally resolving schemes for his injury.

"Curse him!" he said again, "is he to have all and I none? Would that fate were but kind enough to remove him out of my path!"

"Do it yourself!"

It seemed an almost audible suggestion.

He started and glanced around with a shudder, half expecting to see the tempter.

"No, no, I am not so bad as that!" he answered aloud. "I could never stain my hands with blood, but if the Indians should slay him in the woods, as they did Capt. Herrod, or if his horse should happen to stumble and he fall and break his neck, well, it would not grieve me very deeply, ha, ha!

"I suppose the girl wouldn't have me even then," he continued with a gloomy scowl, "but I'd have undisturbed possession of—But nonsense! I must deal with things as they are."

He continued his cogitations, but had not yet succeeded in arranging any definite plan when he arrived at his lodgings and dismounted, giving his horse in charge to Hans.

However, the knowledge casually gained in the course of the evening, of Kenneth's intended departure early the next morning for the East, and with no companion but his negro servant, brought a sudden suggestion to his mind which filled him with fiendish delight.

A letter from England, like Clendenin's received by that evening's mail, furnished a plausible pretext.

Hans was summoned and given orders to make everything ready to leave Chillicothe at once.

"Dish night, mynheer?" queried the man in astonishment.

"Yes, this night; there is a moon and we can travel by her light. I have news from England and must return thither with all speed."

"De horses pe not shtrong enough to go day and night, mynheer," remarked Hans, scratching his head and looking not over pleased; for he was loth to lose his night's rest.

"That's my affair; you have nothing to do but obey orders," was the haughty rejoinder.

Lyttleton knew that Nell was out of town, and now was glad that it had so happened, as he did not care to meet her again, yet felt that it would not look well for him to leave the place without a parting call on the family.

He met Clendenin coming away, passed him with a cold bow, and joined the major who was still on the porch, its sole occupant as before.

"What you, too, sir?" he exclaimed, when Lyttleton had explained the object of his call. "The doctor was in but now to say that he leaves unexpectedly in the early morning; but it seems that you are making even greater haste to forsake us. Coming back again, I hope."

"Doubtful, my good sir, and I must leave my adieu to the ladies with you, regretting deeply that I could not deliver them in person," Lyttleton said, lying with a glibness that was the result of long practice.

He tarried but a few moments, and again the major was left to his solitary meditations, which now ran upon the question whether Nell had aught to do with the sudden migration of these two admirers of hers. He could not tell, for the girl had kept her own council in regard to her feelings toward them, and Lyttleton's offer of the previous day.

CHAPTER XXVI.

Dale was in his office, very busy with some writing, when Lyttleton looked in.

"Excuse the interruption, Mr. Dale," he said, holding out his hand, "but I did not like to go without saying good-bye to you and the doctor. He, however, I find is not in."

"Good-bye! you're not going to leave Chillicothe to-night, are you?" cried Godfrey in surprise, as he laid down his pen and took the offered hand.

"Yes; immediately, Hans has everything packed, and the horses saddled and at the door. Had a letter from home to-night, and find I must tarry no longer. Please give my respects and adieus to the doctor," he added, as he hurried away.

"I wonder he's not afraid to risk travelling with only that rascally looking servant, who might rob and kill him and nobody any the wiser," thought Dale. "Well," he remarked aloud, resuming his pen, "I suppose it's no affair of mine."

Was it a haunting doubt of Hans's fidelity or some other motive that led Lyttleton to turn to him, as they left the town, and bid him ride by his side instead of behind him?

However that may have been, he kept a sharp watch upon his valet's movements.

Presently he took him into his confidence in some degree, partially unfolding a plot to get Clendenin into his power, and securing the Hessian's co-operation by the promise of a bribe.

They pressed forward all that night and the next day, pausing only for a short rest when their horses showed signs of exhaustion.

The greater part of the way was very lonely; they had met no one since early morning, when toward the close of the day they overtook a man mounted on a sorry nag and jogging along in silence and solitude; a villainous looking fellow, in whom Lyttleton at once recognized one of his intended tools; whose acquaintance he had made on the outward bound journey of some months ago, and whom he had casually discovered to be an enemy to Dr. Clendenin.

It was in fact Brannon, who had never forgotten or forgiven the part Kenneth had had in his conviction of the theft of the great-coat, handkerchief, and shirt, abstracted from the dwelling of the Barbours.

Lyttleton hailed him with, "Hello, Brannon, you're the very man I was wanting to see."

"And who may you be?" returned the fellow surlily, showing a scowling face as he glanced back over his shoulder at the speaker; then suddenly wheeling his horse across the narrow path so as to bar their further progress, "What do you want with me?" he demanded in a tone of one who feels himself at enmity with his kind.

"To furnish you with a bit of employment very much to your taste," answered Lyttleton.

"And what may that be? Ha, I remember you now, the English gent that was a goin' out to Chillicothe some months back, and had so many questions to ask about Dr. Clendenin. Curse him! Well, did ye find it all out?"

"It?"

"Yes, it, whatever you wanted to know."

"Yes; I found out, what I suspected before, that he is very much in my way: and—but before I lay my plans open to you I must have your promise, your oath of secrecy."

"Them's easy given," the fellow answered with an unpleasant laugh; "I promise and swear never to tell no tales consarnin' what you're agoin' to say."

"Very well. Clendenin is travelling in this direction, with no companion but a young negro servant who, I take it, is neither very brave nor strong."

A malicious gleam of satisfaction shone in Brannon's eyes.

Lyttleton noted it with pleasure.

"We could not have a better opportunity," he went on; "you who have an old score against him, and I who find him as I just said entirely too much in my way."

"What are you at, mister, out with it plump and plain," Brannon said with an impatient gesture and a volley of oaths, as Lyttleton came to a pause and looked hesitatingly at him. "I ain't no fancy for this 'ere beating about the bush. Is it his life you want, or not?"

"No, no; I'm no murderer!" Lyttleton exclaimed with a shudder and a fearful glance from side to side. "But patience, man, and I'll explain in a few words. We'll call this doctor a mad fellow, perhaps it isn't so very far from the truth, ha, ha, and we'll take him prisoner, and keep him such somewhere in these woods until I can make arrangements to remove him to a mad house."

Brannon listened with a grim smile.

"But look ye here, stranger," he interrupted, "what if he should get free and peach on us?"

"We must take care that he doesn't; and I'll make it worth your while to take the risk. Can you get help in capturing him?"

Brannon nodded. "Here comes one now that'll bear a hand willingly if you give him his price;" and as he spoke he waved his hand toward a tall, burly figure just emerging from the wood a few paces from them.

"Dree of us," muttered Hans, watching its approach; "dat ish pooty goot; and mynheer, too; dree, four against two. We takes dem brisoner mitout fail."

The last comer was drawing near with long and rapid strides.

"What's that?" he asked sharply and bringing his rifle to his shoulder. "Ah, is it you, Jack! what's up?"

"Yes, it's me, Bill Shark," answered Brannon. "Come on; here's a gent as has a job suited to the likes of us."

As the fellow came near enough for a distinct view of his features, Lyttleton involuntarily shrank from him, so brutal and forbidding was their expression.

But recovering himself instantly, he repeated substantially, and under the same promise of secrecy, what he had been saying to Brannon.

"I'm your man, if we can agree on the terms," was the rejoinder. "I'll want a pretty stiff price, mind ye, stranger, for it's like to be a risky business, more so than if ye wanted him put clean out o' the way; for 'dead men tell no tales,' you know."

Lyttleton shook his head.

"No, no, I can't stain my hands with blood, his or that of any other man."

The ruffian regarded him with a brutal sneer and a muttered sentence, of which the only audible words were "white livered coward."

Lyttleton writhed under the charge but dared not resent it. In fact he began to feel himself in a perilous position; darkness was already settling down over the forest, he had not full confidence in his valet, and these others were evidently unscrupulous scoundrels.

"How much ahead are you, did ye say?" queried Shark.

"I think we have the start of him by from six to eight hours," replied Lyttleton. "Besides, we have pushed on more rapidly than he would be likely to, as you may judge by the condition of our horses."

"H'm! then he'll most likely be along here about this time, or a trifle earlier, to-morrow, stop fur his lodging at Brannon's, just above here, a little back in the woods, or at my shanty five miles furder on. 'Twont make much difference; whichever he stops with, the other'll help entertain him. And, stranger, we kin turn out purty strong on occasion. I've two strappin' sons and a nevvy, and the old woman can lend a helpin' hand too, when she's wanted.

"S'posen' you and Brannon and this other feller come over home with me now, and let's talk it over. We'll determine just what's to be done, and I'll set my price."

Lyttleton had felt a cold chill running down his spine during this speech and at the moment would gladly have put many miles between him and what he began to suspect was an organized band of robbers and cut-throats.

But evidently it would not do to show fear. Carefully steadying his voice, he courteously thanked Shark for his invitation, but declined it on the plea that they all, himself, Hans and both their horses, were in sore need of rest; for which reason they would stop for the night with Brannon; his house being so much nearer. This seemed satisfactory and thither they all went.

CHAPTER XXVII.

The sun had not yet risen, and few of the townspeople were astir, when Kenneth and his faithful Zeb set forth upon their journey.

They rode slowly through the almost deserted streets, the master in seemingly absent mood, quiet and thoughtful even to sadness, the servant glancing briskly from side to side with a nod and grin for each visible acquaintance with whom he felt himself upon terms of something like equality.

"Good-bye, Tig; dis heyah niggah's off for Glen Forest," he shouted as they passed the major's.

Tig, who was cutting wood in the kitchen door-yard, dropped his axe to gaze after them in wondering incredulity.

"Oh, you go 'long wid yo' tomfoolin'," he muttered, as he stooped to pick it up again, "'taint no sech ting; and the doctah ain't never goin' so fur, 'tout sayin' good-bye to our folks; and Miss Nell she's away whar he can't git at her. 'Spect I knows who's powerful fond of her, and who tinks he's mighty sight nicer'n any ole Britisher."

They were early risers at the major's, and Mrs. Lamar having retired the previous night several hours before her usual time, had slept off her fatigue and found herself ready to begin the day earlier than was her wont.

From her chamber window she, too, saw Kenneth and his attendant ride by.

"Why, there goes Dr. Clendenin equipped as for a journey, valise, saddle-bags and servant!" she exclaimed, addressing her husband who was still in bed.

"Yes, he's off for Pennsylvania."

"For Pennsylvania, it's very sudden, isn't it?"

"Yes; he had bad news last night, sickness in the family I believe, that hurried him off in great haste. He called to bid us good-bye, but found no one but me."

"But you will be more surprised to hear that Lyttleton left town last night in obedience to a summons from England. He, too, called and left his adieus for you and Nell."

Mrs. Lamar faced round upon the major a face full of astonishment, not wholly unmixed with disappointment and vexation.

"Gone!" she cried, "actually gone for good! I must say, Percy, that I am completely out of patience with Nell."

"With Nell, pray what has she to do with it?"

"She has rejected him. I suspected it before; now I am sure of it. News from England indeed!" and she turned away with a contemptuous sniff.

"Possibly you are correct in your conjecture," the major remarked, recovering from the surprise her words had given him; "but if she has rejected Lyttleton, she had a perfect right to do so, and I am inclined neither to blame her nor to regret her action."

"Why it would have been a splendid match, Percy, and such a chance as she is not likely to see again."

"Not in my opinion. He seems to be wealthy, but I do not admire his character. And it would have robbed me of my little sister, taking her so far away that I could hardly hope to see her again in this world. I should far rather see her the wife of Clendenin."

"I gave that up long ago," returned his wife in an impatient tone, as she hastily left the room.

"I believe something has gone wrong between them; I wonder what it can be," soliloquized the major while making his toilet, and at the same time taking a mental retrospect of such of the interviews of Nell and Dr. Clendenin as had come under his notice.

But having no proclivity for match-making, and no desire to be relieved of the support of his young sister, whose presence in his family he greatly enjoyed, he shortly dismissed the subject from his thoughts.

Not so with Kenneth; as he passed the house he involuntarily glanced toward the window of her room, half expecting to catch a glimpse of the face dearest and loveliest to him of all on earth, then turned away with an inward sigh, remembering sadly that each step forward was taking him farther away from her.

Very much cast down he was for a time, having had in Hans's story to Zeb, that his master was but going away temporarily for the purpose of making suitable preparations for his approaching nuptials, what seemed confirmation strong of the truth of Lyttleton's assertion that he was Nell's accepted suitor. But ere long he was able to stay himself upon his God, and casting all care for himself, and those dearer than self, upon that almighty Friend, resumed his accustomed cheerfulness and presently woke the echoes of the forest with a song of praise; Zeb, riding a few paces behind, joining in with a hearty goodwill.

They had left Chillicothe far in the rear and the nearest human habitation was miles away.

They made a long day's journey and bivouacked that night under a clump of trees on the edge of a prairie, and beside a little stream of clear dancing water.

It was Clendenin's intention to be early in the saddle again, and great was his disappointment on the following morning to find Romeo so lame that a day's rest just where they were was an imperative necessity.

It was a strange and perplexing dispensation of Providence; yet recognizing it as such, he resolutely put aside the first feeling of impatience as he remembered how sorely he was needed at Glen Forest; how the dear ones would be looking and longing for his coming. There must be some good reason for this apparently unfortunate detention, so he submitted to it with resignation and passed the day not unpleasantly or unprofitably in reading; it was his habit to carry a pocket volume with him while travelling, or wandering through the adjacent wood.

They were able to move on the next day, but only slowly, as the horse had not fully recovered; and while halting for an hour's rest at noon, they were, to their great delight, overtaken by the other party from Chillicothe.

It consisted of three merchants, Messrs. Grey, Collins and Jones, and a stalwart backwoodsman and hunter, Tom Johnson by name.

They also were much pleased at the meeting, which they had desired but hardly hoped for, though they had set out a day earlier than had been expected, the merchants hastening their preparations when they found that by so doing they would secure the company of the hunter, who for fearlessness, strength, and skill in the use of fire-arms, was a host in himself.

Each merchant carried his money in his saddle-bags, and the whole party were well armed.

Greeting Clendenin with a glad, "Hello!" they hastily dismounted, secured their horses, and joined him, producing from their saddle-bags such store of choice provisions as made Zeb's eyes dance with delight, for the lad was in his way quite an epicure.

The sight of the goodly array of weapons of defence, and stout arms to wield them, gave him scarcely less pleasure, for Zeb's courage was not always at fever heat.

"Golly, massa doctah!" he exclaimed, showing a double row of white and even teeth, "I 'spec's we needn't be 'fraid no robbahs now. Gib um jessie ef dey comes roun' us."

"Best not to be too jubilant, Zeb," said his master; "you and I may have to fall behind because of Romeo's lameness."

"No, no, never fear," said the others, "we are not going to forsake you, doc, now that we have joined company."

They did not linger long over their meal and were soon in the saddle again, riding sometimes two abreast, at others in single file, but always near enough for exchange of talk.

Kenneth bore his own burden bravely, was quite his usual cheerful, genial self, and no one suspected what a load of sorrow and anxiety was pressing upon him.

They journeyed on without mishap or adventure, and late in the afternoon came to a two story log dwelling standing a little back from the road, or rather trail, for it was nothing more.

There was nothing attractive about the aspect of the house or its surroundings, but the sun was near his setting, the next human habitation was in all probability ten or fifteen miles further on, and the way to it lay through a dense forest where, doubtless, panthers, bears and wolves abounded.

A moment's consultation led to the decision that they would pass the night here if they could get lodging in the house.

An elderly woman of slatternly appearance, hair unkempt, clothing torn and soiled, had come to the door.

"What's wanted?" she asked in a harsh voice.

"Shelter for the night for men and beasts," returned Clendenin, who had been unanimously chosen leader of the party.

"Well, I dunno 'bout it, I haven't no man about, but if ye'll 'tend to yer beasts yerselves, yer can stay."

They agreed to the conditions. She pointed out the stable, and they led their horses thither, curried and fed them, remarking to each other, meanwhile, that they did not like the woman's looks; she had a bad countenance.

She had gone back into the house, and as she moved here and there about her work, muttered discontentedly to herself,

"There's too many o' 'em. Bill, he won't like it. But I wonder if the right one's among 'em. Wish I knowed."

Hearing their voices outside again, she stepped to the door.

"Ye'll be a wantin' supper, won't ye?"

"Yes, let us have it as soon as you can, for we're tired and hungry."

"She mout put some pizen in de wittles, massa doctah, don't you tink?" whispered Zeb, close at Kenneth's ear, and shuddering as he spoke.

"If you think so, it might be as well to watch her," was the quiet half-amused answer.

"Dat I will, sah!" and Zeb bustled in and sat himself down between the table and the wide chimney, where he could have a full view of all the preparations for the coming meal.

The woman scowled at him and broadly hinted that he was in the way, but Zeb was obtuse and would not take a hint.

He watched her narrowly as she mixed corn-bread and put it to bake, as she made the rye coffee, and fried the ham and eggs. It would have been impossible for her to put a single ingredient into any of these without his knowledge.

Nor did he relax his scrutiny until he had eaten his own supper, after seeing the gentlemen safely through theirs.

"She mout put sumpin into de cups wen she pours de coffee," he had said to himself.

It did not escape him that she listened with a sort of concealed eagerness to every word that was said by her guests, and that she started slightly and looked earnestly at Dr. Clendenin the first time he was addressed by name in her hearing.

"What shall we call you, mother?" asked the hunter, lighting his pipe at her fire for an after supper smoke.

"'Taint perticlar, ye can just call me that, if ye like," she returned dryly.

"You don't live here alone," he remarked, glancing at a coat hanging on the wall. "Where's your man now?"

"Off a huntin'. Where's your woman?"

"Don't know, hain't found her yet," he laughed, taking the pipe between his lips and sauntering to the door, outside of which his companions were grouped.

The air there was slightly damp and chill, but far preferable to that within, which reeked with a mixture of smells of stale tobacco, garlic, boiled cabbage and filth combined.

It was growing dark.

The woman lighted a candle and set it on the table, muttering half aloud, as Zeb rose and pushed back his chair:

"I'm glad you're done at last."

Then she bustled about putting the food away and washing her dishes.

Johnson finished his pipe and proposed retiring to bed, as they wanted to make an early start in the morning.

A general assent was given and the woman was asked to show them where they were to sleep.

She vouchsafed no answer in words, but taking from the mantel a saucer filled with grease, in which a bit of rag was floating, she set it on the table, lighted one end of the rag, picked up the candle, and motioning them to follow her, ascended a step-ladder to the story above; letting fall drops of melted tallow here and there as she went.

Reaching the top of the ladder, they found themselves in an outer room that had the appearance of being used as a depository for every sort of rubbish.

Crossing this, their conductress opened a door leading into a smaller apartment, communicating, by an inner door, with still another.

There was a bed in each and a few other articles of furniture, all of the roughest kind. Dirty and untidy in the extreme, the rooms were by no means inviting to our travellers, but it was Hobson's choice, and they found no fault to the hostess.

"You white folks kin sleep in them two beds," she said, with a wave of her hand toward first one and then the other, "and the nigger, he kin lop down outside on them horse blankets, if he likes."

And setting the candle down on top of a chest of drawers, she stalked away without another word.

"Massa doctah, and all you gentlemens, please sahs, lemme stay in heyah," pleaded Zeb in an undertone of affright. "Dat woman she look at me down stairs 'sif she like to stick dat carvin' knife right froo me."

No one answered at the moment; they were all sending suspicious glances about the two rooms, and Zeb quietly closed and secured the door.

"Ki! massas, jus' look a heyah!" he cried in an excited whisper, and pointing with his finger.

"What is it?" they asked, turning to look.

Zeb sprang for the candle, and bringing it close showed a small hole in the door.

"A bullet hole, sure as you live," exclaimed Grey, who was nearest.

"And exactly opposite the bed," added Jones, stepping to it and beginning to throw back the covers.

In an instant they were all at his side, and there was a universal, half suppressed exclamation of horror and dismay, as a hard straw mattress, much stained with blood, was exposed to their view by the flickering light of the candle, which Zeb in his intense excitement had nearly dropped.

They looked at those tell-tale stains and then into each other's faces. A trifle pale at first most of them were, but calm and courageous.

Clendenin was the first to speak.

"We have evidently fallen into a den of thieves and murderers, but by the help of the Lord we shall escape their snares."

"Yes, we'll trust in God, boys, and keep our powder dry," said Grey.

"And Heaven send us a more peaceful end than some poor wretch has found," added Collins, pointing with a sympathetic sigh to the gory evidences.

"We must keep a sharp lookout, for we may depend that thar hunter'll return to his wife's embraces afore mornin'," remarked Johnson, grimly.

They at once set about making a thorough examination of the rooms, but found nothing more to arouse uneasiness, except the fact that the window of one opened out upon the roof of a shed, by means of which it was easily accessible from the ground.

Then their plans were quickly laid. They would all occupy that one room, and take turns in watching, two at a time; thus giving to each about two-thirds of the night for rest and sleep.

The arms were examined and every man's weapon laid close at his hand, ready for instant use.

These preparations completed, Grey turned to Kenneth, saying softly:

"Doc, we seem pretty well able to defend ourselves in case of attack, but it wouldn't hurt to ask help from a higher Power."

"No," said Kenneth, kneeling down, the others doing the same; then, in a few appropriate, low-breathed words, he asked his Father to have them in his kind care and keeping, and if it was His will grant them safety without the shedding of blood.

CHAPTER XXVIII.

Down-stairs the woman was moving about her work, stopping now and then for a moment to listen to the sounds overhead.

"Why don't they get to bed and to sleep!" she muttered at length with an oath. "Bill and the boys must be sharp set for their supper and will come in most ready to take my head off. 'Tain't no fault o' mine, but that'll not make no difference. Well, I'll call 'em anyhow, for them fellers ain't comin' down agin to-night."

So saying she set her light in the window and hurried her culinary operations, for she was getting ready a second and more plentiful meal than the one she had set before the travellers.

Ere many moments four men, great broad-shouldered, brawny, rough looking fellows, on whose faces ignorance, vice and cruelty were plainly stamped, came creeping stealthily in at the open door.

"Well, old girl, what have you bagged?" asked the eldest, in whom we recognize Bill Shark, the confederate of Brannon and Lyttleton. "I conclude it's somethin', since we've been kept a starvin' till this time o' night."

His tone, though suppressed, was savage, and his look angry and sullen.

She held up a warning finger.

"Hush-sh-sh! they're up and awake yit. More quiet, boys. Let up now, and go to work. The vittles is all on table."

"Are ye a goin' to tell me what I asked?" demanded her husband in a fierce undertone, as he sat down and began helping himself liberally to the smoking viands, but looking more at her than at them.

"It's him," she answered, with a slight chuckle; "and he's as nice lookin' and soft spoken a chap as ever you see."

"An' what o' that?" sneered one of the sons. "His purty face ain't a goin' to save him."

"Maybe not, Abner; but I'm afeard they're too strong fur ye."

"How many?"

"Six, countin' the nigger, and one on 'em's Tom Johnson."

This announcement was received with a volley of oaths and curses, not loud but deep, Bill adding:

"He'll count two at least."

"The other two fellers'll have to come and lend a hand whether or no," said Abner gloomily. "Don't you let 'em off, dad. With them and Brannon we'll be seven. And if we come on 'em asleep, why, we'll not have such hard work, I take it."

"Time they were asleep now. How long since they went up there?"

There was an angry gleam in Bill's eyes as he turned them upon his wife.

"Long enough to have got to sleep twic't over, I should think. But they hain't done it. Hark! they're a movin' about, and talkin' too, I believe."

"Then you didn't mind my orders, and ought to be licked."

A volley of oaths followed, and he half rose from his chair and seized her by the arm.

But his sons interfered.

"Are you mad, old man?" pulling him back into his seat; "we'll not have a ghost of a chance if you kick up a row now."

He yielded, though with an ill grace, and the woman, not in the least disconcerted by his brutal behavior, said in her ordinary tone, as she replenished his empty cup:

"'Twasn't no fault o' mine, Bill; I'd a drugged 'em, every one, if that nigger would a took his eyes off o' me for a single moment; but it did beat all, the way he watched me back and forad and all the time. I hadn't the least mite of a chance."

This explanation seemed to appease the man's wrath, and the meal was concluded without further disturbance.

A whispered consultation followed; then two of the younger ruffians went out and plunged into the forest in the direction from whence they had come.

At no very great distance they came out upon a little clearing where stood a tiny cabin, roughly but strongly built of unhewn logs, no window save an aperture scarce a foot square near the roof, and the one door, of solid oak planks, furnished with heavy bolts and bars upon the outside.

This was the prison intended by Lyttleton for the safe keeping of Clendenin, the man to whom he owed his life.

Heretofore it had been used by the Sharks as a depository for their ill-gotten gains.

Near at hand, but concealed from view by the thick undergrowth, the

Englishman and his valet lay sleeping upon the ground, wrapped each in his blanket, and with sword and gun within reach of his hand.

A few minutes' search disclosed their whereabouts to the Sharks, and it was no gentle waking that ensued.

"Ho! rouse up, I tell ye, and wake your master!" growled Abner, touching Hans with his foot. "You're both wanted at the house."

"Yaas," grunted Hans, sleepily, "but I dinks you petter leaves mynheer to dake his sleep."

"What is it? What's wanted this time of night?" demanded Lyttleton, starting up and glancing about him in no amiable mood.

"You're wanted," was the gruff, unceremonious reply. "Game's bagged, but such a lot we must come on 'em as strong as possible."

"What! you've got Clendenin?"

Lyttleton's tone was jubilant.

"Humph! he's there, but he ain't took yet, and there's four more stout fellows beside the nigger, and one on 'ems ekal to any two o' us. So come along, both o' ye."

"No," said Lyttleton, "you have undertaken the job, and it's no part of my plan to assist in the fray. I'll pay liberally when it's done; but as I told you in the first place, I can't have Clendenin get sight of either my face or that of my valet."

"Black your faces, or tie a handkercher over 'em," suggested Abner's brother.

"No; he'd recognize our voices."

"You're a—— coward," sneered Abner. "No use argufying with the white-livered critter, Josh. He won't git his job done, 'tain't likely, if he don't help, that's all. Come on back. P'raps Brannon's there by now, and if the fellers'll only quiet down to sleep, I for one am willin' to try it for the sake o' the plunder, and the cash we'll have in hand afore we let these ere chaps have their way with the one they're wantin' to git shut of."

"What a vulgar wretch!" muttered Lyttleton, in a tone of extreme disgust, as the two ruffians turned and left the spot to make their way rapidly back to the house.

They found Brannon there, waiting with the others for the slight occasional sounds overhead to cease, as they dared not make the desired attack with their intended victims awake and prepared to meet and repel it.

179

But they waited in vain; our travellers hearing men's voices, conversing in subdued tones in the room below, understood for what they were waiting, and not wishing for a fight, took care to let them know that they had not all succumbed to sleep.

In fact the hunter, listening intently with his ear to a crack in the floor, heard the woman say, "Not yet, they're not asleep yet, for I hear 'em movin'."

"Ye do, eh?" he growled in undertone, "well, ye'll likely keep on a hearin' it till them he wolves o' yourn goes back to their den in the woods."

At last as a faint streak of dawn began to show itself above the eastern horizon, the ruffians drew close together and held a whispered consultation, the result of which was the decision to give up attacking here, leave at once, and hastening on ahead of the travellers, post themselves at a certain spot favorable for an ambuscade, where they would play the highwayman, "relieving the fellers o' their plunder," as they expressed it, and letting them go with their lives if they were wise enough not to show fight, but taking Clendenin prisoner for the sake of slaking Brannon's thirst for revenge and obtaining Lyttleton's offered reward.

The first part of their plan was at once put into execution, and with no small sense of relief our travellers heard them depart.

"Up, boys, now's our time," said the hunter; "day's breakin', the thieves has left for the present, and we'd best git out o' this instanter."

The others being of the same opinion, they hastily gathered up their guns and saddle-bags, unbarred the door, and as nearly in a body as might be, the hunter taking the lead, descended the step-ladder to the room below.

The woman nodding in her chair beside the smouldering embers of the fire, was its only occupant.

She started up, saying, "Why you're airly, ain't ye? I hadn't thought of gettin' breakfast yet."

"Never mind, we don't want any, mother," said Johnson dryly.

"Why, ye ain't goin' a'ready? ye'd better stay for breakfast. I'll not be long gettin' it."

"No," they answered, "we must start at once."

"Ye didn't sleep much, I think," she remarked sullenly, following them to the door.

"How do you know?" queried Johnson, giving her a sharp look.

"Oh, I was up myself, and I heard ye movin' around."

Clendenin stepped back to enquire, and pay her charges for the entertainment of the party, and thought she eyed him strangely during that transaction, with a sort of repressed eagerness and cupidity, and somewhat as if she were trying to estimate his strength, and calculate whether she dare measure it with her own, and would gain anything thereby.

He puzzled over it for a moment as he hastened to rejoin his companions, who were at the stable busied in saddling their horses, then dismissed it from his thoughts with the conclusion that it was his purse she wanted to secure.

It was now quite light and the sun began to show his face above the treetops, as they mounted and away, felicitating themselves on their fortunate escape.

"I see now," said Kenneth in tones of thankfulness, "why that seemingly unfortunate delay was sent me. It was certainly a special providence."

"Ho, comrades!" cried the hunter, suddenly reining in his steed across the path so as to bring the whole party to a halt. "I have a thought!"

"Better keep it for a nest egg then, Tom," laughed Collins, overflowing with animal spirits in view of their recent deliverance.

"No, I hadn't, Sam; I'd better by half use it to save our plunder, if not our lives. You must know, lads, that Tom Johnson's no stranger to these here woods, and knows the trail better'n the doc there, and the rest o' you readin' men, knows a book."

"Now, Tom, my boy, that hasn't an over modest sound. But what's that thought of yours? Let's have it at once."

"Listen then. About six or seven miles furder on, there's a place where the trail runs through a little valley, between two hills that's covered thick with trees and bushes; and now I tell you them cut-throats is just lyin' in wait there, Injun style, to ketch us between two fires as we come along."

"Then what's to be done?" was asked in various tones of inquiry and dismay.

"Why, we'll just keep out o' the trap. I'll take ye round it. I know the way, and though it'll give us a few more miles, and hard ones at that, it'll be better than makin' ourselves a target, or rather half a dozen of 'em, for those scoundrels to shoot at. Won't it?"

"Yes, yes," from all the voices in unison.

The hunter wheeled his horse and galloped on, the rest following in single file.

He kept the trail for a while, then struck off into the thick woods, and for a couple of hours they had a toilsome time, pushing their way through thickets, leaping logs and fording one or two streams; then taking the ordinary trail again, beyond the point of danger, they were able to go forward with comparative ease and comfort.

With the purpose to make his assaulting party as strong as possible, Bill Shark sent Brannon to urge Lyttleton and his valet to join them where they were to lie in ambush.

Lyttleton once again roused from slumber, received the messenger surlily, declined to go with him, but fearful of the consequences of utter refusal to comply with the demand, for the message was couched in terms that make it such, promised to join them shortly, after refreshing himself with food; and made Brannon describe the locality and manner of reaching it so particularly as to enable him to find it without a guide.

The moment Brannon was out of earshot, Lyttleton turned to his valet.

"What say you, Hans, are those fellows to be trusted not to turn on us, if it happens to suit their fancy, after they have finished with the other party?"

"Mynheer, I dinks dey is von bad lot."

"Then we won't put ourselves in their power. Listen; we will not join them, but will hide in some place where we can watch their proceedings unknown to them; and if events don't turn out as we could wish, we will slip away through the woods and continue our journey, and so escape their hands. Now kindle a fire and prepare me a cup of strong coffee."

With no small difficulty, and damage to their clothing from thorns and briers, master and man at length succeeded in taking up a position advantageous for the carrying out of Lyttleton's plans. Shark's party had divided, posting themselves three on one side of the little valley, three on the other, and less than half way up the hills.

Lyttleton's ambush was on the eastern of the two hills, considerably higher up, where from behind a screen of bushes and interlacing vines he could see all that might occur in the valley below.

He found, to his satisfaction, that he could also overhear whatever was said by the ruffians in an ordinary tone of voice.

The first sound that greeted his ear was a sullen growl from the elder Shark, familiarly styled Bill.

"What's a-keepin' that thar confounded Britisher and his Dutchman? I tell you, lads, they're a brace o' cowards and don't mean to take no share o' this here fray. I'd go after 'em and give 'em a lesson if I was sure o' gettin' back in time, but the other fellers may be along now any minnit."

"I likes to send de lie de droat down off dot von pig schoundrel!" muttered Hans, laying his hand on the hunting-knife in his belt.

An imperative gesture from Lyttleton commanded silence.

Brannon was saying something in answer to Bill's remark, but the tones were so low that Lyttleton could catch only a word here and there, not enough to learn its purport.

A long silence followed, broken occasionally by a muttered oath or exclamation of impatience, then a low-toned consultation, which resulted in the despatching of one of the younger villains to reconnoitre and try to discover why their intended victims delayed their appearance.

Another long waiting, and then the scout returned.

"Been all the way back to the house," he reported, loud enough for every word to reach the listeners above, "and not a sign of 'em to be seen. The old woman says they left thar at sun-up, so if any o' you kin tell what's become of 'em it's more'n I kin."

"Must ha' smelt a rat somehow, and pushed through the woods another way," cried Bill, pouring out a volley of oaths and curses so blasphemous, and in tones so ferocious, that Lyttleton's blood almost curdled in his veins.

Then his heart nearly stood still with affright as the ruffian went on, in the same savage tones:

"Well, there ain't no use in waitin' here no longer. They've got off safe and sound, and we not a penny the richer; but there's that Britisher, with a pocket full of tin that'll come as good to us as the other fellers'. Let's hunt him up and help ourselves. Easy work it'll be, six agin two."

Hans and his master exchanged glances. Lyttleton held up a finger in token of silence, and again they strained their ears to hear the talk going on below.

The ruffians seemed to be of one mind in regard to robbing him, impelled to it by their cupidity and their indignation at his failure to join them according to promise.

Fortunately for him they had no suspicion of his vicinity, and presently set off in a body to search for him at the scene of his late bivouac.

The moment they were out of sight and hearing he and Hans rose, scrambled down the hill, mounted their horses, which they had left at its foot, concealed in the thick wood, and striking into the trail at the nearest point, pushed on their way eastward with all possible despatch.

CHAPTER XXIX.

Clendenin's heart beat quickly between hope and fear. He was nearing the home of his childhood and knew not in what state he should find the dear ones there, for he had had no later news of them than that contained in the letter written so many weeks ago, and received the night before he left Chillicothe.

He had pressed on as rapidly as circumstances would allow, yet the journey had been long and tedious, made to seem doubly so by his haste and anxiety; for faith was not always strong enough to triumph over doubts and fears.

He had passed the previous night some ten miles west of Glen Forest, and taking an early start entered the little valley two hours before noon.

It was a sweet, bright summer day, trees dressed in their richest robes of green, wild wood flowers scattered in lavish profusion on every side, fields clothed in verdure, the air filled with the music of birds and insects, the bleating of sheep, the lowing of kine, and the fretting, gurgling, and babbling of the mountain stream, as it danced and sparkled in the sun.

Each familiar scene had charms for Kenneth's eye, yet he lingered not a moment, but urged Romeo to a brisk canter, until, as he came in sight of the house, his eye was suddenly caught by the gleam of something white among the trees that bordered the rivulet.

He halted, looked more closely at the object, then hastily dismounted, and, giving the bridle into Zeb's hands, bade him go on to the house and say that he was with Miss Marian, and they would both come in presently.

Marian had wandered out an hour ago to the spot where she and Lyttleton had sat together for the last time, on the day he bade her a final good-bye.

It had been her favorite resort ever since. Thither she would carry book or work, or go to sit with folded hands and dream away the time that seemed so long, so very, very long till he would come again.

That was all she was doing now, seated on the grass with her arms clasped about Caius's neck, her cheek resting on his head, and her eyes fixed with mournful gaze upon the rippling water at her feet.

Kenneth drew near with so noiseless a step that she knew not of his coming, and he had leisure to study her face for several minutes while she was entirely unconscious of his scrutiny.

His breast heaved, his lip quivered, and his eyes filled as he gazed; for a sad change had come over the fair, young face since last he looked upon it, the bloom was all gone from cheek and lip, the temple looked sunken, the eyes unnaturally large, and, oh, the unfathomable depth of sadness in them! And the slight girlish figure had lost its roundness; the small, shapely hands were very thin and white.

A bird suddenly swooped down from a tree and skimmed along just above the stream. Caius uttered a short, sharp bark and made a spring toward it, and with a deep sigh Marian awoke, released him, and turning her eyes in Kenneth's direction gave a joyful cry.

In a moment she was clasped in his arms, her head pillowed on his breast, with convulsive sobbing and floods of tears, while he held her close and soothed her with tender words and caresses.

"O, Kenneth, how glad I am you have come at last!" she said when she could command her voice. "It seemed so long, so very long that we had to wait; and yet you are here sooner than mother thought you could come."

"I made all the haste I could, dear child," he answered, "starting early the morning after the letter reached me with the news that you were not well. What ails you, Marian, dear?"

"I'm not sick, Kenneth," she said, a vivid blush suddenly suffusing her cheek.

"But you have grown very thin and pale, and do not seem strong," he said, regarding her with tender, sorrowful scrutiny. "Something is amiss with you, and surely you will tell me what it is, that I may try to relieve you?"

She only hid her face on his shoulder with a fresh burst of weeping.

A terrible fear oppressed him as he went on questioning her about the symptoms of her disease, she still insisting that she had no pain and was not sick, though she could not deny loss of appetite, weakness and palpitation of the heart upon slight exertion.

At length her reserve gave way before his loving solicitude; for she had been wont to confide her childish joys and sorrows to him in the old days before he went to Ohio, and could tell him now what she would not breathe to any other creature.

"O, Kenneth!" she cried, "can't you see that my body is not sick, that it's my heart that is breaking?"

His very lips grew white.

"What can you mean, my poor, poor child?" he asked huskily, drawing her closer to him with a quick protecting gesture, as if he would shield her from the threatened danger.

"Oh," she cried in bitter despairing tones, "I thought he loved me, he said it with his eyes and with his tongue; he said I was the sweetest, fairest, dearest girl he ever saw, and he promised to come again in a year at the very farthest; but more than a year has gone by and never a word from him."

His first emotion as he listened to this burst of anguish was utter astonishment; the next the fear that she was not in her right mind, for he had every reason to suppose that she had never met other than to exchange the merest civilities of life with any man.

Her mother had no suspicion of the real cause of her child's suffering. Marian had not confided in her, had never mentioned Lyttleton's name; and the death of the Misses Burns, followed very shortly by the removal to a distance of their maid Kitty, had left no one in the neighborhood who had been cognizant of even that small part of the intercourse between Marian and Lyttleton of which Woodland was the scene.

But the ice once broken, the pent up waters of the poor child's anguish speedily swept away every barrier of reserve, and the whole sad story was poured out into Kenneth's sympathizing ear.

It brought relief from the fear for her reason, but filled his heart with grief and pity for her, mingled with burning indignation against the author of her woe.

"And who is this wretch?" he cried in tones quivering with intense emotion.

The answer was so low that he bent his ear almost to her lips to catch it.

"Lyttleton!" he exclaimed, "Lysander Lyttleton? I know the man; and Marian, my poor deceived and wronged little sister, he is utterly unworthy of even your friendship; 'twould be the consorting of the dove with the vulture."

She gave a sharp cry of pain.

"O, Kenneth, Kenneth, you can't mean it?"

It was hard to see her suffer, but best that she should know the truth at once. In a few brief sentences, carefully worded to spare her as much as possible, he told of Lyttleton's approaching marriage.

She did not cry out again, but asked, in a tone of quiet despair, to whom.

It cost Kenneth an effort to speak Nell's name, and something in his voice thrilled his listener with an instant consciousness of what she was to him.

She lifted her face to his, the wet eyes full of tender pity.

"You, too, Kenneth, my poor dear Kenneth?" she said in low, tremulous tones, "has he wronged you too? Then he is cast out of my heart forever. I cannot love one so base, so unworthy."

But with the last words her head went down upon his shoulder again with a passionate burst of weeping.

A storm of feeling swept over Kenneth as he held her close, not speaking, for he could find no words, but softly smoothing her hair, gently pressing one of the small, thin hands which he had taken in his.

He could not forgive Lyttleton at that moment, he felt that he could crush him under foot as he would a viper that had stung this precious little sister, and poisoned two other lives. His own must be dark and dreary without sweet Nell, and what better could hers be, passed in the society of such a wretch, nay, more, in the closest union with him.

Alas! alas! hers was the saddest fate of all, and none the less to be pitied because she had in some measure brought it upon herself.

In some measure? Ah, was he utterly blameless, Kenneth Clendenin?

The question came to him with a sharp pang of self-reproach. He had won her affection, his lips had never breathed a syllable of love. Then who was he that he should be so fierce against this other transgressor?

The tempest of emotion had spent itself, and Marian lay pale and exhausted in his arms, trembling like a leaf.

Very gently he raised her, and bidding her cling about his neck, bore her in those strong arms to the house, Caius running on before to announce their coming.

Mrs. Clendenin met them in the porch, her face full of anxiety and alarm.

"Kenneth! what is it?"

"She is wearied out now, mother, but will be better soon. Let me lay her in her bed."

She had already fallen into the sleep of utter exhaustion. He placed her comfortably on the bed, while the mother drew down the blinds and Caius stretched himself on the floor by her side.

"Kenneth, my dear boy, oh, what a comfort to have you here again!" whispered Mrs. Clendenin, as they clasped each other in a long, tender embrace.

Leaving Caius to watch the slumbers of their dear one, they withdrew to the sitting-room.

"What do you think of her?" There was another, an unspoken question in the mother's pleading anxious eyes.

Kenneth's answer to it was, "Let your poor heart be at rest, mother, it is not that."

A cloud of care, of deep and sore anxiety lifted from her brow, and she wept tears of joy and thankfulness.

"Anything but that," she sighed, "any other burden seems light in comparison with that. But, Kenneth, the child is certainly ill, have you discovered the cause of her malady?"

"Yes," he said, "and have brought her a cure which, though it must be painful at first, will, I doubt not, prove effectual in the end."

Then he repeated Marian's story, having won her consent that he should do so, and added his own knowledge of Lyttleton.

The mother's surprise was not less than his had been, and her tears fell fast over the sorrows of her sweet and gentle child.

"I take blame to myself for leaving her alone," she said, "and yet it was what seemed best at the time."

"I would not have you do so, mother, dear," he said, gazing tenderly into the patient yet troubled face whereon sorrow and care had left their deep and lasting traces, "no blame rightfully belongs to you; and let me say for your consolation, that if I read her aright, there is one drop of sweetness in this otherwise bitter cup, she will never love again."

She gave him one earnest look, then dropping her eyes, seemed lost in thought for several minutes.

"Yes," she said at length, "I think you are right. And she has passed this trying ordeal safely?"

"Yes."

Clasping her hands in her lap and lifting her eyes to heaven, "I thank thee, oh my Father, for that," she murmured in tones so low that the words scarcely reached Kenneth's ear.

He stood looking down upon her with loving, compassionate eyes. Ah, if it were but in his power to remove every thorn from her path!

That might not be, but her face had resumed its wonted expression of sweet and calm submission. She glanced up at him, her fine eyes full of affectionate pride.

"You have told me nothing yet of yourself, Kenneth. How fares it with you, my boy? Sit down here by my side and open all your heart to me as you used to do. I see you have something to tell," she added, watching the changes of his countenance as he took the offered chair, "something of joy and something of sorrow."

"Yes, mother, I have learned that long sought secret, and it brings me both gladness and grief," he answered with emotion.

"You have found her?" she asked in almost breathless, half credulous astonishment.

"Yes, mother, Reumah Clark, and—"

"Wait one moment," she faltered, pressing her hand to her heart.

He knelt at her side and threw an arm about her waist. She laid her head on his shoulder, heaving a gentle sigh.

"Now," she whispered, "tell me all. Oh, that terrible, terrible day. I can never recall it without a shudder."

His story did not go back to the scenes of that dreadful day on which he first saw the light. He merely gave a brief account of his interview with Reumah Clark, confining himself chiefly to her explanation of the mark which proved his identity, and her assertion that she had looked for and seen it at the time of his birth.

Mrs. Clendenin raised her head, showing a face radiant with joy and thankfulness.

"Oh, my dear boy, what glad news for you, what a burden removed! And yet —Ah, I am not the happy mother of such a son!" and her eyes filled with tears.

"No, that is the bitter drop in the cup, sweet mother, for I must still call you so, unless you forbid it. And, thank God, we are of the same blood."

"Yes, yes, my own mother's child by birth, mine own by adoption, we are very near and dear to one another," she whispered, clinging to him in a close and tender embrace.

For a moment there was utter silence between them, then she spoke musingly, as if half talking to him, half thinking aloud.

"I have often wondered over that mark, but could find no clue to it, for my mother never mentioned the occurrence to me, and I knew nothing of the mark upon Clark's arm. Ah, had I known, how much of anxiety and mental suffering might have been spared us both!"

"Yes," he assented with almost a groan, thinking of his lost love.

She saw the anguish in his face and with tender questioning at length drew the whole story from him.

"Do not despair," she said when he had finished, "I think the man has told you a falsehood. I understand woman's nature better than you can, and such a girl as you have described would never give herself to such a man. And now the seal is taken from your lips and you may declare your love and sue for hers in return. Ah, my dear boy, I trust happy days are in store for you even on this side of Jordan."

She looked into his eyes with hers so full of loving pride, tender sympathy and joyful anticipation, that hope revived in his desponding heart.

CHAPTER XXX.

"One thing more, mother, before Marian joins us," Kenneth said, breaking a pause in the conversation; "she surely need know nothing of the discovery we have made. I once at her earnest request told her of the doubt, and she was sorely distressed by it; to use her own expression, could hardly endure the thought that I might not be her very own brother! Shall we not let her remain in ignorance of that which could bring her nothing but sorrow?"

"You are right, Kenneth, we will bury it in our own hearts, so far as she is concerned, along with that other, terrible secret," sighed the mother in low, tremulous tones.

They were silent again for a little, there was so much food for perplexing thought in the circumstances that surrounded them; then, "Who is this Lyttleton?" she asked. "Coming first here, taking pains to ingratiate himself with Marian, asking many questions about you, afterward appearing in Chillicothe, having in the meantime visited Virginia, very possibly Tennessee also; does it not look as if he had a design in it all, a purpose to carry out?"

"It does indeed!" cried Kenneth in surprise and perplexity; "and if so, doubtless he will cross my path again; perhaps Marian's also; but woe to him if he attempts further harm to that dear child!" he added with stern and angry determination.

"O Kenneth, beware!" exclaimed the mother half frightened at such vehemence in one usually so self-controlled, "if he have evil designs toward our darling, we must baffle them by keeping her out of his way."

"We must indeed," he said in quieter though not less resolute tones; "and while I am here she shall be my special care."

A few days later light was thrown on this dark question by a letter forwarded by Dale from Chillicothe, enclosed in one from himself stating that he now had Reumah Clark's evidence in proper shape.

The enclosure was from England, and brought news of the death of a brother of Kenneth's own father, the last of that family.

He had left a very considerable property, to which Kenneth was the rightful heir, both by law and the provisions of his uncle's will, in case he could prove his identity; failing that, Lyttleton, though only very distantly related, would inherit for lack of a nearer heir. He had therefore a strong motive for wishing to destroy whatever proof of Kenneth's real parentage might exist, unless he could make sure that such proof would be in favor of the supposition that Kenneth was the child of his reputed parent, the younger of the two Clendenins of the Tennessee tragedy.

Hence his efforts to bribe Reumah Clark to silence. He had visited the neighborhood of the tragedy and learned just enough to assure him that if any living person could supply the missing link in the evidence, it was she and she alone.

If he could prevent her doing so, Kenneth's claims must inevitably fall to the ground, and by its failure his own succession be secured.

In his interview with the woman he was made aware of the fact that one of the children bore a distinguishing mark, but it was impossible to discover whether Kenneth were that one or the other.

In these letters, written by the attorney of the deceased gentleman, Kenneth was informed of the antagonism of his own and Lyttleton's interests, warned that the latter might be supposed to entertain designs against him, and informed that he had gone to America.

These letters and the answers to them were shown to Mrs. Clendenin and quietly discussed with her when Marian was not present.

It seemed, in the light of these revelations, almost a foregone conclusion that Lyttleton was the man who had so nearly succeeded in preventing Kenneth from gaining the all-important evidence of the white squaw of the Indian brave; and while the discovery of the Englishman's perfidious character gave Clendenin increased hope that his boast of having won Miss Lamar was false, it also augmented his anxiety for her in case it should prove true.

The impulse to return at once to Chillicothe and seek an interview with her was often strong upon him. Yet he put it resolutely aside for Marian's sake; so all-important to her seemed his watchful care just at this crisis.

And most wisely, tenderly, lovingly was the duty performed. They were seldom apart in her waking hours, and he exerted himself to the utmost to comfort and soothe, to amuse, to entertain, and by interesting her in other matters, to keep her thoughts from dwelling upon her grief and disappointment.

It was no longer unrequited love, for she had, as she said, cast Lyttleton out of her heart the moment she had discovered his utter unworthiness; but the heart was sore, nevertheless, and the niche once filled by the now broken idol, an aching void.

Her newly awakened woman's pride, too, was deeply wounded, and yet it came to her aid, helping her to bear up with resolution against the crushing sense of loss and humiliation; deceived and wronged she had been, but none should know how deeply; none, save the two to whom she was so dear, suspect that any such calamity had befallen her.

Kenneth kept his patient much in the open air. The days were long, warm and bright, and the two, or sometimes it was the three, when household cares could be laid aside by the mother, taking an early start, and carrying lunch, books and work with them, would seek out one or another secluded spot, some little glen among the hills, or some level place along their sides, or on their summits, that gave them a fine view of the lower country, and where tree or vine or towering rock shielded them pleasantly from the too fervid rays of the sun, and there while away the hours, till the lengthening shadows warned them it was time to return.

From her earliest recollection Marian had loved Kenneth with well-nigh passionate devotion; he was to her the impersonation of all that is good and noble.

Her father had been a perplexity and at times almost a terror to her; silent, gloomy, his presence ever like a dark shadow in the house, ever imposing a vague restraint upon all manifestation of mirth and gladness. Her mother had heart and mind so intent upon him, that, while loving her child very dearly, she had little time or opportunity to study her disposition or win her confidence. She was one indeed respected, honored, looked up to as counsellor and guide, an authority never to be questioned, but it was Kenneth, her one brother, who was her closest intimate and confident of all her childish joys, sorrows and perplexities.

In his early childhood the father had been a different man, bright, cheery, pleasant tempered and genial; the mother able to do all a mother's part by him.

He understood the change and its cause; understood also Marian's needs, and earnestly strove to supply to her whatever was lacking by reason of the strange and sad vicissitude that had come upon the family.

Angus, born in the same hour with Kenneth, was the eldest child, Marian the youngest and the last of the four or five who filled the gap between, and who had passed away from earth while she was still a mere babe.

Thus everything conspired to make Kenneth all in all to her in the early days before he left home to pursue his medical studies.

Since that he had been in all his absences her one correspondent; and except in the one matter of her acquaintance with Lyttleton, she had been wont to pour out to him, in that way, her thoughts and feelings without reserve.

During the last year she had written but seldom, and the alteration in the tone of her letters, the few that he had received being short and constrained, had greatly puzzled and troubled him. Now he comprehended the cause.

But the old unrestraint and confidence had returned, and the poor girl found the greatest consolation and support in Kenneth's presence, Kenneth's sympathy and love. "Her dear, dear brother," she called him, and he did not intend she should ever learn that he was not.

Thus cheered and comforted, she soon began to regain strength, flesh and color; spirits too, till at times her silvery laugh rang out quite merrily.

One morning, several weeks after Kenneth's return, he and Marian were out among the hills at no great distance from home, where they had left Mrs. Clendenin busied with some domestic duty.

Marian ambled along on her pony, Kenneth walking by its side, Caius leaping and bounding, now before, and now behind, now in silence and anon waking the echoes with joyous bark.

The sagacious creature evidently rejoiced over the improvement visible in his young mistress.

"Here is Prospect Hill," remarked Kenneth; "do you feel equal to climbing it? The slope is very gentle on this side, and I think your pony will carry you full two-thirds of the way up. For the rest you shall have the support of my arm."

"Oh, yes," she answered almost eagerly; "we have not been there together for years, and I always enjoy the view so much."

They made the ascent slowly, stopping now and again to take in the view from different points.

When the way grew too steep for the pony Kenneth tethered him to a tree, and lifting Marian from the saddle, half carried her to the top of the hill.

The prospect here was very fine; looking off from a precipice two hundred feet high, they could take in the whole extent of their own little valley and many miles of country lying beyond it, beautifully diversified with hill and dale, meandering streams, forest and cultivated fields, farm-houses and villages stretching away far as the eye could reach, toward the west and north; while on the south and east the lofty Alleghenies shut in the view, seemingly at no great distance, though in reality miles away.

With a folded shawl laid over the roots of a tree Kenneth made a comfortable seat for Marian within two or three yards of the edge of the cliff; then threw himself down beside her, and they fell into cheerful chat, calling each other's attention to the varied beauties of the landscape spread out before them, and talking of other days when they had gazed upon it together.

Neither of them had cast a look behind as they came up the hill, so they had not seen a man who stepped out of the woods into the road below just as they began the ascent, and stood for a moment gazing after them, then stealthily followed, not by the path they were pursuing, but creeping along a little to one side, under cover of the bushes and trees that thickly clothed that part of the hill.

Reaching the top, still unnoticed, for their faces were turned from him, he concealed himself behind a clump of evergreens whence he could take cognizance of both their movements and their talk, without danger of discovery.

It was Lyttleton, who had followed Kenneth into this neighborhood and was prowling about with no very settled purpose, but with a vague idea of finding some means of removing him from his path. It might be that with the assistance of his valet alone he could, if circumstances should favor the design, carry out even yet the plan which had so signally failed under the auspices of Bill Shark and Brannon.

He had spent many an hour in watching the brother and sister and listening to their mutual confidences, when they little dreamed of his vicinity.

Thus he had learned of Marian's changed feelings toward himself and how he had sunk in her estimation.

His vanity was sorely wounded, and as blessings brighten as they take their flight, he began to grow very desirous to win back her esteem and affection.

Suffering had spiritualized her beauty, and watching the play of her features and her changing color as she conversed so unreservedly with Kenneth, he sometimes pronounced it superior to that of Miss Lamar.

Yes, he began, now that it was beyond his reach, to covet the jewel he had won, then carelessly and heartlessly thrown aside.

She had never looked lovelier than on this particular morning, and the impulse came strongly upon him to go to her and make an effort to recover lost ground. Why should he not present himself as having just come, after unavoidable detention, to fulfill his promise of return, he queried with himself, forgetting for the moment that he had told Kenneth he was engaged to Miss Lamar; thus proving that he was false to Marian; and only remembering that Kenneth could know nothing of the plots against his liberty and his inheritance to his uncle's estate.

He would have preferred to see Marian alone, his inordinate self-esteem assuring him that in that case he would have little difficulty in re-establishing himself in her good graces; but Clendenin was always with her. Therefore no time could be better than the present; and just then, as if to favor his design, Kenneth rose and left her; going to the very verge of the precipice, where he stood for several minutes gazing down into the little valley at its foot.

Lyttleton approached her with quick but noiseless tread, and happening to raise her eyes they encountered his as he stood close at her side intently scanning her features.

She uttered a little cry of mingled surprise and alarm, at which Kenneth turned instantly and flew to the rescue.

"Don't be alarmed, sweet one," Lyttleton said; but the words had scarcely left his lips when he found himself confronted by Kenneth, who with form erect and flashing eyes, sternly demanded of him, "How dare you, sir, venture to address my sister after the shameful manner in which you have acted toward her?"

"She is your sister, is she, sir? That is good news for me," Lyttleton said, with a malicious gleam in his eyes. "I am most happy to hear it."

"I am her natural protector and intend to prove myself such in good earnest," returned Kenneth. "As for you, sir, I have lately become aware of, not only your perfidious conduct toward this poor innocent child, but also who you are and your probable errand to this country."

Lyttleton grew pale with anger and fear. He did not think at the moment of Clendenin having received news from England, but supposed Shark, Brannon or Hans had betrayed him; or perhaps Reumah Clark; though she could have told nothing save that he had bribed her to silence.

A moment he stood shamefaced and irresolute, then anger getting the better of fear, he turned furiously upon his antagonist, heaping the most virulent abuse upon him, calling him coward, villain, supplanter, accusing him of robbing him of fortune and lady-love, and vowing sleepless revenge.

He drew nearer and nearer to Kenneth, as he spoke, using violent and threatening gesticulations; and the latter confronting him with calm, quiet, yet sternly determined face, kept constantly stepping back to avoid a collision, till again he stood on the very verge of the precipice; but with his back to it, and in the forgetfulness caused by excitement, utterly unconscious of his danger.

Whether Lyttleton was aware of it is uncertain, but he struck him a blow that sent him toppling over, and with a wild cry, echoed by Marian, the terrified witness of the whole scene, he disappeared from sight.

Lyttleton shrieked, fell on his knees and crawling, shuddering and trembling, to the edge looked over.

There down at the bottom of the steep descent of two hundred feet, lay something, indistinctly seen because of the distance and intervening trees, that looked like a confused and lifeless heap.

"Oh my God, have mercy! I have killed him!" he cried, springing to his feet. "I've killed him! I've killed him!" he repeated clenching his hands and groaning aloud in an agony of terror and remorse. "I've killed him, but God knows I didn't intend it!"

He glanced at Marian.

She lay in a little white heap apparently as dead as the one at the foot of the precipice.

Then with flying footsteps he fled down the hill, by the way he had come, nor paused, nor looked back till he reached the spot, some half mile distant, where he had left Hans and the horses.

The valet, spite of all his natural stolid indifference under ordinary circumstances, was startled into an exclamation of wonder and dismay at sight of his master's pallid, terror-stricken countenance.

"Mine Gott! mynheer, vat ish happen you, to see von pig ghost?"

Lyttleton shivered with the thought that he had evoked a ghost that would haunt him all his days.

"Nonsense," he said in a hoarse whisper and glancing fearfully behind him; "there's been an accident; Clendenin has fallen down a precipice and is probably killed, and I may be suspected of having had something to do with it. I must mount and away in haste. I shall take yonder road and travel east. Do you go and settle our bill for board, and follow me with the luggage.

"All haste, we must be miles away from here before the thing is discovered! Fortunately I had expressed my intention of leaving to-day or to-morrow, so that our sudden departure need excite no suspicion.

"Not a word of the accident to any one, remember; be discreet and prompt, and you shall not fail of your reward."

With the last words he vaulted into the saddle, put spurs to his horse and galloped away at the top of his speed.

What cared he for the helpless girl whom he had left lying insensible and alone upon the hill top? Ah, he cursed her between his clenched teeth, and wished she might never wake again to tell of his foul deed; she, its only human witness.

CHAPTER XXXI.

No, Marian was not quite alone; her four-footed friend and protector would not forsake her, though for a time he seemed divided between the duty of watching over her and succoring Kenneth. When the latter fell, Caius sprang forward with a loud bark, as with the double purpose to save him and to avenge him upon his cowardly assailant; but Marian's cry recalled him instantly to her side.

He stood over her, gazing into her white, rigid face with a low whine, then he gently tried to rouse her, pulling at her dress, then licking her hands, and then her face.

At last she opened her eyes, sat up and looked about her.

Where was she? What had happened? Where was Kenneth? It all came back to her, and with an anguished cry she staggered to her feet, drew tremblingly, shudderingly near to the edge of the cliff and looked down.

Nothing to be seen but rocks and trees and the little stream quietly wending its way through the valley below.

"Kenneth!" she shrieked wildly, "Kenneth! Kenneth!"

But there was no answer, and now her eye caught that little confused heap. Was it he? She seemed to recognize the clothing he had worn. Oh, he was dead, how could it be otherwise after that fearful fall!

She swooned again and Caius dragged her away from the perilous spot and renewed his efforts to revive her.

How long it was before he succeeded she could never tell, or how, when at last consciousness returned, she made her way to her pony, untethered him and got upon his back.

She left him to his own guidance, and he took the right road for home.

She seemed to see nothing but Kenneth lying cold and dead at the foot of the precipice, to know nothing but that he was gone from her forever, and that Lyttleton, the man she had once loved, was his murderer.

The pony stopped at the gate; Marian lifted her head.

What, who was that coming slowly and with limping, halting gait to meet her from the other direction?

She looked again, and a cry of joy, so intense that it was near akin to pain, burst from her pallid lips.

Torn, bruised, scratched, disheveled, clothing hanging in tatters, the difficult, awkward, evidently painful and toilsome movement, as different as possible from his accustomed free, manly, energetic carriage, it was yet, without doubt, Kenneth himself.

Caius bounded toward him with a joyous bark of recognition, and Marian sprang to the ground and rushed with outstretched arms to meet him, crying, "O, Kenneth, Kenneth, is it, can it be you? Oh, I thought—I thought—"

The rest was lost in a burst of weeping, as she clasped him close, then, holding him off, gazed shudderingly into his face, so bruised, wan and bloody that she might well have doubted if it were indeed he.

"Yes," he gasped, staggering and catching at the fence for support, "I have had a wonderful deliverance. And you, darling? Oh, the Lord be praised that you are here safe and sound!"

Their approach had been seen from the house, and mother and servants now came running to ask what had befallen, every face full of agitation and alarm at sight of Kenneth's condition.

But seeing that he was half-fainting, the mother stopped all questioning till he could be got into the house, laid upon a bed and his wounds dressed.

There were no bones broken, he presently assured her of that, but the jar to the whole system, the bruises and cuts, would confine him to his couch for some days.

Great was her astonishment when told whence he had fallen.

"How is it possible you can have escaped alive?" she exclaimed, her usually calm face full of emotion; "it seems nothing short of a miracle!"

"Yes," he said, with deep gravity, and a far away look in his eyes; "my thought, as I felt myself falling, was that I was going to certain, instant death; but there was a joyful consciousness that all would be well."

"But what saved you?" she asked, in almost breathless excitement.

"The trees and the sand, joined to my light weight, were my heavenly Father's instruments to that end," he answered with his grave, tender smile. "The bank of the stream just there is a deep bed of soft sand; that is overhung by waterwillows with very thick, very pliant branches; and towering above them, from fifty to seventy feet high, are oaks and other varieties of trees. I must have fallen first into those, and without striking any large branch, from them into the willows, and from them on to the bed of sand.

"I was there when I came to myself; how long I had lain there insensible I cannot tell, but it must have been a good while. I had a good deal of difficulty in dragging myself home; could not get to Marian by any shorter route, and thought to send Zeb for her.

"Poor child! I was very anxious about you," he added, with an affectionate glance at her, "for I did not know but the Englishman might have carried you off."

"He's bad enough, no doubt, if he had wanted me," she cried indignantly; "but it seems he did not, fortunately."

She alone, of the three, showed any feeling of bitterness toward Lyttleton; with the others resentment was swallowed up in thankfulness.

They made no effort for the apprehension of the criminal, and indeed let it be supposed by their friends and acquaintances, and even their own servants, that Kenneth's fall was accidental.

They heard casually, in a day or two, that Lyttleton had been a boarder for several weeks past at a solitary farm-house some miles distant, but had left on the day of Dr. Clendenin's accident, travelling in an easterly direction.

The sudden turn affairs had taken proved a decided benefit to Marian. Her thoughts were turned from herself and her sorrows to her suffering brother. She was his nurse; quite as devoted and affectionate as he had been to her, and, in her detestation of Lyttleton's crime, she lost the last vestige of regard for him, of regret of his desertion.

She could never again be quite the careless child she was of yore, but grief and disappointment had lost their keen edge, and she would one day emulate the calm, placid resignation of her mother.

The change that came over her greatly lightened the hearts of the two who loved her so dearly.

For Kenneth, too, clouds and darkness were breaking away, and the star of hope shone brightly.

He at first thought Lyttleton's accusation against him, that he had robbed him of his lady-love, referred to Marian; but on reflection he felt convinced that it was Miss Lamar the man meant; the admission being unguardedly made while half maddened by anger and resentment.

It seemed very unlikely that he would have left Chillicothe just then, so suddenly and for such a length of time, and without bidding adieu to Nell, if they were really engaged.

Beside, Dale in his last letter had expressed in strong terms his conviction that Lyttleton's boast was utterly false.

As Kenneth thought on these things and remembered that he was now free to win the long coveted prize, if he could; as he talked it all over with her whom he still called mother, his impatience to get back to Chillicothe grew apace.

A visit to England would be necessary for the settlement of his affairs there, but the business which called him to Chillicothe was of far more importance in his esteem, and must be attended to first.

He took Marian into his confidence as far as might be without causing her sorrow and distress, and with the promise of a visit to Glen Forest both on his way to the sea-board when about to set sail for England, and on his return, reconciled her to his departure for Ohio as soon as he was sufficiently recovered from his fall to be able to travel.

CHAPTER XXXII.

Evening was closing in upon the Scioto valley after a day of incessant rain often accompanied by sharp flashes of lightning and heavy peals of thunder; the streets were flooded, the trees, shrubbery, all things not under shelter, were dripping with moisture; and still the rain fell in torrents and at intervals the thunder crashed overhead, waking the echoes of the hills and frightening the timid and nervous with its prolonged and angry roar.

It was just as it had grown too dark for those within doors to distinguish passers by, who, indeed were very few and far between, and during one of the heaviest showers, and the most terrific discharge of thunder and lightning, that Dr. Clendenin and his attendant, Zeb, came dashing into the town and hastily alighted at the door of the doctor's office.

Hearing, between the thunder peals, the sound of horses' hoofs, and Clendenin's voice giving directions to Zeb, Dale rushed to the door to greet his friend; in his great delight more than half inclined to embrace him after the fashion of womankind.

"Hello, doc! are you actually here *in propria persona*? Well I must say this is a most agreeable ending of an intensely disagreeable day. I am glad to see you; think I was never gladder in my life!" he went on, shaking Kenneth's hand again and again; "but I wonder how you had the courage to push on in spite of such a storm. Must have had trouble in crossing some of the streams, hadn't you?"

"Yes, we had to swim our horses several times," Kenneth answered, beginning to divest himself of his wet outer garments.

"I'd have taken refuge in some hospitable farm-house till the storm was over," said Dale, helping him off with his overcoat.

"We stopped and had supper at Shirley's, and I was strongly urged to stay till morning; but really felt it impossible to sleep within five miles of Chillicothe," Clendenin said with a gayety of look and tone that struck Dale as something new in him.

"Hello! old fellow, you seem in rare good spirits," he remarked in a tone of mingled surprise and pleasure.

"I believe I am; and yet a little anxious too," Kenneth answered, his face growing grave. "How are all our friends here?"

"All flourishing at the major's," laughed Dale, with a quizzical look. "Ah ha! I believe I have an inkling of the reason why you couldn't stop short of Chillicothe. But you'll not think of making friendly calls in such weather. They'd think you crazy, man."

Clendenin's only reply was a quiet smile.

Truly he meant to be knocking at the major's door within the next half hour. What, live in suspense till another day, while within three minutes walk of her who held his fate in her hands? Impossible! 'twould take a severer tempest than the one now raging to keep him from her side.

Dale, watching him with curious scrutiny, read all this in his speaking countenance, yet was morally certain he would not enter the major's doors that night—duty would erect a more impassable barrier than the fiercest war of the elements.

"Doc," he said with rueful look, as he perceived that his friend was nearly ready to sally forth upon his eagerly desired errand, "I hate most confoundedly to have you disappointed, but the truth is—"

"What! Godfrey, you surely said they were all well? Has—has anything—"

"No, no, you needn't turn pale, or be in the least alarmed. It's only thatyou're called another way. Fact is Flora Barbour's lying at death's door; Buell's given her up, and Barbour's been round here several times to-day, knowing that I'd got a letter and you were expected, and made me promise over and over again to get you there as soon as possible in case you came. You see they have the greatest confidence in your skill, and can't give up the hope that you can save her yet."

Without a word, but scarcely able to suppress a heavy sigh, Kenneth at once began preparations to obey the unexpected call.

"I declare it's a shame!" cried Dale, "I wouldn't be a doctor, to come and go at everybody's beck and call, for a mint of money."

"It's a noble profession, Godfrey, spite of some serious drawbacks," returned Clendenin, constrained to smile at his friend's vehemence, albeit his disappointment was really very great.

Protecting himself as well as might be from the deluge of rain that as yet knew no abatement, he hurried on his way.

The Barbours had, like most of their neighbors, exchanged their log cabin for a comfortable two story dwelling, and from an upper window the light of a candle gleamed out upon the darkness of the street.

Kenneth glanced up at it with the thought that there the sick girl was lying.

Mr. Barbour met him at the door.

"Thank God you have come; though I'm afraid it's too late," he said in a hoarse whisper, wringing Kenneth's hand.

"Don't despair, while there's life, there's hope," Kenneth answered feelingly. "Shall I go to her at once?"

"Yes; but maybe you'd like to see Buell first. He's in here," opening an inner door.

Dr. Buell, who was seated at a table measuring out medicines, rose and came forward to meet Dr. Clendenin.

The two shook hands cordially, Buell saying, "I am very glad to see you, sir! You are the family physician, and I trust will now take charge of the case."

"I should like to consult with you, doctor," Kenneth said. "What is the disease?"

In answer Dr. Buell gave a full report of the symptoms and the treatment thus far; the two consulted for a few moments, then went together to the sick room.

They entered noiselessly. The room was silent as the grave. The patient lay in a deathlike sleep; and beside her, motionless as a statue, watching intently for the slightest movement, sat, not the mother, she was too nervous, too full of real or imaginary ailments of her own, to be a fit nurse for her child, but Nell Lamar, sweeter, fairer, lovelier in her lover's eyes than ever before.

His heart thrilled with ecstatic joy at the sight, but her eyes remained fixed upon the deathlike face on the pillow, and a slight deepening of the rose on her cheek alone gave token of a consciousness of their entrance.

They lingered but a moment, withdrew as noiselessly as they had entered, and held a second consultation.

Both pronounced it the crisis of the disease and thought that the next few hours would decide the question of life or death.

"Miss Lamar has proved herself an excellent nurse," said Dr. Buell, "and has promised to stay with her through the night. I meant to share her vigil, if you had not come, Clendenin, but I have lost a good deal of rest lately and have a very sick patient of my own."

"It is my turn," was Kenneth's prompt reply, "and I shall not leave her till the crisis is past."

Dr. Buell now took his departure and Dr. Clendenin found himself compelled to spend some time in attendance upon Mrs. Barbour, and in comforting and encouraging the distressed husband and father.

At length he was free to return to the sick room, and in another moment was standing close beside her who had for years held dominion over his noble, manly heart, and into whose ear he longed with inexpressible longing to pour out the story of his love.

Yet must he remain mute, for no word might be spoken to break the silence of the room where life and death were trembling in the balance.

But he stood gazing down upon the loved face till some magnetic spell forced the beautiful violet eyes to lift themselves to his.

Ah, words were not needed! His eyes now spoke joy and entreaty too, as well as love, and she knew that the barrier which had so long separated them, whatever it might have been, was swept away.

Her eyes dropped beneath his ardent gaze, a vivid charming blush suddenly suffusing her cheek, then again yielding to that magic spell were timidly raised to his.

He held out his hand, she laid hers in it and found it held fast in a warm tender clasp that would not let it go, that seemed to speak proprietorship; and strangely enough, considering how highly she had always valued her liberty —she did not care to resist the claim, nor did she repulse him even when, presently, he bowed his head and pressed a passionate kiss upon the white fingers.

The patient slept on; the family retired to rest and utter stillness reigned through all the house; outside there was the incessant drip, drip of the rain, but not a solitary footstep passed; it seemed as though they two were alone in the world save for that motionless form on the bed.

There came another terrific peal of thunder, yet the sleeper did not stir, but Nell instinctively drew nearer her companion, while he with the impulse to protect her, threw an arm about her waist and drew her close to his side. Neither intended it, but the next instant their lips met and they knew they were betrothed.

Blushing deeply, though her eyes shone and her heart thrilled with an exquisite joy, Nell would have withdrawn herself from his embrace, but he gently detained her; she was his and he could not let her go yet; and again she yielded to his stronger will.

She wondered at her own submissiveness as she realized to-night that it was a positive pleasure to be ruled.

The hours flew by on viewless wings; it was no hard task to keep that vigil, yet the physician was not forgotten in the lover.

Toward morning the patient awoke and recognized her watchers with a pleased smile. The crisis was safely passed. Nell knew it instantly by the glad look in the doctor's face.

He held a cup to Flora's lips, saying in a low quiet tone, "Swallow this, my child, and go to sleep again."

She obeyed. He drew a long sigh of relief. He had been bending over her in intense anxiety for the last half hour.

"Saved! The Lord be praised!" he whispered, turning to Nell with shining eyes. Then, taking her hand, "My darling, my own, is it not so?"

She astonished herself and him by bursting into a passion of tears.

It was simply overwrought nerves. She had been exceedingly anxious about Flora and had watched beside her day and night for nearly a week. After months of mental disquietude because of apparently unrequited love, the revulsion of feeling was too sudden and too great for the worn out physical frame, and this was the result.

He understood it in a moment.

"Let the tears have their way," he said tenderly; "it will do you good. I will leave you for a little, while I carry this good news to the anxious parents."

By the time he came back Nell had recovered her composure, but was too shamefaced to look at him.

"Well, fair lady, will you vouchsafe an answer to my question now?" he asked, kneeling before her and taking both hands in his, while he looked into her eyes with his own brimful of tenderness, love and joy.

"I'm not worth having," she answered with unwonted humility, speaking in the whispered tone that he had used.

"That is for me to judge," he returned, with laughing eyes. "But do be kind enough to answer my question. Or let me put it in another form. Will you have me, have me for protector and provider, lover, husband and friend?"

"Yes, if you will take me in exchange, and not think it a bad bargain," she said with a sudden impulse, and hid her blushing face on his breast as he folded her close with a glad solemn "God bless you, my darling! I shall be the gainer a thousand fold!"

CHAPTER XXXIII.

The storm was over and the rain drops on tree, shrub and flower, glittered like untold wealth of diamonds in the bright rays of the newly risen sun, as Clendenin and Nell walked down the street together.

There was nothing in the looks or manner of either to excite curiosity or suspicion in those who saw them pass.

He left her at her brother's door with a half playful order, not from the lover but the physician, to take some breakfast and go directly to bed and to sleep.

"I shall not promise," she answered saucily, lifting a a pair of bright, roguishly smiling eyes to his face, "I have not resigned my liberty yet, you know."

"Ah well, I think I may count on obedience," he said with the grave, tender smile that had first won her heart.

"I want you to rest all day and let me come to you this evening," he whispered, bending down to speak close to her ear, "I have much to tell you, my darling. You have a right to know what so long prevented my lips from repeating the story you must have read a thousand times in my eyes, if they spoke the true language of my heart."

"Never mind, I am quite content without the knowledge if, as your face seems to say, it is something painful," she said with generous confidence, and sudden gravity of looks and tone.

"Nay, dearest, you shall hear it. I will have no secrets from her who is to be 'bone of my bone and flesh of my flesh,' the nearest and dearest of all created beings," he said, lifting her hands to his lips.

Her eyes filled with happy, grateful tears, as from the vine covered porch where they had had their chat, she watched him hurrying away down the street, then turned and went into the house.

"Was that Dr. Clendenin?" asked Clare, meeting her in the hall.

"Yes."

"Why didn't he come in and take breakfast with us?"

"I didn't ask him."

"You didn't? Nell Lamar, I'm ashamed of your rude behavior to that man! If he treats you henceforward with the coldest politeness, I am sure it will be no more than you deserve."

A curious smile trembled about the corners of Nell's lips for an instant, then was gone.

"Flora has passed the crisis," she remarked, "and the doctor says will get well if she has proper care."

"Oh, I am glad!"

"Can you take my place for to-day? He wouldn't let me stay, and her mother would kill her with the fretting and worrying."

"No wonder he wouldn't let you stay. You look wretchedly tired. Yes; I'll go over presently. You'd better eat your breakfast at once and go directly to bed."

"I will," Nell answered with unaccustomed meekness, and proceeded to redeem her promise without delay.

Kenneth, too, needed rest after his wearisome journey and long night vigil, but did not seek it till a letter telling of his great happiness had been written to the dear ones at Glen Forest, and sent to the mail by Zeb.

Nell came down at tea-time to find the major alone in the parlor. He looked up on her entrance, with a smile that brought swift blushes to her cheek, then rose and came to meet her.

"I know all about it, Nell," he said, giving her a brotherly kiss. "You have made me very happy by the wisdom of your choice; I shall be proud of my new brother. Ah, here he is just coming in at the gate! You must let me share the pleasure of his society now, and after tea I will take care that you have the parlor to yourselves."

Kenneth's eyes shone at sight of his betrothed. Sleep had refreshed her and restored her bloom, and her simple white dress with no ornaments save a few delicate, sweet-scented blossoms at her throat and in her hair was very becoming.

The major kept his word, and early in the evening they found themselves sole occupants of the parlor.

Then, seated by her side, with her hand in his, Kenneth told the story of his birth and the accompanying tragedy; then went on to tell of the removal of his supposed parents to Glen Forest, and of the life there.

He described his childhood as bright and happy. Angus and he believed themselves, and were believed by others to be twins. They were devotedly attached and almost inseparable. The parents made no difference between them, and indeed, had no reason for so doing, as they were entirely unable to decide which of the two was their own child.

The boys knew nothing about the circumstances attending their birth except that at or near that time there had been an attack by the Indians in which their mother's stepfather had been slain, and that the shock had killed his wife; she being just then very ill and weak.

They could perceive that their mother was at times oppressed with sad memories of that fearful past, but for the most part she was very cheerful, and they found her ever ready to sympathize with them in joy as well as grief.

The father was inclined to be somewhat strict in his discipline, but kind and genial, a parent whom they sincerely loved and respected.

Nell listened with intense interest; wondering within herself too, why the doubt as to which of the two couples were his true parents should have been, as she began to perceive that it had, a reason why Dr. Clendenin should feel that marriage was not for him; in either case his birth was not ignoble.

He paused, seeming for a moment lost in painful thought, then casting it off with a slight sigh, went on.

"Yes, ours was a very happy childhood till we, Angus and I, were about twelve years old. Then sickness and death came into the family, two little sisters being taken away within a few weeks of each other.

"The heart of the tender mother seemed well-nigh broken; but alas! the time came when she was unutterably thankful for their early removal to a better land.

"There were still two little ones, a brother and sister, left, and within the next two years Marian was born.

"Troubles came thick and fast during the first year of her life. There was a great and sudden change in our father. He had received a package of letters and papers from England, and from the hour of their perusal was a strangely altered man; silent, morose, disinclined to mix with his fellows, or even with his own family, and at times looking haggard and wretched in the extreme.

"It was a sad mystery to us boys, but mother, who seemed to have a sorrowful understanding of it, hushed every enquiry into its cause, and would suffer no allusion to it in her presence.

"A few months later came one of the sorest trials of my life," continued Kenneth, his voice trembling with excess of feeling. "Angus, my twin brother, my second self, was accidentally drowned. I cannot dwell upon the particulars, but shall never forget my mother's look of woe, her white despairing face, as the dripping corpse was borne and laid down before her, nor the strange unnatural laugh, the expression of mingled agony and triumphant pleasure, with which the father bent over his dead son, saying, 'It's better so! Wife, why do you grieve? I've no tear to shed for him.'

"I was inexpressibly shocked and very angry at what I deemed his heartlessness.

"This mother saw, with deep sorrow; she loved her husband devotedly, and could not bear to have him unjustly blamed. She felt, too, that it would be necessary at some time for me to know the fatal secret. So one day, after the grave had closed over all that remained of our loved one, she sought me in my room and told me all.

"Her husband was an only child, had lost his father by death shortly before coming to this country. Of his mother he had no recollection, but had always understood that she had died soon after his birth.

"That, however, was not the case, and those letters from England had revealed to him the fact that she had only just died, at the time when they were written; died in a mad house, a furious, raving maniac, having been in that condition for many years; also that such had been her mother's fate, and that of several others of the family; in short, insanity was undoubtedly hereditary.

"From the moment of learning all this he had felt that his doom was sealed, and that of each of his children also.

"I cannot describe to you the horror and fear that came over me as I listened to the tale. Then mother told me, oh, so gently and tenderly, of the mystery that hung over my birth; leaving, while it almost orphaned me, a faint hope that that fearful curse was not mine.

"And now you know, sweet one, why, when I would fain have poured into your ear the story of my love, my lips were sealed. I could not ask you to link your life with that of one for whom so sad a fate might be in store. I dared not risk the transmission to future generations of a curse so fearful.

"But God, in His great mercy, has sent me the knowledge that it is not mine," he added, with a look of deepest gratitude and joy.

"And I was at times shamefully angry with you," murmured Nell, penitent tears shining in her eyes.

"I cannot blame you under the circumstances," he said, smiling tenderly upon her.

"And this was the explanation of the rumors that reached us of some white woman, living among the Indians, giving testimony before the squire in regard to some matter of importance to you?"

"Yes, it was Reumah Clark." And he went on to give a narrative of his interview with her, then to finish his story of the life at Glen Forest.

The two remaining little ones older than Marian, had followed Angus to the better land in the course of a few months, leaving her sole inheritor—after her father—of that terrible curse.

He described, in moving words, his own and the mother's anxiety for her, and for the wretched husband and father; the wife's life of devotion to him, the long years of fear and care, of untiring sympathy and love, of faith and submission; rewarded at last by seeing him pass peacefully away to another and happier existence, for he had gone trusting in a crucified and risen Saviour.

Marian, still spared to them, was now their one great anxiety, but he was hopeful for her. She had stood some severe tests of late, and it might be, he trusted it was the case, that her mental powers and peculiarities were inherited from her mother's side of the house, or her father's paternal ancestors; all of whom were free from that dreaded taint.

"We have endeavored, and thus far with success, to keep the fatal secret from her," he said, "deeming that her danger would be greatly enhanced by the knowledge.

"She has long known there was a grievous thorn in the Clendenin nest, but what it is she does not know, and I trust never will. Her mother and I have also another innocent concealment from her. She still believes that I am her brother by right of birth; and we do not intend that she shall ever be undeceived."

"No; it would be very cruel to rob her of the blessedness of believing that," Nell said, with the sweetest look in her beautiful eyes, "to be your sister would be the greatest happiness, except to—"

But she stopped short, blushing and confused.

"Except to be something far nearer and dearer? Ah, tell me that was what you were thinking," he whispered, his eyes shining, as he bent his head for a closer look into the sweet, blushing face.

"Now, don't be too inquisitive, Dr. Clendenin," she said, in pretended vexation and pretty confusion.

"Never mind the doctor," he returned gayly. "Kenneth is three syllables shorter and easier."

"But not so respectful."

"Quite sufficiently so, however. It is Marian's and my mother's name for me, and I hope will be my wife's also," he whispered. "Oh, dearest, how soon may I claim the right to call you by that sweetest of names?"

"Ah, don't speak of that yet!" she said, hastily, her cheeks crimsoning, her eyes drooping.

"Forgive me, I am very selfish," he replied, "but it must be very soon or not for long weary months, while an ocean will roll between us; to say nothing of the hundreds of miles of land that will separate us besides."

"What can you mean?" she asked, with a start and look of surprise and dismay.

Then he told her of his inheritance in England and the unfortunate necessity it entailed of a speedy visit there. It could not well be deferred till the ensuing spring, and must therefore be undertaken soon if he would avoid the dangerous storms likely to be encountered in the fall.

"And you must go?" she said, struggling to keep back her tears.

"Yes," he sighed. "I cannot tell you how hard it is to think of leaving you just now, or how sweet it would be to call you mine before I go; and to know that, if anything should befall me, you would—"

"Oh, don't, don't!" she cried, the tears coming now in good earnest, "I can't bear it! I—I think you might ask me to go with you."

"Would you, oh, would you?" he exclaimed joyously. "My dear girl, how very sweet and kind in you to propose it."

"Did I?" she asked, smiling through her tears, as she gently released herself from his enraptured embrace. "I thought I only suggested the propriety of your asking me."

"I feel very selfish in so doing, dearest Nell," he said, "but will you go?"

"Yes, if you really want me and will take me."

"Only too gladly, ah, you cannot doubt that, but have you thought of the long, tedious journey overland, and the dangers of the voyage?"

"Yes; and how can I let you meet them alone?"

"Ah, my darling, you are the most unselfish of women," he exclaimed, regarding her with tender, loving admiration, "and I the happiest of men."

"But," said Nell presently, "you will have a poorly attired bride. I shall have no time to get new dresses made."

"Very much wiser to wait for that till we reach New York, London or Paris," he answered, with his grave, tender smile. "'Tis the bird I would secure, sweet one, and I care not for the color or quality of the feathers she may wear."

So it was all settled, after a little more talk, and in a week they would be setting off for Europe on their wedding tour.

Great were Clare's astonishment and delight when she heard the news.

"Just the match I've always wanted for you, Nell, even when I'd no idea he was going to be so rich."

"He didn't say it would be riches," returned the young lady, supremely indifferent to such trifles.

"But I dare say it will. At all events you are going to Europe for your wedding trip. Won't the other girls envy you? Yet I don't know, Nell, I should be afraid of the sea. What if you should be drowned?"

"I hope we shall not," Nell answered gravely, "but even if we should, I'd rather die with Kenneth than live without him. And as to the envy the other girls may feel, I should think it would be because of him rather than anything else," she added, her cheeks glowing and her eyes shining.

"Oh, I suppose so!" laughed Clare. "It's a great shame, though, that we can't have a grand wedding and elaborate trousseau. Still the means can be provided for that last, all the same; and it will be lovely to have it bought in Paris."

THE END

Lightning Source UK Ltd.
Milton Keynes UK
UKHW041041100820
367987UK00004B/844